The Beast Takes a Bride

"Alexandra," he said softly. "Do you think I'm actually made of stone?"

There was a sort of tender, amused menace in the words.

But it sounded like a serious question.

He could do anything he wanted to her in this moment, should he choose. They both knew it.

But around the edges of those words shimmered something like a plea.

As if, despite everything, he was still at her mercy.

God help her, she wanted him to do things to her.

Anything he wanted.

What madness was this?

Her lips trembled toward each other, desperate to form the word that meant surrender, that word that would let him know he'd won, that would betray to him that she would do anything he wanted: *please.*

Also by Julie Anne Long

The Palace of Rogues series

The Pennyroyal Green series

Julie Anne Long

The Beast Takes a Bride

The Palace of Rogues

AVON

An Imprint of HarperCollinsPublishers

First Avon Books mass market printing: October 2024

Print Edition ISBN: 978-0-06-328117-2
Digital Edition ISBN: 978-0-06-328098-4

Cover design by Amy Halperin
Cover illustration by Chris Cocozza

Avon, Avon & logo, and Avon Books & logo are registered trademarks of HarperCollins Publishers in the United States of America and other countries.

HarperCollins is a registered trademark of HarperCollins Publishers in the United States of America and other countries.

FIRST EDITION

24 25 26 27 28 BVGM 10 9 8 7 6 5 4 3 2 1

To all the members of the Pig & Thistle After Dark

Acknowledgments

❧❧❧

My GRATITUDE to my ever-supportive editor, May Chen, and the hardworking team at Avon; to my agent, Steven Axelrod, and his wonderful staff; to my delightful community at The Pig & Thistle After Dark Facebook Group, with special thanks to our read-along ringmistress Helen Kunic-Davis; to my Street Team and Instagram Community for such warmth and enthusiasm— you make me feel blessed; to Julia Quinn, for her extraordinary generosity, enthusiasm, and support—it means more than I can say; and to the incredibly kind authors and readers who had shared their love of my books with their own communities: may your kindness return to you a thousandfold.

The *Beast*
Takes a *Bride*

Chapter One

⤬⟆⟆⟆⟆⟆⤬

THREE OF them were thieves (a silver candlestick, a half dozen handkerchiefs, a wheel of cheese, respectively), another one was a forger, and the fifth one had stabbed her husband in the leg. Alexandra was the only one wearing a gold shot-silk ball gown, which was probably why the others had circled her like wolves around a lame deer when she'd been brought into the cell.

The matrons had taken her hairpins from her lest she decide to impale someone with them—this notion had never once occurred to her in her life, but was apparently often taken at Newgate—and this left Alexandra with only one defense. She was going to have to charm them.

She'd leaned forward and confided conspiratorially, to Agnes, the husband stabber, "I've a wonderful receipt for getting bloodstains out of your clothes. Lemon juice and kerosene."

Two hours later they were all cozily clustered about her like guests at a dinner party. She had learned their first names, their alleged crimes, and three verses of "The Ballad of Colin Eversea," a bawdy song in which the word "cock" liberally featured. No doubt because so many things rhymed with it.

Alexandra's crime was the group favorite because they all thought she was making it up.

Because the light in the prison ranged from sludgy gray to sludgy pitch, it was difficult to know how many hours had passed since she'd been brought in—perhaps twenty-four?—but she hadn't closed her eyes since she'd arrived. Her neck felt sticky; her loosely knotted hair sat heavily on her nape. She was certain the entirety of her person was coated with an invisible layer of filth, which hung in the atmosphere the way fog hung over London. All of her senses were excruciatingly heightened, which was both necessary and a pity, as the smell was an unholy potpourri of human effluence, and the cacophony (sobs, curse words, bitter arguments, shrieks, snores, farts) was ceaseless.

Straw had been strewn on the floor, as this was where they were meant to sleep. If it was good enough for cows, apparently it was good enough for them. There wasn't enough room for mattresses.

She understood viscerally now why people spoke of "the fibers of their being." For the first time she was acutely aware of hers, and they were all perilously stretched.

The warden—whose appearance was usually heralded by a jingle of keys and shouted invective and obscene suggestions from all the women locked in the cells—had just installed a new prisoner in their cell and departed. That made seven of them now crammed into the space.

"Bunty," she announced. This was apparently the new prisoner's name. "I clouted me employer in the head."

"Alexandra stole an entire *carriage*," Agnes proudly informed the newcomer, essentially declaring her allegiance. "Horses and all. A carriage belonging to a *duke*." She elbowed Alexa whimsically and winked.

Bunty assessed Alexandra through unimpressed, narrowed dark eyes.

"Cooorrrr, Alexandra, is it? Ain't ye a *rascal*, then." The words were flatly ironic. She flexed hands the size of pitchforks. "They'll 'ang ye for stealin' a carriage."

Everyone had, in fact, already pointed this out to Alexandra.

"Thankfully, I did *not* steal a carriage, so there will be no hanging," Alexandra replied lightly. Her mouth had gone sandy; her voice was hoarse. "It was all a silly misunderstanding."

"Doesn't she talk pretty? *Misunderstandin'*," Agnes imitated loftily, and everyone laughed, including Alexandra, because she wasn't a fool.

"Never ye mind, lass. Ye've a wee skinny neck, and t'will snap like a twig when they yank the noose." Lizzy, the cheese thief, gave Alexandra's thigh a reassuring pat. "Ye'll doubtless not feel a thing."

She was absurdly touched. She knew this was what passed for kindness here. "Thank you, Lizzy."

Lizzy normally stole handkerchiefs and watch fobs. She had given Alexandra a lot of advice on how to do both (men are easily distractible idiots; "when in doubt, show 'em yer teats" is what it boiled down to, she claimed) and even a pantomime demonstration. She'd stolen a wheel of cheese because she was pregnant and therefore always ravenous, and she'd gotten caught trying to smuggle it out of a shop under her dress.

How outlandishly studded with blessings Alexandra's life was. She supposed she'd always known that. When she was free from here—surely she would be?—she would count them over and over, like a miser with his gold.

But now her head felt light as blown glass. So far she'd been given one lumpy beige meal in a bowl, because it was apparently important to keep criminals alive until the court said they could go ahead and kill them. She was ashamed that she hadn't been able to eat it. Nerves had obliterated hunger pangs, and revulsion had done the rest. She'd given her meal to Lizzy.

"Tell Bunty your story," Lizzy urged.

Alexandra obligingly turned to Bunty. "My dear friend, Lord Thackeray, who is my third cousin, was given permission to borrow the carriage of the duke, with whom he is acquainted—"

"Ha! A duke! That there is my favorite part of the story!" Agnes gleefully interjected.

"—who is up in years and quite forgot that he'd loaned his carriage and alerted the authorities and they took us away. It's merely a mistake and I'm confident all will be resolved soon."

She had told this story three times. They loved it. They all thought it was a fairy tale.

Alexandra was half beginning to believe it was, too.

The "resolved soon" part of it, that was.

Because not one of the prison officials seemed to believe she was who she claimed to be. Then again, there were moments she found it difficult to believe, too.

She had given them the name of her solicitor, and her sister's husband, who was a viscount, though her sister and her husband were currently on holiday in Italy.

No one had yet come for her.

This seemed impossible. Unreal. Nearly the whole of her life someone had always known precisely where she was at any given time.

Her brother and father were currently in America, in New York, visiting. She was meant to travel to New York in a week in the company of a couple she knew from her childhood parish, Mr. and Mrs. Harper. She ought to be finishing up packing right at this moment.

It seemed nothing in her life, and yet everything in her life, had prepared her for being abandoned in a prison. She was three people at once in this moment: the one who was comprised of pure terror; the one floating over her body with a sense of unreality; and the diplomat, who, despite

herself, remained curious, kind, respectful, and
sparkling, adroitly managing the circumstances
without anyone quite realizing that this was precisely what she was doing.

"Ye mun 'ave a lot of time on yer 'ands if ye can
waste it on words like misunnerstannin'." Bunty
spat on the floor, as if the word was an insect
she'd accidentally ingested.

"Oh, no, she's right busy," Agnes defended
stoutly. "Getting blood out of clothes and the like."

Bunty's eyes traveled Alexandra speculatively
from head to toe.

"I'll just 'ave them shoes off yer, will I?" she decided to say threateningly, at last.

"Oh, I don't think so," Alexandra replied pleasantly but firmly. She tucked her satin-slippered
feet beneath her skirt.

Would she fight for her slippers if she needed
to? She decided she would. She was fit enough.
What she lacked in size she could perhaps make
up for in stamina. Even if Bunty's biceps looked
like little cannonballs tucked under her sleeves.

Agnes had shared with her that a previous cell-
mate had managed to hide in her skirts the leg
of a broken stool, which she'd patiently, surreptitiously sharpened to a lethal point over a period
of weeks. She'd used it to attack the warden. But
Alexandra didn't have weeks to fashion a weapon.

How had her life come to this? How had her life
narrowed to a single point? At least prison was *definitive*. For the past five years, she'd lived in a sort
of in-between world, a sort of pampered purgatory,

admittedly of her own making. She had recently taken steps to break away from it: she was meant to begin a journey to New York to visit her brother in about a week's time, traveling from Liverpool on a Black Ball packet. She had no real desire to spend six weeks at sea. But she needed a change, and she wanted to be with people who loved her, to be reminded that she was a person who could be loved.

And while Bunty stared at her with her flat, dark eyes, Alexandra's overtaxed senses, pitched like a small prey animal's for new dangers, sensed almost at once that something had disturbed the usual rhythms of the prison.

Along the block of cells, a hush was creeping toward them. A bit like a slow, oily tide.

The volume of the ceaseless human sounds was tapering, gradually, into murmurs.

And then into silence.

The notion that something—or someone—existed who could actually put the fear of God into this desperate place ramped Alexandra's ambient terror. Her heart, which had not beat at a normal pace from the moment she'd arrived, punched the walls of her chest.

Presently it was so quiet through the whole prison ward that she could hear, for the first time, both the jingle of the warden's keys and the echo of his footfall.

It was accompanied by another footfall.

This one was heavier than the warden's and quite obviously boot-heeled.

Twice she detected the slightest of hesitations

in one of those steps. It was almost, but not quite,
a limp.

Suspicion clubbed her.

It must be. Oh, dear God. But how?

Surely not?

For a maniacal instant the gallows seemed
preferable.

Because she knew of only one other person
who could cause such a hush. One other person
with that hesitant gait.

Salvation and damnation in the flesh.

In other words: her husband.

She hadn't seen him in five years.

COLONEL MAGNUS BRIGHTWALL peered into the
cage in which his wife was being held. His eyes
seemed bright as windows in the gloom.

He found her at once.

Alexandra's breathing had gone shallow. She
was sorely tempted to duck, but she refused to
allow her gaze to drop from his. Damned if she
would ever appear abject before him. Even as her
heart pummeled away inside her.

She vividly recalled her very first sight of him
almost five years ago, standing amid his luggage
in the foyer of her family home. In the blazing
light of noon his shadow had fallen nearly entirely across the circular marble expanse, like a
giant compass needle.

He turned to the warden. "I assume she told
you she was my wife."

By rights, one would expect such an imposing

man's voice to boom like a cannon. But it was an elegant, smoky-edged bass. The first words he had ever said to her were *A pleasure, Miss Bellamy,* just after her father had introduced them.

Never had the word "pleasure" sounded so profound.

The warden's Adam's apple bobbed when he swallowed.

"It's . . . it's . . . just that so many of them claim to be your wife, Colonel Brightwall, we took it quite for granted she was lying. They all lie. About everything."

"Coorrr, look at the *size* of 'im!" Agnes whispered gleefully. "Ye're just *full* of surprises, Alexandra. *Brightwall* the Beast hisself."

Alexandra stared at him. Her mind was static. She felt as though she'd never learned how to form words. Her heart was now beating so hard the blood rang in her ears.

"Let her out." Brightwall's voice was calm.

The warden cleared his throat. "Colonel Brightwall. As a man all too familiar with bureaucracies, surely you understand we have a formal process. I fear we cannot just allow an inmate to stroll out of the . . ."

His ability to speak apparently evaporated when Brightwall fixed upon him an expression of scathing amazement.

"The process is this, sir." He said it almost tenderly. It was the tone one might use to administer last rites. "You unlock the cell. I depart with my wife. Her name is forever struck from your rolls, thereby also eliminating the record of the appallingly grave error made in incarcerating her. Do you require further clarification?"

"*Brrr.* Has anyone else's nips gone hard?" Agnes murmured.

The warden shook himself out of the trance of Brightwall's icy gaze and pivoted. The keys frantically jingled in his now-trembling hand. He stabbed at the keyhole and missed for a few torturous seconds.

Finally it fitted in.

The fateful clunk was heard as the cell door unlocked.

Everyone exhaled.

Alexandra surreptitiously pressed clammy palms against her skirt and stood from her spot on the floor. Black spots scudded in front of her eyes and she nearly swayed. She took a last long, deep breath of fetid prison air, gathering courage for another kind of ordeal. She knew she would never forget the smell.

The warden stepped aside so she could exit and then at once slammed the cell door and turned the key.

And for the first time in five years, she tipped her head back to take in the dizzying view that was her husband.

He'd always seemed to her hacked from granite in stark, almost brutal, lines: a jaw made of severe, hard angles, a bold nose, battlement cheekbones, legs like pillars, a shoulder span nearly twice the width of her. A few tiny pinprick scars were scattered in the hollow of his cheeks. Another thin, white scar bisected a thick, dark eyebrow. He had survived both illness and combat.

When she'd first met him, she'd been unable to decide whether he was ugly or magnificent.

But even in the gloom of Newgate, he looked indestructible.

I do think we'll suit, Alexandra, he'd said gently, the day he'd proposed.

Two months after they'd met.

He had brushed his lips across her knuckles.

She was fairly certain he was seething now. It was difficult to tell. He excelled at cool inscrutability.

He'd been seething the last time she'd seen him, too. But then, she'd given him a good reason.

In her current dazed state, she could almost imagine he'd seethed nonstop for the nearly five years he'd been in Spain.

She turned to the warden. "Thank you," she told him. As though he'd been her host for the evening. Because she was well-bred, and the social niceties were what knit the world together.

"Madam." The warden bowed ironically.

Brightwall did not extend his arm to her.

Ah. So he *was* seething.

She supposed she could hardly blame him, given the circumstances of their reunion.

But she was certain the warden would notice that sort of thing, and he would likely happily tell everyone of his acquaintance who would listen that Brightwall refused to touch his estranged wife.

Her husband opted for a subtle, ironic "shall

we?" gesture with his chin instead. Clearly the outside of a jail cell wasn't the place for the get-reacquainted chat.

She smoothed her palms down her skirts and rearranged her shoulders and took her place by his side.

Thusly, much the way she'd been installed into a cage by a man, another man retrieved her from it, as if she was a parakeet with clipped wings.

Lack of sleep and the steady diet of terror and acute, constant alertness made her feel as separate from her body as a kite aloft on a string. As though she did not belong to herself anymore.

"Fare thee well, Alexandra! I'll name me bairn for you!" Lizzy called after her.

She turned around. Suddenly, bizarrely, her heart ached at the sight of those eyes staring at her through bars.

She was reminded of something Magnus had once said to her on a sweet, breezy spring day, about heroes, scoundrels, and boors, and how applying a label to someone could be a foolish tactical move. She hadn't realized then that he saw the whole of life the way a chess master saw a chessboard.

And that included people.

And that included her.

"Oh, thank you, Lizzy," Alexandra called. "I'm honored. Godspeed and good luck, ladies." She paused a beat. "And Bunty."

Bunty spat again on the floor.

"Good luck to *you*," Agnes called. "I think ye was safer in 'ere."

Chapter Two

❧❧❧

THE LANDAU to which she'd been led seemed startlingly, sparklingly new. Blissfully comfortable, seats plump, redolent of leather and polish. Worth two hundred pounds, if she had to guess. Four matched bays pulled it.

No crest was apparent on it. Did it belong to Brightwall?

If so, when had he commissioned it?

Magnus hadn't spoken since the driver had assisted her aboard and closed the door upon them. And he hadn't said a word to her.

"Thank you for coming for me," she said to her husband, finally. Subdued.

Her raspy voice shocked her. It was shredded from shouting over the prison noise.

For long seconds he didn't reply.

Perhaps words couldn't possibly struggle through the thundercloud of his thoughts.

"Are you sound?" His voice was gruff. His eyes remained fixed on the carriage wall ahead of him.

"Yes. Thank you. I didn't know hairpins were considered a weapon. Or the leg of a stool."

She had no idea why these were the first things she would say to her husband in five years. She was apparently too tired to filter her thoughts before they emerged as words.

"Anything can be a weapon." He sounded faintly surprised. As if this was something everyone ought to have been born knowing.

Silly Alexandra. Then again, he supposed he'd been forced to view the whole of life that way.

She cleared her throat. "Are . . . *you* . . . sound?"

He snorted softly.

And he still didn't turn his head to look at her.

With a sense of unreality, she surreptitiously studied the profile of this familiar stranger to whom she was bound for life. The sun revealed shadows of sleeplessness beneath his eyes. Lines, earned through years of peering across battlefields or into the souls of enemies or squinting at maps and dispatches by firelight, rayed from the corners.

Seconds after they'd first been introduced, he'd held her fast in his cool, remote gaze for several potent seconds, during which she could have sworn he didn't draw a breath.

And then his eyes had kindled to the warm blue at the center of a flame, and a wry, intimate smile had tipped one corner of his mouth. As if he knew things about her even she had yet to discover, and liked them all.

She wondered if he'd ever anticipated then there would be a time he couldn't bear to look at her, let alone speak to her.

Perhaps she reeked of the prison. Or appeared haggard from sleeplessness.

Her vanity stung at the thought.

What a luxury it was to worry about how she looked, she realized. Despite its strifes, heartaches, and upheavals, her entire life, end to end, was comprised of luxuries such as those. From now on, no matter what happened, she would never let herself forget it.

And besides, she could hardly smell worse than the soldiers he'd lived with for months on end.

She tried again. "I wasn't aware you had returned from Spain."

He'd been there for nearly the whole of the last five years; they'd made him a diplomat after the war.

As his new wife, she was supposed to have gone with him. Destiny had thrown a flaming grenade into those plans.

Well, *she* had. She was the one who'd thrown the grenade.

It occurred to her then: What if he'd actually been in London for weeks and hadn't bothered to tell her? Her stomach twisted at the implications.

But would it have really mattered?

"I arrived only a day ago. I sent word to you of my arrival via Mr. Lawler."

Mr. Lawler. The solicitor through whom they had conducted all matters between them for the last five years. He administered to Alexandra her reasonable allowance and approved and paid all of her expenses, including clothing, servants, household furnishings, travel, like her upcoming trip to New York, and entertainments.

Like the opera she was supposed to have attended when she was arrested.

In all of that time she had not exchanged one word directly with her husband, written or spoken. She had been kept apprised of whether he was alive or not, and she assumed Mr. Lawler had likewise reported on her continued existence to Brightwall. All Brightwall had asked in return was that she discreetly conduct herself in a way becoming of the wife of a man of his stature.

And it ought to have been so easy: she'd been raised to do, and be, exactly that, her entire life.

How had she failed?

"Lawler would have conveyed word of my presence to you had you been available to receive it," he added.

Oh, so very dry: In other words, if you had not been in prison due to a lark, Alexandra.

"How did you hear that I was in . . ." She couldn't quite bring herself to say it.

"I was awakened at my lodgings just past dawn by a distraught Mr. Lawler, who held in his hand a copy of *The Times.*" He paused. "Imagine my delight when the word used to describe my wife was 'accomplice.'"

Oh, dear God.

"The gossip columns?"

"The front page."

Worse and worse. She squeezed her eyes closed.

"I understand Ackerman's is already selling the Rowlandson illustration accompanying the article entitled 'The Beast Takes a Bride.'"

Oh no.

Oh no oh no.

No wonder he was furious.

Her husband had been found as a baby squalling in a sack on the back garden steps of a Yorkshire manor, next to a delivery of potatoes. His name, Magnus Brightwall, was how the servants who found him had interpreted the barely legible scribble on the scrap of paper pinned to his swaddling clothes. He had triumphed over incomprehensible odds. He was extraordinary by any definition of the word. All of England considered him a hero.

She was one of the few who knew his ambivalence about the word "hero."

It seemed a cardinal sin to do anything at all to tarnish the name of such a man. The gossip sheets had no such compunction about it, of course. Their fealty was to profits.

She wondered if she'd unwittingly been doing it in increments. Perhaps if she hadn't gone out to that performance of *Artaxerxes* at King's Theatre that one night a few years ago, for instance, a drunk young man she'd never seen in her life might not have stumbled into her opera box and loudly declared his love for her during the first aria. It transpired her sparkly tiara had transfixed him ten minutes earlier in the lobby, so he'd followed her. The gossip sheets had christened her "the mysterious Juliet" until they'd discovered the opera box belonged to Colonel Brightwall and that "Juliet" was in fact Brightwall's allegedly even more mysterious wife. That was when the fun really began.

She ventured out rarely into public after that. Her social circle remained primarily her extended family. This hadn't been easy. She was a fundamentally social creature.

After that, from time to time, speculation about the nature of their marriage had sprung up in the gossip sheet like noxious little weeds. But both she and Magnus remained tight-lipped about the reasons they lived apart, and absolutely no one besides the two of them knew the real reason.

She wondered if Mr. Lawler had sent newspaper clippings to him in Spain.

She could not find it in herself to protest her innocence in this latest instance. It would have been an almost macabre echo of their last conversation.

"Magnus, I do not yet know what the newspaper printed," she said carefully, her voice graveled. "And I expect I shall learn presently. But I should like to tell you that this all was merely misunderstanding which escalated horribly. Thackeray swears he was offered the use of the Duke of Brexford's phaeton. Brexford was away when Thackeray retrieved it from the duke's mews, and apparently no one in the stables questioned him about it. He then retrieved me from the town house for our visit to the opera with other friends. But when the duke arrived home and learned his phaeton was missing, he sounded the alarm because he'd forgotten the arrangement . . . and . . . and soldiers descended upon us, and . . ."

She stopped.

"And . . ." Magnus prompted, with great irony.

Which is when she realized Brightwall had probably, somehow, already heard the whole story.

"And Thackeray may have swung his fist at a soldier who seized him," she said quietly.

Admittedly, this was a deeply stupid thing to do. Then again, while Thackeray was diverting company, he was hardly known for his sense, which life seldom required him to use. He took after her father's side of the family. She'd tried to intervene by speaking up on his behalf to the soldiers. She'd scarcely raised her voice. But they were having none of it.

Her husband was one of the most famous military officers in all of English history. She knew exactly how he felt about civilians attacking soldiers doing their jobs.

Which meant she was aware of the futility, even the foolhardiness, of what she was about to say next.

But time was of the essence, and she couldn't live with herself if she didn't try.

"In light of the circumstances, I am aware that what I am about to ask is presumptuous in the extreme." Her voice trembled. "Thackeray won't survive long in Newgate, Magnus. He hasn't the funds or influence to get himself out. You've met him, at our house party five years ago. You have a sense of him, I believe. He means well, even if he is a bit rash on occasion, and this is what will get him hurt in jail. If you could . . . that is, he truly didn't intend to . . ."

She trailed off when she realized Magnus was studying her as if he'd never seen her before. With a sort of hard, closed curiosity. Wondering, perhaps, what she had become. What on earth he had ever seen in her.

"Lord Thackeray might be your cousin, but he is a feckless idiot who recklessly endangered you, himself, my reputation and yours." He explained all of this slowly, with great, amazed patience, as if this was something elementary she ought to have learned with her numbers and letters. "Thackeray can rot in prison."

She stared at him. And as she did, toxic bubbles of fury rose through her exhaustion and unease and layers of grace and control, *always* control, so carefully cultivated. *Do not* ever *speak to me in that tone. No matter what I've done. No matter how angry you might be.* She wanted desperately to say it. And she could have.

It wouldn't have mattered.

He could, of course, say or do anything he liked to her. She was his wife. His property in the eyes of the law.

She gave up and turned away from him, aiming her face toward the window, her eyes half closed, and said nothing more until the carriage came to a halt.

"MAYBE A LITTLE sherry would help," Angelique suggested, tentatively.

The proprietresses of the boardinghouse by the docks known as The Grand Palace on the Thames had just settled in with a basket of mending in their little room at the top of the stairs to discuss an odd little problem: For the past week, the after-dinner discourse in their sitting room had been less spirited than . . . moribund.

And they both felt a little responsible.

Delilah laughed. "Are you suggesting we ought to get our guests foxed?"

But they both knew Angelique was only partly jesting.

The rules of The Grand Palace on the Thames required all guests to gather at least four nights out of the week, which they believed helped foster what they liked to think of as the boarding-house's warm, familial atmosphere. The room had been the scene of impromptu dancing; sultry innuendo; feelings both hurt and soothed; passionate debate about apple tarts, ghosts, the nature of love and death and phallic flora; and once, enthusiastic sex (at night, however, after everyone else had gone to sleep). Bawdy songs had been composed on the spot there. Mr. Delacorte had made many trips to the Epithet Jar, which presided over everything, and maintained civility. Anything could happen in that room.

But currently, almost nothing was happening in that room.

It had to do with their current mix of guests.

The very young Corporal Simon Dawson and his new bride, Cora, had been in residence for four days of the fortnight they intended to stay, and though they had obediently reported to the sitting room after dinner, they had thus far seemed impervious to every attempt to draw them into conversation. It didn't help that Corporal Dawson had a tendency to go mute from awe when the legendary smuggler-catcher Captain Tristan Hardy, Delilah's husband, was in the room, which amused Captain Hardy and didn't bother him a bit. Cora had freckles and Simon had a cowlick and both had big brown eyes and somberly deferential manners, all of which made everyone else present feel ancient. Corporal Dawson was sweetly solicitous of his shy little wife. They were, in a word, adorable; it was like hosting a pair of baby field mice. The Epithet Jar was in no danger of seeing a contribution from either of them.

And then there was Mrs. Prudence Cuthbert, who had come to London from Norfolk to visit her childhood friend, Mrs. Pariseau, a longtime resident of The Grand Palace on the Thames. Mrs. Cuthbert was polite but nervous, and though she and Mrs. Pariseau were both widows in their middle years, she seemed older, perhaps because her lips were so often compressed in a disapproving line. She had confided to Mrs. Pariseau that Mr. Delacorte reminded her of a dog she'd once owned who found it amusing to insert his snout into strangers' behinds, and then stand back and wag his tail. While this was a fair description of Mr. Delacorte, Mrs. Pariseau had later said, somewhat apologetically, to Delilah and Angelique, "I didn't realize Prudence had grown up to be so *prim*."

Two nights ago, Mrs. Pariseau's attempt to lead a discussion of Greek myths had veered into chaos when Mr. Delacorte shared that he'd thought "Testicles" was a Greek philosopher the first time he'd seen the word in print. ("Testi*cleez*, like Hercules," he'd explained to his stunned audience.)

Mrs. Cuthbert now went warily stiff every time Mr. Delacorte opened his mouth, and Angelique and Delilah had taken to keeping smelling salts in the sitting room.

Mrs. Pariseau was patently not prim. She was thoroughly enjoying her relatively monied widowhood, and while she had no desire to ever marry again, she adored handsome men as much as arcane discussion. There wasn't a single topic of conversation too controversial for her to enthusiastically embrace, just as there wasn't a single topic of conversation Mr. Delacorte couldn't make more awkward. Angelique and Delilah cherished both of them, and would be quite pleased if they stayed forever.

But both of them now seemed to be languishing. For the past several days, Mrs. Pariseau had read aloud from *The Arabian Nights' Entertainments*, and everyone else had merely . . . listened politely. Even Mr. Delacorte, who had sat near the chessboard, his chin propped on his fist almost disconsolately.

Delilah and Angelique had never thought a day

would come when they would be uneasy about "politely." They had begun to feel as though they were failing in their mission to make The Grand Palace on the Thames a warm, familial place. The alchemy of guests was what had created the magic in the room thus far.

"We could always dose their tea with something from Mr. Delacorte's case," Delilah mused.

Angelique laughed.

Mr. Delacorte imported remedies from the Orient, "ground up herbs and bits and bobs of animal horns and whatnot," as he described them, and sold them to apothecaries and surgeons up and down the coast. Some of them cured fevers and healed wounds and helped slow bleeding and eased pains and headaches, some caused hallucinations or wild dreams, some did all of those things, and some did nothing at all.

"Oh, it feels a bit like tempting fate to say, but I almost wish a more exciting guest would arrive," Angelique admitted. "Perhaps our sitting room recipe is missing just one crucial person to make it come alive again."

Just then a familiar thundering on the stairs made them leap to their feet.

Dot appeared in the doorway, and her flushed, triumphant expression could only mean one thing: she'd triumphed over Mr. Pike, their new footman, in a race to answer the front door.

Answering the door was Dot's favorite thing to do, but Mr. Pike had gotten a taste of it and, unfortunately, decided Dot was right: it was *de-*

lightful, like opening a gift every time, and he wanted to do more of it. Delilah and Angelique had mostly left the two of them to sort it out between them, as an experiment and by way of avoiding crushing Dot's heart by telling her they wanted their strapping footman to do it all the time. Dot had once accidentally trod on Mr. Pike's foot in a race for the door, which made Mr. Pike darkly mutter "bollocks." This they knew because Dot had tattled on him. They were, after a fashion, each other's nemesis. And like all nemeses since the dawn of time, they were fascinated by each other.

Dot needed three gulps of air before she could deliver her news, which she did in a rush, as if she wanted to prevent Pike from beating her to that, too.

"We've a man downstairs who would like a suite!"

"What sort of man? One of means, it would seem, if he wants a suite, instead of just a room." Delilah began to untie her apron.

Dot's expression fleetingly clouded, as she apparently pondered this question, then cleared, as though she'd swiftly resolved some troubling internal debate.

"Well, we have had other alarming guests before," she said cheerfully. "And they turned out just fine, didn't they?"

Delilah and Angelique froze.

Angelique ventured, "Are you suggesting this man is alarming? And if so, what sort of alarming?

Is he swinging a shillelagh in the foyer? Is our chandelier at risk?"

She felt she could afford to be somewhat glib given that Captain Hardy and Lucien Durand, Lord Bolt (Angelique's husband, the formerly infamous illegitimate son of an awful duke), would make short work of any alarming man. Their husbands were in the smoking room at the moment, which was lovely, as they'd been so frequently away recently, traveling up the coast to supervise repair of their damaged ship and the outfitting of their new one, Delilah and Angelique were beginning to ironically feel as though they and their husbands were ships passing in the night. Their absence, too, was part of the reason the sitting room had been less spirited at night.

As for Ben Pike, if they had to guess, he was likely doubled over, catching his breath and scowling after losing a race to the door. He was also perfectly capable of thumping a man in the jaw, should the need arise.

"Dot?" Delilah pressed worriedly, when Dot didn't reply.

Delilah reached over to right Dot's cap, which had collapsed over her brow.

She discovered Dot's enormous blue eyes had gone starry.

"What is a . . . what is a . . . sillylaylee?" she breathed.

"ShiLAYLee. It's an Irish word for a versatile sort of cudgel. A cudgel is a club." Angelique made a swinging gesture. "The sort you hit people with in order to defend yourself. It can also be used as a walking stick."

Angelique was a former governess who had never lost the impulse to instruct, and Dot's mind was a vast, fertile plain (or a howling tundra, or an attic full of cobwebs and mysterious, broken toys depending upon whom one asked). Dot considered every new word a gift to be displayed proudly and liberally in her sentences for weeks thereafter, the way someone else might set out their best china plates.

"I think it's the most beautiful word I've ever heard. ShILLAAAYLEEE."

"Dot, please. Is this gentleman *truly* alarming? Is he truly a gentleman? Did you feel alarmed as you spoke to him? Do we need to get a pistol? Is he that sort of alarming?"

Delilah hung up her apron on the hook inside the door. Her husband had made sure everyone knew how to shoot, including Dot, even though she had not yet mastered the aiming part of shooting.

"Well, no. It's more about how he looks. But he's also a bit friendly. Polite, like."

"Alarming and friendly could conceivably describe Mr. Delacorte," Delilah pointed out.

As they both tacitly agreed this could also easily describe Dot, Angelique and Delilah carefully did not meet each other's eyes.

"Well, he's not the jolly sort of friendly, like Mr. Delacorte. But he said 'thank you' to me when I said I would need to go and fetch you for an interview.

And men don't usually say that to the people who open doors, do they? Especially the men who have engraved buttons on their waistcoats."

This was both inarguable and a poignant glimpse into the world as seen through the eyes of the former worst lady's maid in the world, current valued member of The Grand Palace on the Thames staff, even if she had dropped a tea tray yesterday because she'd seen a ladybird land on the flowers in the sitting room and wanted to wish on it before it flew away.

"And he's taller even than Mr. Pike."

Angelique and Delilah exchanged a swift glance. This marked the third time they'd heard Dot use her nemesis, the gray-eyed, hard-jawed, vast-shouldered Mr. Pike, as a unit of measurement. And while "He's tall enough to reach the sconces, like Mr. Pike," could conceivably be excused as a fair way to describe a guest, idly commenting that the fire screen was only half as wide as Mr. Pike's shoulders (as she had done yesterday) worrisomely suggested her brain was so brimful of Mr. Pike that he would now be sloshing over onto everything she saw.

"And the gentleman's expression is very—" Angelique and Delilah took involuntary backward lunges when Dot glowered as blackly as the little gargoyles that lined the roof of The Grand Palace on the Thames. "He stands very straight, like Captain Hardy. And he has a skinny white scar right here." Dot touched her eyebrow. "I think I would say that he's the sort of man you would turn to stare at on the street because he doesn't look at all like anybody else."

The beloved bodies of their own husbands bore the marks of battles fought before they'd found their way to The Grand Palace on the Thames. And that ramrod posture was often a giveaway of a military man—as was (possibly) the glower and the "thank you." Taken together, they suggested a man who had achieved some stature and wealth—hence, the engraved buttons—and had acquired manners but had not been raised a gentleman.

Dot was a savant when it came to noticing such things, and Delilah and Angelique indeed liked to be prepared before they ventured downstairs to confront someone who could either become a cherished fixture in their lives or someone who would need to be forcibly removed by the British army. The latter had happened only once before, however, and they liked to think that surely, like a lightning strike, it couldn't happen to them again.

Still, it never hurt to be too prepared.

"And the lady with him looks as though she wants to be anywhere else and with anyone else," Dot concluded.

They stared at Dot.

And then Angelique pulled in a long, long breath, which Delilah knew from experience was the sound of her patience unraveling.

"The lady seems to be a new character in this narrative, Dot," Delilah suggested carefully.

"Well, she looks like a lady, only a bit . . ." Dot

leaned toward them and whispered, ". . . worse for wear."

Delilah and Angelique exchanged glances. This story was really beginning to interest them.

"She's wearing one of the finest ball gowns I've ever seen—gold silk with gauze over it. Very dear or I'll eat my cap. And it looks as though she's slept in it."

Dot would know what a slept-in ball gown looked like, too. As a former lady's maid, she'd tended to foxed women who collapsed drunkenly straight into bed after balls.

Angelique exchanged a glance with Delilah.

"Dot, you're certain she's a *lady* lady? You do recall the man and woman whom we were forced to send away the other day . . ."

Pink bloomed in Dot's cheeks. She'd been forced to describe those two to Angelique and Delilah in a single, scandalized, whispered sentence: "They are both giggling, and he's got hold of her left bottom and hasn't let go since they arrived."

The Grand Palace on the Thames's previous unruly incarnation still haunted the sign outside in the form of the ghostly outline of the word "rogues," and every now and then someone appeared at the door, bearing a yellowed menu of prurient services such as the Vicar's Wheelbarrow or the Archbishop's Piccolo, and would be sent away, dejected, the admonishment "read the sign!" ringing in their ears.

"Oh, no. This one is a lady, just like you and Mrs. Durand," Dot said with conviction. "Just . . ."

"Bedraggled?" Angelique suggested.

"Yes. Draggled," Dot agreed confidently.

Dot did indeed know at almost a glance her ladies from her not-ladies. They were convinced she was correct.

"Did you happen to get this gentleman's name, as well as his coat, Dot?" Delilah asked.

"His name is something to do with a wall, I think, which fits, because he's a bit like a wall, only human. And he said he would keep his coat, as he was going right back out again."

Delilah gasped as realization settled in. "Oh, good heavens. Could it be Colonel Brightwall?"

It certainly sounded like him. He'd been away from London on diplomatic duty in Spain since the end of the war.

"Wasn't his wife arrested for allegedly stealing Lucien's father's carriage?" Angelique whispered. "It was in the newspaper."

Dot gasped theatrically and clapped her hands over her mouth. Aghast and thrilled.

"Well. Perhaps we should be careful what we wish for," Delilah said brightly.

They went down to meet their exciting new guests.

Chapter Three

❦

COLONEL MAGNUS Brightwall—for it was, indeed, he—and his wife, Alexandra, sat side by side, but a significant span of settee remained visible between them. Their thighs seemed in no danger of touching, even if one of them exhaled, or should Colonel Brightwall take a notion to sprawl. He didn't look like a man who had ever taken that notion in his life. Dot was right about his posture.

Lavender arced beneath Alexandra's red-rimmed eyes. Her gold ball gown was crushed and rumpled and her bright hair had slumped to the nape of her neck. She was both "draggled" and beautiful, by anyone's definition.

Delilah and Angelique liked her immediately. Alexandra's face lit when she saw them, as if she recognized friends, and they saw in her at once a kindred spirit, someone who had been raised gently and now found herself married to the last man on earth she'd ever expected to marry, a man who was astonishing in some way.

"It is such a pleasure to make your acquaintance, Mrs. Hardy and Mrs. Durand, but I'm distressed you are compelled to meet me when I'm clearly not at my best. Perhaps you can tell I've had a rather eventful evening." She smiled valiantly.

"Dot will be here soon with tea," Delilah assured her. "And we'll have you in a room as soon as possible."

Angelique nodded her agreement. As proprietresses of The Grand Palace on the Thames from the beginning, Delilah and Angelique were so often of one mind now they had developed a sort of shared, silent language. They were both usually comfortable speaking on each other's behalf.

As for Colonel Brightwall . . . well, "liking" was beside the point when it came to someone who was a revered English institution. One did not like or dislike the London Bridge, for instance. Perhaps they would come to know him; such men, when exposed to things like Mr. Delacorte and the sitting room or irresistibly attractive guests, had proved to be human, after all.

But quite apart from his imposing presence, they found Colonel Brightwall had that otherness they had learned often characterized Great Men: a weighty reserve combined with an unsettling intensity born of seeing and accomplishing things no other human ever had, or ever could. He had legendarily saved the life of General Blackmore, now the Duke of Valkirk, who had once been their guest, and in so doing had nearly lost his own.

And he was polite. Just as Dot had said.

But when he'd politely introduced his wife, he hadn't looked at her.

Nor had she looked at him.

They in fact appeared to be studiously avoiding each other's gaze.

But Mrs. Brightwall didn't seem the least frightened or cowed. Her posture was erect; she held her head high. She was clearly well-bred. But both the Brightwalls seemed distracted and darkly absorbed. This, and a certain palpable simmering tension, were the only things suggesting the two of them were linked at all.

Perhaps it had to do with whatever nonsense had allegedly happened the previous evening. The bit with a stolen carriage.

But Delilah would wager that this was not a happy marriage.

Had it ever been? They had been apart for five years.

A cold, superstitious little wind whistled through her soul. She immediately desperately wanted to feel Tristan's familiar, beloved rough palm against hers, and to twine her fingers through his. They were so happy now. But life was long. She felt she didn't want to bring an unhappy marriage into their house any more than she wanted to bring the plague in, and she knew this was neither completely rational nor compassionate.

Dot had assessed this correctly, too. Delilah kept a mental list of Dot's unique talents, just in case someday some exasperated person wanted to know why Delilah and Angelique kept Dot. She was also conscientious, loyal, kind to a fault, and in some ways surprisingly pragmatic.

"The Grand Palace on the Thames was recommended to me by the Duke of Valkirk," he told them. "And I of course am acquainted with your husband, Captain Hardy, a fine man, indeed."

"That is very kind of you to say, sir, and I, of course, concur," Delilah said pleasantly.

"I'm given to understand yours is a very exclusive establishment, and an interview is required to determine whether we are suitable for admission."

Was she imagining the challenging—even somewhat roguish—glint in Colonel Brightwall's eyes?

Angelique cleared her throat. "The Duke of Valkirk's is of course an unimpeachable reference, and we are so pleased that we were able to make him comfortable for the duration of his stay. We are particularly gratified that he met his wonderful wife here. And yet I hope you know no reference at all is required, Colonel Brightwall. We are delighted for you and Mrs. Brightwall to stay with us. You honor us with your presence."

He nodded, graciously.

Mrs. Brightwall appeared to be studying the flowers in the vase on the mantel. It was anyone's guess whether she was actually listening.

"We feel you should know that guests from many different walks of life stay with us—we find this enriching and interesting. We also have a list of rules we cannot waive for any guests. We like to be certain they feel comfortable abiding by them before we formalize our arrangement. For we enforce them scrupulously."

Angelique delivered this information with a gently ingratiating smile.

They had nearly evicted the Duke of Valkirk for rudeness to another guest. She wondered if Valkirk had mentioned this. They would do it again if they had to.

If the notion that he would not be exempt from rules amazed Brightwall, not an eyebrow flicker betrayed it.

He did smile, faintly. "I cannot wait to see them."

Delilah obligingly placed the little cards upon which the rules were printed into the Brightwalls' hands, and they bent their heads to read.

All guests will eat dinner together at least four times per week.

All guests must gather in the drawing room after dinner for at least an hour at least four times per week. We feel it fosters a sense of friendship and the warm, familial, congenial atmosphere we strive to create here at The Grand Palace on the Thames.

All guests should be quietly respectful and courteous of other guests at all times, though spirited discourse is welcome.

Guests may entertain other guests in the drawing room.

Curfew is at 11:00 p.m. The front door will be securely locked then. You will need to wait until morning to be admitted if you miss curfew.

If the proprietresses collectively decide that a transgression or series of transgressions warrants your eviction from The Grand Palace on the Thames, you will find your belongings neatly packed and placed near the front door. You will not be refunded the balance of your rent.

Gentlemen may smoke in the Smoking Room only.

A little silence elapsed. From a distance, faintly, came the clink of the tea tray traveling up from the kitchen with Dot. Delilah and Angelique had learned to pitch their ears for it. To the end of their days their hearts would begin to hammer at that sound, in anticipation of a crash.

"A warm, familial atmosphere," Colonel Brightwall quoted slowly from the card. With just a frisson of irony.

He hadn't yet lifted his head from the card. He seemed to be pondering it.

Mrs. Brightwall looked up then, her expression inscrutable.

"Indeed," Angelique said brightly. "Our guests seem to relish it."

He finally lowered the card.

Delilah and Angelique smiled at him encouragingly.

"Yes. We will abide by these rules," he said shortly.

He bothered to neither look at nor consult his wife.

Whereupon Alexandra finally shot him a

glance fleeting in duration, but which seemed capable of leaving a bleeding puncture wound.

Angelique and Delilah were both tempted to give him a little kick, too.

"I'm given to understand the suites are comprised of two rooms," Brightwall said.

Delilah stopped herself from glancing at Mrs. Brightwall. "They are."

"Thank you, Mrs. Durand and Mrs. Hardy," Alexandra said. "These rules are wonderfully civilized. Yes, I can abide by them."

Brightwall's jaw tensed slightly.

"We're glad you agree, Mrs. Brightwall. Mr. Benjamin Pike will show the two of you to your suite, if you'd like to see it now. We'll have Dot bring the tea up to you."

Alexandra stood, followed, more slowly, by her towering husband. He was momentarily very still, as if suppressing a twinge of pain.

And suddenly both Angelique's and Delilah's hearts went out to them.

Tea could solve nearly every ill, but they didn't think it was going to do much to fix whatever was ailing the Brightwalls.

Perhaps spirited discourse would. One could hope.

THE SUITE TO which the boardinghouse's strapping young footman brought them was located in what their proprietresses referred to as the annex. Blue velvet curtains poured to the floor from tall windows, through which the very tops of the spires of ships were visible. A long blue settee presided over the center of the room, and comfortable chairs surrounded two little tables—one for dining, one for games. On the mantel a decanter of what appeared to be brandy glowed in the reflected light of the leaping fire.

All in all, Alexandra conceded it was a handsome room.

But why the devil were they here?

"Magnus, if I may ask a question?"

Magnus turned to her coolly, eyebrows upraised, as though she were a footman who had made an inquiry.

"This seems like a lovely place. The Grand Palace on the Thames . . ."

"That strikes me as more of a comment than a question."

She clenched her teeth against a spurt of anger. "May I ask why we have we come here, instead of to the town house on St. James Square?"

Which is where she had lived since shortly after their wedding.

He'd owned it for years.

He absently peeled a glove from his hand as he glanced around the room, taking inventory of their furnishings.

"I am selling the town house." He stuffed his gloves into his coat pocket.

She went airless.

Her heart contracted into an icy knot.

"But . . . but . . . it's my home. That is . . . it's . . . it's where I live."

He settled upon her the whole of his attention then. It still required an inward adjustment whenever he did that. That first connection with his eyes had always been a bit like staring into the sun.

"The town house is mine to do with as I please."

And then he merely waited, as a cat would wait to see what a mouse would do next.

His expression revealed to her nothing.

Panic welled in her chest, shortening her breath.

"But . . . the . . . the furnishings . . . the . . . the canopy bed . . ."

Why on earth would she mention the canopy bed specifically? Except that it was pretty and she loved it and she had carefully chosen it. Never once had she abused her allowance.

And she had slept alone in it for nigh on five years.

"The money used to purchase the furnishings was mine," he explained with what felt like hateful patience. "Therefore the contents of the house also belong to me."

She was inwardly quaking now; it was the feel, she thought, of the strands of her soul giving way, one by one.

"So I expect my clothes belong to you, too. Since your money purchased them." Her voice was deceptively calm.

"If you like, yes."

They stared at each other.

His face was cold, implacable as stone.

Her breath was a roar in her ears now.

She could almost hear a "plink" as the last fiber holding her being together finally snapped.

She clawed off one glove with violently shaking hands. "Take this, then." She flung it at him. She had the satisfaction of seeing him blink. "Since it's yours."

She stripped off the other and whipped it at him. "Take this one, too."

"Alexa—"

"And this." She kicked off a slipper and punted it. It sailed toward him.

He dodged nimbly.

She kicked off the other, sending him dodging in the other direction.

Then she scrabbled at the laces on the back of her ball gown.

She roughly yanked it off over her head and whipped the dress at him. *"TAKE IT!* Since it is yours, too. Since *nothing* is mine. Not my skin, my clothes, not my life, not the air I breathe. Nothing in this world is mine. It's all yours. You bought it. So take it. Do what you want! Take it all. Take it, *take*—"

She ducked and reflexively threw her hands up over her head when he lunged toward her with shocking speed.

Suddenly all was enveloping warmth and soft darkness.

She staggered backward. Somehow the backs of her knees met the settee.

She sank down onto it, shivering, and dropped

her face into her hands. Half naked but engulfed by her husband's greatcoat. He'd whipped it off and surrounded her with it.

She could feel him gently adjusting it, tucking it around her shoulders.

She submitted to being tended to by her tormentor.

And then he must have stepped away.

The ensuing silence seemed to ring interminably.

She could hear her own breath, shuddering in and out into her palms. *This must be what it feels like to be mad. I've gone mad*, she thought. How horrifying. How humiliating.

How *liberating*.

It was all that was left to her. She had no weapons, no resources at all of her own. And more's the pity, it simply wasn't in her to just surrender. Her downfall would clearly be messy and protracted.

What was he doing now, in this silence?

Staring at her in horror?

After what seemed an endless amount of time, she heard the unmistakable sound of the bung being pulled from the little decanter.

Then the gurgle of brandy into a glass.

"I don't want brandy," she said into her hands.

"I see."

He paused.

"Whiskey, then?"

This was almost funny. She had never forgotten that about him: the flashes of dry, incisive, irreverent humor. It took one by surprise. She had once found it as unexpected and delightful as a sudden brisk breeze in a closed room.

"I don't need to be *medicated*."

"Fair enough," he said almost equably. "But I don't suppose there's any dishonor in numbing the shock of being reminded you have a husband."

And what a husband. An imperious, unyielding bastard of a husband.

"Or in taking the edge off of spending a night in less than hospitable accommodations. Despite the clear benefit of the fact that a number of children named Alexandra will likely be picking pockets in St. Giles in the near future."

This was sounding perilously close to conciliatory.

"*Dishonor.*" The word was muffled by her hands. "Of course. My greatest concern at the moment."

But then, for Brightwall, she thought cynically, honor was never a small concern. And why should it be? He was an edifice. An institution. He had earned every bit of it.

He'd protected her dignity and modesty immediately with his coat. Likely he'd suspected she could hardly sustain more regret.

But then, wasn't he renowned for always knowing what to do? For thinking and acting quickly?

Another silence stretched.

It was blessedly, blessedly quiet here at The Grand Palace on the Thames, she would give it that.

She was loath to look up from the safe darkness of her own palms.

"Inside coat pocket," he informed her.

She sighed heavily and reached into his large coat. Her searching fingers brushed over a little collection of the kinds of homely things men carried about: something made of stiff paper, perhaps a theater ticket, a tiny box that might have been for snuff, or perhaps a flint and steel—did he take snuff? Surely not. A few shilling coins.

How terribly odd and sad it seemed that she didn't know the kinds of things her husband tucked into his coat pockets.

It smelled of tobacco and woodsmoke, a hint of cloves, and perhaps a touch of horse. She didn't know why all of this together should be comforting. Somehow it was.

Her hand emerged holding a handsome little silver flask. His initials were engraved upon it in fancy curlicues. It was the sort of thing men were given as a gift.

She pulled the bung, took a breath as though she were about to wade into freezing water, and recklessly took her first-ever gulp of whiskey.

She immediately coughed and spluttered.

Dear God. She might as well have poured fire down her throat.

Eyes streaming, she stared him, half in amazement, half in betrayal.

She'd had *no* idea about whiskey.

The corner of his mouth twitched upward. "It gets better in a moment."

Even as he said that, a blessed warmth was

stealing through her solar plexus, and into her veins, it seemed, flowing like satin over the raw, jagged edges of her nerves.

"Oh, I understand whiskey now," she breathed.

His smile was fleeting, but real.

And so they sat together quietly.

She didn't apologize for throwing things.

He didn't apologize for being the icy, imperious bastard who had inspired her to throw things.

She supposed they tacitly agreed they were both entitled to be somewhat awful, given the circumstances.

A weighted detente of some sort seemed to settle. She tucked the whiskey back into his pocket.

Then again, over the course of his life, he'd been shot at by bullets and cannonballs, a few of which famously had not missed. A hurled slipper or dress was child's play. If anything ever truly shook him, it was impossible to tell. Impassivity seemed to be his special skill. Revealing vulnerabilities could get one killed in battle, she supposed. Perhaps it went bone deep. Perhaps, despite his flashes of humor, he was merely an iceberg in Weston-cut clothes.

After all, a man had to be assumed invincible if he wanted to get men to follow him into battle and do all that fighting.

This was what she told herself, anyhow.

It was easier to believe this.

Because she sometimes awoke from fitful dreams of turning around that fateful night in that twilit garden, to find him standing there. A silent witness to her perfidy.

He'd been utterly motionless. His face white and stunned as if he had just taken a cannonball to the gut.

Chapter Four

⤷⤶⤷

"*W*HY DO you have whiskey so readily to hand?" she wondered, almost conversationally, into the elongating silence. "In case you need to subdue hysterical women? Or is it for fortifying *yourself* against hysterical women?"

"For pain," he said shortly. Absently. His expression was thoughtful. But he wasn't blinking.

She leveled a searching gaze at him. Damn it all. Despite everything, she didn't like the notion of him being in pain.

"So in other words, yes to both," he added, a second later. With a flickering ghost of a smile.

She eyed him cautiously. Though she did indeed find this rather blackly funny, she was disinclined to reward him with anything like a laugh. It seemed inadvisable to betray any sort of weakness to this man. To relent in any way. Though she wasn't precisely entitled to it, she had her pride, too.

"Alexandra . . ." He paused, seeming to consider what he was about to ask. This hesitance struck her as unusual; she'd known him as a man who bluntly came out with things. "Are you afraid of me?"

She went still. The question surprised her.

She regarded him warily.

How to answer?

Five hours after they had spoken their marriage vows, two hours after she had broken those vows in a way she had neither planned nor anticipated, he had demonstrated to her why his enemies found him terrifying. He'd done it without raising his voice.

Before that time, he had never been anything other than solicitous and gentle with her.

The clearheaded, ruthless, cold efficiency with which he had outlined the nonnegotiable terms of her fate—and therefore, his fate—as a consequence of her actions had shocked her, then numbed her, then settled on her soul like a killing frost. Until her heart felt like a rattling black husk in her chest.

It was how it had felt ever since.

That was, until today. Her heart had gone through a lot of things today.

She had trembled throughout that whole horrible conversation that night. But she hadn't groveled or lied or sobbed or hidden her face.

She had never planned to wrong him.

But she uncontrovertibly had.

Her own stubborn, inconvenient integrity refused to allow her to do anything like dodge away from the truth, or attempt to rationalize the choice she'd made. As far as he was concerned, she'd sealed her own fate that night.

"Why do you ask?" she finally asked.

She saw his features darken and tighten as if her words had entered him like a dart.

It was a long moment before he spoke.

"I would never harm you." He sounded tired. He landed tautly on "never."

She merely nodded, humoring him. Men said a lot of things they didn't mean.

His eyebrows dove. "Has any other man ever harmed you?"

She stared at him, stunned. Her cheeks went warm.

Any other man. She was unprepared for the almost dispassionate acknowledgment that in the five years they'd lived apart she might have taken a lover or two, any one of whom might have knocked her around a bit. For his apparently cold acceptance of their very unorthodox, yet not uncommon among the aristocracy for all of that, arrangement.

Doubtless he'd had lovers in the interim. He was a man.

She felt this possibility now like a weight on her chest.

It had been so easy not to think about it when she was occupied. Which is why she'd made certain she was always occupied.

Which was part of how she'd ended up in a Newgate cell. Trying so very hard to remain occupied.

"No," she answered quietly. "No other men have harmed me." She wasn't going to expound. It was true. She paused. "What would you do if

they had?" She made the question sound casual.
It emerged slightly defiant.

She found she was genuinely curious.

He studied her. But the faint smile lifting the
corners of his mouth did not light his eyes, and it
made the little hairs prickle at the back of her neck.

"Make them rue the day they were born," he
explained with great patience.

Long before she'd ever met him, her father
had told her an anecdote about Colonel Brightwall: the mail coach upon which he'd been traveling one night had been waylaid by a pair of
highwaymen, who had forced the passengers to
disembark at musket point. Brightwall had at
once put himself between the other gentlemen
and the two lady passengers. Quick as a snake
he'd lashed out and snatched the musket from
the grasp of the nearest robber and swung it like
a cricket bat at the man's skull. The man had
gone down like a ninepin. Then Brightwall had
pivoted and rammed the musket stock into the
other robber's chest, sending the man's shot—
aimed right at Brightwall—well wide of the
mark. That rogue had crumpled, too. Over in
seconds, the whole thing. As efficient as if he'd
practiced doing all of that at Manton's.

"Why waste good gunpowder?" he'd allegedly
remarked absently as he worked with the other
gentleman passengers to tie them up. He hadn't
even reached for his pistol.

They'd left the robbers bound hand and foot on
the side of the road and carried on their journey

within minutes. Brightwall had taken the robbers' weapons. He still owned them.

It was what he was built for: inspiring *rue* in anyone who dared cross him.

"So it's just the general . . . fact of me." He swept a hand vaguely about his vast person. "That made you flinch away, as one might from any alarming thing. A dragon, for instance."

She'd always known him to be economical with words. But she recalled how now and again out came something so intriguingly, delightfully vivid it had made her restless to know the other thoughts that milled about in his mind, unspoken.

"The sudden appearance of a dragon *would* be alarming," she agreed politely.

And for a breathtaking, vanishing instant, shared amusement arced between them.

They had liked each other, once. Though they'd known each other for so short a time before they wed.

Of course, it had become all too clear they hadn't truly known each other at all.

Even now she could probably charm him.

To what end? He would soon resent her for it. For it would remind him of what a fool he'd been to be charmed once before, and this had led to what he surely now considered the one great folly of his brilliant, storied life: marrying her.

Well. He had bought her.

Or her father had sold her.

However one preferred to look at it.

Caveat emptor, Colonel Brightwall.

Did he think the notion she *might* genuinely fear him outlandish? Had he never stood in front of a mirror?

And then she had it: likely it was simply a matter of honor for him. For if she'd been a man, he might have killed her with pistols at dawn or some such for what she'd done five years ago. The rules were different for women.

And what did a military man understand better than rules?

Her father, Lord Bellamy, was a widower who loved to entertain, and when he held house parties, it was Alexandra's habit to circulate through the gathered guests like a breeze, making certain everyone felt comfortable and welcome and seen. The night of the reception in honor of Colonel Brightwall, sweet, shy Mary Hotchkiss had been sitting alone near the hearth, pushing her sliding-down spectacles back up her nose at intervals and trying to disappear into the wallpaper, valiantly pretending she was not suffering. Alexandra had gone to sit with her. Soon she had Mary laughing, and one by one guests were drawn to their effervescence, until they were the center of a small, merry crowd.

Whereupon Alexandra melted away to the arched window that looked out over the back garden of the house they might soon lose forever thanks to her father's bad luck with investments, and admired Mary's face shining amidst her new friends. Her own world was rife with concerns. She knew life to be both beautiful and pocked with injustices and hurts. But there was such relief to be had in making it all just a bit easier for someone else, if only for a moment or two.

"You're a kind person, Miss Bellamy."

With a start she turned to discover Colonel Brightwall leaning against the wall near her.

She studied him. Hanging in the British Museum was a painting of Brightwall atop a rearing, wild-eyed horse, his leonine head wreathed in the smoke of battle. Defeated enemies were heaped all around like cordwood. She'd thought it an exaggeration bordering on parody. She was not so sure now.

He looked exactly like the sort of man who would swing a musket at the skull of a highwayman.

His entrance into the party tonight had precipitated a hush. Jaded adults with glittering pedigrees craned their heads, staring mutely up at him like bashful children. The air was practically misted with awe.

Brightwall was clearly accustomed to this. Her proud father had led him about the gathering. The colonel apportioned to each introduced guest a few gruffly gracious words and brisk nods of thanks for what were clearly compliments. He clasped both hands behind him when he listened. His bearing recalled the mast of a ship. He left in his wake eased postures and glowing faces, as though he'd bestowed benedictions.

He moved, and occupied space, with utter self-possession. There wasn't a single tentative thing about him. Alexandra found him thoroughly intimidating.

Another person might have said "you are kind" as a matter of rote, as one might say "please" or "thank you." But he'd said this almost gravely. As though he was imparting something significant he felt she should know.

She soon learned that almost nothing he said sounded casual.

She was not a shy person. But what she saw in his eyes then made her cheeks warm. She found she could think of nothing to say, which was a rare occurrence, indeed.

"Thank you, sir," she said politely, finally. "I do hope you are enjoying your evening."

Worrisomely, he seemed to actually be contemplating whether he was.

"Mr. Perriman went on at great length to me about pigeons and I fear I may have merely stared at him with my brows drawn together." He paused, pensively. "I couldn't think of a single thing to say. I seem to be struggling a bit to regain a knack for light conversation."

She was amused speechless at the thought of him glowering while Mr. Perriman nattered on about pigeons.

He turned to her, his eyes creased with rueful amusement.

All at once she felt peculiarly light, as if she'd stumbled across something unexpectedly magical. A gemstone embedded in a rock.

"If it helps at all, Colonel, Mr. Perriman never

seems to require a response. Just an audience. I've found that nodding along and interjecting an occasional 'ah' or 'you don't say' usually suffices. And then a polite excuse to retreat when the opportunity arises. If it happens again, touch your ear and I'll rescue you."

Eyes glinting, he nodded as somberly as if she were Aristotle imparting wisdom.

He appeared to be looking for someone as he watched the milling gathering.

And then her father saw him, and Brightwall straightened alertly.

"When I was stationed in Spain, a huge striped cat by the name of Oliver lived in our camp," he said suddenly.

"A cat?" She was startled and enchanted by this non sequitur.

He nodded. "During a lull in action, my subaltern took a notion to sew a wee uniform coat for him and stuff him into it. You've never seen a more confused, resigned expression on an animal. We all had a laugh at the poor beast. And that"—he turned to her with a roguish, conspiratorial smile that transformed his face so utterly it made her breath hitch—"is a bit how I feel walking about in civilian clothes at a house party instead of on a battlefield in my uniform."

And off he'd gone with her father.

But she remembered this conversation now because Magnus was the first person to ever outright tell her she was kind, as though he saw this as a precious and rare quality.

She could not recall the last time she'd extended any charity to herself, or thought of herself as possessing a redeeming virtue. The last five years her life had been strung together by sleep and diversions designed to keep her from dwelling on a thing she had done which could not be undone.

And even though her pride warred with her instinct to soothe him, this was simply how she was made: she could not seem to help caring.

Gently, she said, "If I flinched, Magnus, it was less to do with you than with how . . . everything during my visit to . . ." She closed her eyes. *Visit?* It wasn't as though she'd left an engraved calling card there. She cleared her throat. "Everything at Newgate made me flinch and I suppose I've acquired a sort of flinching reflex. I'm certain it will pass."

She met his eyes bravely. It was an appalling thing to admit to her war hero husband. But now it, too, was part of her personal history. Which had been spotless for most of her life and then had taken an abrupt turn into the catastrophic, where it seemed to have settled in comfortably.

Would a day come when she could blithely say at a dinner party, "This blancmange is such a nice change from prison food!" and everyone would laugh and laugh over the lark of it all?

Perhaps it would even be the sort of thing considered spirited discourse in the sitting room here at The Grand Palace on the Thames.

Magnus took this in, and his fingers twitched reflexively on the arms of the chair, as if he was flinching away from all those things, too. Or itched to combat them.

He deliberately flattened his hand and patted it once, thoughtfully, on the arm of the chair.

Finally he rose, somewhat stiffly, and surprised her by pacing slowly to the crumpled dress on the floor and lifting it gently. It looked like so much bright scraps in his big hands. He gazed down at it, his expression bemused and almost weary in a way that sliced right through her.

She wondered if he was thinking: *In another life, in other circumstances, I might know this dress, and all my wife's clothes.*

Her throat suddenly felt thick.

"Please do not let it trouble you any further," she urged softly.

He met her eyes again and held them. His did not precisely soften, but with a short nod he indicated he was apparently satisfied that she was telling the truth.

"I expect you're exhausted." His voice was gruff. "And hungry."

The moment he said it she fully realized she was almost too weary to even agree. As if she could melt into the settee, become one with it, vanish from existence.

The *bliss* of that notion this moment.

"And perhaps you'd like a bath, as well," he added.

Her face must have registered surprise, even wariness, because a screen of cynicism moved across his eyes.

"To be clear: you are safe with me, Alexandra. And from me."

In other words: not even the prospect of her nude in a bath would tempt him to touch her.

Fair enough.

"Yes," she said quietly. "I should like to sleep. And eat. And I would like a bath."

Baths were not included with room and board at The Grand Palace on the Thames, their charming and genteel proprietresses had delicately informed them. There would be an additional cost.

And so of course, that meant the bath was his, too. She was wildly, wildly tempted to say it. Why not continue to court catastrophe? What did she have to lose? Perhaps with enough practice she could field catastrophe with the panache of Brightwall swinging a musket at a highwayman.

He draped her dress on the back of the settee as gently as if it was a living thing. "I'll speak to the proprietresses about preparing one for you. And a meal."

He turned toward the door, then paused with his hand on the knob, and turned back to her. "We'll talk when you've rested."

It sounded like a warning.

Chapter Five

ALEXANDRA CATAPULTED awake, her heart pounding, limbs flailing.

Oh no! She'd fallen asleep! Her shoes! Bunty would take her shoes!

Memories clattered into place like falling dominoes: A carriage ride. Prison. And the last one: Brightwall.

Whereupon her heart gave a hard, sharp lurch. Not unlike an allegedly stolen carriage being pulled to an abrupt halt.

She gulped in steadying breaths and in came sweet, clean air, scented with hints of blossoms and linseed oil lovingly applied to furniture. She exhaled in relief.

Not her own bedroom, with its canopy bed. She was now in a room at a boardinghouse improbably named The Grand Palace on the Thames.

Thank God.

Albeit in a suite she would apparently be compelled to share with her erstwhile husband.

She had clearly gotten as far as the bed, but she didn't remember anything that had happened between that moment and this one. She must have toppled into a black and dreamless sleep straightaway.

She was still buried beneath her estranged husband's wool coat and . . . what was this?

Her fingers skimmed another layer she seemed to have acquired. A pink knitted coverlet.

She didn't recall pulling it over herself.

She tentatively gathered a handful of its dense, soft weight. She knew it represented hours of careful feminine labor and it smelled faintly of lavender. Which reminded her of her mother, who had died when she was thirteen years old.

And something about that coverlet made her feel more cherished than she had in longer than she could remember.

Her eyes began to sting. She gave her head a rough, admonishing shake.

She was not a child anymore. She was just tired.

Another blessing to count: her mother would never know she'd shared the family's blood-stain removal receipts with a husband stabber at Newgate.

She could think of no reason yet to leave this almost outlandishly comfortable bed. She wasn't certain how long she'd been asleep, but neither her meal nor her bath had yet arrived, so she propped herself up on the bosomy soft pillows and had a look around the room.

Despite the little thundercloud of dread hovering on the horizon, dawning pleasure was difficult to suppress. Everything about the room seemed designed to soothe and comfort.

Alongside the bed, a rag rug braided in soft shades of pink and gray and green invited her toes to test it.

Neatly lined right in the middle of it were the satin slippers she'd kicked at her husband.

The gloves she'd peeled off and flung at him rested on the corner of a little writing desk, next to a vase from which sprang a tiny riot of wildflowers.

Most of the men she knew would never have dreamed of picking a woman's shoes up off the floor, let alone ones she'd hurled at them. A woman's shoes on the floor would have, in fact, been all but invisible to a man raised with servants.

She was tempted to ascribe significance to the neatly arrayed slippers.

It was an odd sensation, to know he must have seen her sleeping. She'd never spent a single night alone with him.

Feeling only a trifle guilty, she slipped her hands into his coat pockets again, and inspected the artifacts she found in there.

A folded ticket, in Spanish—he'd gone to an opera in Spain. This, for some reason, surprised her. He'd lived a whole life in Spain for the past nearly five years, just as she'd lived her life in London, and apparently this included amusements. And why shouldn't it? He didn't seem the sort who would have much patience with opera.

She thumbed open the tiny silver box, wondering if she would find lavender pastilles, or tobacco, or rolled cheroots.

Inside was a gleaming little scrap of pink satin.

She stared at it, frowning faintly. Puzzled.

And then her breath left her in a gust.

Goose bumps spangled her arms.

She touched it gently, remembering.

A week into the fateful house party, she'd risen very early, ruthlessly secured her bonnet with pins against a morning wind that was already bending the tops of trees, and took her sketchbook out deep in the grounds, near the gate where she met Paul for her chats at twilight, when he went home to his lodgings.

Paul Carson was her brother's tutor. They were in love. It was the perfect secret affair: forbidden and star-crossed but chaste and sensible, conducted primarily at twilight with the back garden gate between them. He lodged with their neighbor, and a small wooded area separated the properties. He was homesick for his family in Northumberland, her life felt threateningly shambolic, and though neither one of them had stated this in those terms, they had found in each other an oasis. They talked about poetry and mythology and birds and art. They both knew not a thing could or would come from their romance, in large part because he was nearly destitute, and would be leaving for a teaching position in Africa soon. Neither one of them made a fuss about this, but it was a poignant undertone in all their conversations.

She loved the way Paul looked at her with his soulful dark eyes. He was slim and sensitive; his profile would not look amiss etched on a coin. He'd touched her hand only once; this was the limit of the physical affection he dared express. She supposed she was lucky he was so thoroughly a gentleman, but then, she had never been drawn to rakish types. They struck her as exhausting, and her life was complicated enough as it was.

Meanwhile, a few other handsome, titled young men had been orbiting her with caution-tempered ardor, as her depleted dowry and unruly family were as well-known as her charms. She expected she would eventually marry one of them, but on this particular morning that day seemed remote and she'd rather hoped it was. She could not yet imagine falling in love with someone else.

Her favorite part of their vast garden was nearest the little gate; it was semi-wild, and growing wilder and shaggier now that they could only afford an occasional gardener. The signs of decay made her increasingly nervous.

She'd just paused to swiftly sketch a robin posing charmingly high up on the fine twigs of a poplar when the red crayon she was gripping slipped her grip. She scrabbled to catch it, but it fell and promptly rolled into the ivy beneath a wild and tangly cluster of shrubs and twiggy trees.

"Blast," she muttered. Money for things like little luxuries like pastel crayons was increasingly scarce, and the red was so useful.

She ventured into the thicket to fish around in the ivy. She was vaguely aware that her bonnet ribbons had come undone; they softly lashed her face and danced about her head in the stiff wind as she futilely scrabbled in the ivy, dodging the grabby twigs of the trees.

Conceding defeat, she finally stood. And that's when she discovered the wind had whipped her bonnet ribbons up into the twiggy branches of a young tree, where they were almost picturesquely entwined.

She stepped backward in an attempt to tug free of it.

And somehow managed to pull the ribbon into knots.

And since her bonnet was firmly pinned to her head, she was essentially snared in the bushes like a hare.

It was a patently ridiculous and entirely novel predicament.

"Well, bloody hell," she said aloud. It marked perhaps the second time in her life she'd used those words.

She froze at the sound of a footfall crunching.

Colonel Brightwall was standing at the edge of the ivy. Hands clasped behind his back. Hatless, the wind whipping his hair about.

"Colonel Brightwall," she managed faintly. "Good morning."

He bowed. "Good morning, Miss Bellamy. I was just enjoying a stroll about your grounds. My apologies if I'm intruding upon your morning ritual of cursing in the shrubbery."

Judging by the temperature in her cheeks, she was as scarlet as the crayon she'd lost.

"Oh my goodness . . . I *deeply* regret—I am so terribly sorry you were compelled to hear me . . ."

"As well you should be. I'd so hoped to never again hear that kind of language outside of a battlefield."

His expression was pure, grave disapproval.

His eyes were positively brilliant with wicked, wicked amusement.

How peculiar to be trapped in a bush, equal parts mortified and pleased beyond all proportion to be teased by a famous colonel.

She smiled at him.

He craned his head. "It appears as though . . . are you . . . tethered to the bushes?"

He said this as if perhaps loath to insult her if this had been her goal all along.

"I'm . . ." She sighed heavily. "Well, yes. I suppose I am, after a fashion."

He took this in. "Do you . . . want to be?"

What a thoroughgoing rogue. She was hideously embarrassed and absolutely delighted.

She regarded him sternly and levelly for a silent beat or two.

"Do you think perhaps you're having a little *too* much fun with this, Colonel Brightwall?"

His shout of laughter was so warmly, unapologetically impudent she burst into laughter, too.

Then she sighed. "It's simple, really. I dropped my crayon and holder as I was sketching a pretty bird. It rolled into the shrubbery, so I went in to fetch it. I didn't realize that my bonnet ribbons had come loose until I stood up again and discovered they were snagged in the twigs, and when I pulled away, I realized they had tightened into knots, and . . ." She made a sweeping gesture at the result.

He'd nodded along with all of this. "Of course. A similar sequence of catastrophes led to our defeat at the Battle of Dos Montanas."

They smiled at each other again.

"Shall I have a look?"

"I should be obliged, sir."

And so into the shrubbery he waded.

"Good God. I knew trees could on occasion be traitorous fiends," he murmured, his big hands sliding over the ribbon as gently as though inspecting a bone for a break. "But I've never known them to take a hostage."

She laughed. "But they have us surrounded, Colonel," she breathed with great melodrama. "There's a whole battalion."

"Oh, they wouldn't dare try anything dastardly," he said distractedly. "My reputation for mercilessness precedes me."

She fell abruptly quiet, as this was true. *I heard Brightwall ordered deserters shot immediately*, her brother, Theo, had mentioned on a hush over dinner a few weeks ago. It was his misguided attempt to deflect a little of the well-deserved censure aimed his way. He'd been expelled from university.

Well, that's because you can't just go and casually leave the army during a war to drink and carouse with actresses on a whim, her father had said with bitter irony. *Unlike university. Except with university, they don't shoot you, more's the pity, they send you home to be a burden to your father.*

The colonel set to work.

He seemed inclined neither to flirt nor to fill up the silence with words, which is what most men would do when presented with a literally captive female audience.

Perhaps he knew his mere presence was profound enough to transcend the need for speech. A bit like a mountain.

Or maybe he just didn't know what to say to her.

He was no prettier in very close proximity. The sunlight and shadow filtering down through the leaves made him look like some ageless, majestic beast lying in wait in the underbrush. But drama and mystery, even a certain allure, lurked in the crags and hollows of his face. His hair was streaked in a half dozen subtle colors, from brown to sun-bleached gold, like a lion's mane, and dashed through here and there with threads of silver. His eyelashes were flaxen at the tips, like a little boy's. She found this incongruously rather sweet.

"I heard a story about you, Colonel Brightwall."

"Only one?" He sounded amused. He appeared to be struggling a bit with the knot.

"Something heroic to do with highwaymen. It involves you bashing them with a musket and tying them up."

He smiled slightly. "Are you suggesting that if I'd been required to *untie* them rather than tie them, I'd likely still be there on the side of that road to this day?"

"I would *never* imply such a thing," she vowed, with faux wounded sincerity. "Take all the time you need with my little satin ribbon."

It felt bold to tease him. She did it because she felt awe encroaching. Awe was a great inhibitor of conversation, and unlike Colonel Brightwall, she wasn't entirely comfortable with silences.

Thankfully, he did smile again. But he didn't take his eyes from the knot. "What if I told you that every heroic thing you've ever heard about me is both true and untrue?"

"I fear I would then be compelled to ask why you are speaking in riddles. Although I don't mind riddles, on the whole."

"What is perceived as heroism, Miss Bellamy, is often just some poor bloke doing their job."

"Come, Colonel. Surely even you have heroes."

She worried then that she'd been too bold, but he smiled at this, too, thankfully. "Oh, certainly I admire dozens of people for many reasons. I have the privilege of knowing a number of truly great men. But I've learned that the moment we decide someone is a Hero or a Scoundrel or a Boor or what have you—imagine all those words writ with capital letters, like labels—we've a tendency to go blind to qualities that might contradict our assumptions, which can often be a grave tactical error. I'm suspicious of pedestals, on the whole. They just beg to be knocked over. And I'm disinclined to judge."

Briefly she amused herself by imagining him crashing through a museum, swinging a musket at pedestals. But she was, in truth, enthralled at this peek into his mind. She'd heard it said that the few enormous, sometimes controversial, strategic risks he'd taken during the war—promoting talented men from the ranks, demoting other officers ahead of an important battle, for instance—had proved to be the best, and even obvious, choices when viewed after the fact. She knew from playing chess that strategy had its roots in an ability to critically assess every piece's position on the board.

She thought of her charming, loving father, who found it so exhilarating to take wild chances with finances he'd consigned his family to a life lived on a perilous seesaw of uncertainty, and who was in danger now of needing to sell the ancient, unentailed family home lest they face penury. Her older brother, Theo, who had a quick wit, a quick temper, a tender, easily wounded heart, and a reckless streak of hedonism that got him thrown out of university. Her younger sister, Elizabeth, who was recovering only slowly from a long illness from which she'd nearly died, and not doing it that noble way so beloved of novel writers. She was instead peevish, bored, resentful, and jealous of everyone else's good health. Alexandra didn't blame her at all, but keeping the peace often meant coddling her and keeping her own effervescence tamped.

That was her job in the family, ever since her

mother died. She restored peace. She was the smoother of feelings, the tonic for bitter arguments, the adroit manager of upheavals, the jollier out of dark moods. She was a confidante, a rescuer, a nurse, and a friend.

"It seems to me, however, that blindness to certain qualities might be beneficial to maintaining harmony among people." She ventured this gingerly. "Provided harmony is what's desired, of course."

Brightwall paused in his ribbon ministrations to regard her. "Oh, certainly," he said easily enough. "Perhaps. Particularly in families, I should imagine. But is that really blindness? Or is it forbearance?"

This seemed so startlingly close to the bone that she went abruptly silent.

"Well, it's love, I should think," she finally replied, somewhat awkwardly. "And loyalty."

His smile was enigmatic and faint, as if her answer surprised him not at all.

She was unsettled by his astuteness. But perhaps she only felt that way because her family was what she loved best, and was therefore her greatest vulnerability.

"This is all just to say that no mere man is worthy of worship," he concluded simply.

She wanted to return the conversation to its previous lightness. "Are any mere women worthy of worship?"

She met the dry look he cast her way with one of mischievous, utterly feigned innocence.

His little smile informed her he was far too wise to answer that question.

A silence fell again.

It occurred to her that he might be deliberately lingering over the ribbon. She wondered whether she might be the reason, if so. She recalled then that Brightwall's rooms overlooked this part of the garden.

In truth, it mattered little. Being in love with Paul meant she felt disinterested benevolence toward all other men, and that included Brightwall.

"It strikes me as a rather bruising responsibility, being a hero in the public eye. One could get to feeling as though he could never put a foot wrong. And I imagine it would be *crushing* if word got out that one isn't good at . . . well, everything." She tipped her head very subtly toward her knotted ribbon.

To her delight, he laughed.

She never would have guessed that this fortress of a man would be so easily able to laugh at himself. It had to do with his unnerving and absolute self-assurance, she suspected.

"I'm admittedly better with weapons than knots, Miss Bellamy. In my defense, the point of knots is to secure something one doesn't want to escape, and this one is performing its job exceptionally well. Perhaps what you need is a sea captain, instead."

"Sea captains are particularly good at knots?"

"Yes."

"We neglected to invite one to the party, alas."

"Mr. Perriman would likely have found him more stimulating company."

She laughed.

But all at once an epiphany swooped in. How disorienting it must be to step from the ceaseless clamor and tension and violence of war into a country house party teeming with pampered strangers. How did one pretend to care about pigeons after the brutal things he had witnessed and endured? The friends and compatriots he had lost?

She supposed anyone would stagger a bit to regain balance after laying down a heavy load. Even Brightwall the Beast.

Perhaps this accounted for the silences in their conversation.

And now his brow was furrowed over the puzzle of a pink ribbon.

An almost painful rush of sympathy swelled her heart.

"As your hostess, I hereby declare you entirely exempt from any expectation to amuse anyone for the duration of your visit. I would imagine that nearly everything seems trivial or even foolish in comparison to what you've recently experienced. A bit like a strange dream, I expect."

He went still, then lifted his eyes to hers. They were surprised and almost wary, as though she'd uncovered a secret. He was not a man who would tolerate gushing, she suspected.

He seemed to be considering how to reply.

"I say this in all seriousness, Miss Bellamy: we fought that war in large part so women can worry about ribbons and Mr. Perriman can natter on about pigeons. It is in fact a privilege to stand in a shrubbery with you, fighting instead with a satin knot. I am grateful to do it."

"Thank you," she said shyly, after a moment. "For all of it."

He nodded almost curtly.

There was a little silence.

"But when in doubt, just tell the story about the cat in a coat."

He gave another little shout of laughter, then sighed. "Miss Bellamy, if you'd like to be freer sooner rather than later, I've a knife that will do the trick. But I did hope to save your ribbon." He glanced up at her. "I know such things as ribbons and bonnets and crayons do not come cheaply."

This concern for a ribbon was almost touching.

Or . . . perhaps it was more that he was familiar with her family's financial straits.

At once this likelihood made her cheeks go hot.

He was here, after all, on a matter of business to do with her father.

She fell abruptly quiet.

Neither of them spoke for a second or two.

"Ah. Very well. There's one knot undone," he muttered.

She cleared her throat. "Perhaps you'll have an opportunity to target shoot while you're here," she ventured. "We often get contests up during house parties."

"Oh, it would hardly be fair to the other gentlemen," he said offhandedly. "I always win, which is rather dull for everybody, including me. A man's pride is his armor, and there's no real pleasure for me in stripping a fellow of it for the sake of recreation."

There wasn't a shred of arrogance in this remarkable statement. It left her momentarily speechless.

She understood then she had never been in the presence of this sort of confidence: the . . . *embodied* sort.

When she said nothing, he flicked his gaze up to hers.

This time it lingered, as if snagged, like the ribbon in the branches.

She had a strange, disorienting conviction then that the essence of the man shone from his eyes, as strangely beautiful and dangerous as the sun glinting off the barrel of a rifle.

And in that moment she was held fast between two confusing warring impulses: to take a step back, away from him, as he suddenly seemed too compelling, like a wild wood she'd never explored. Or to take a step toward him, as if he was the only refuge from all of life's vicissitudes. Neither impulse seemed particularly rational.

Her cheeks were considerably pinker than her ribbon now, she expected. They certainly felt that way.

As if making her cheeks pink had been exactly what he'd set out to accomplish, he finally freed his gaze and returned to the ribbon, his face gone carefully expressionless.

"Mind you," he added, a moment later, "if I see no other way to make a point, I've no compunctions about pride-stripping. But since you're such a conscientious hostess, you'd be run ragged doling consolation out to the losers, and we can't have that."

"Oh. Well. We've plenty of liquor. And what is it for if not consoling the defeated?"

He gave a soft laugh.

Overhead, birds hopped from twig to twig, and the trees shook restively in the wind.

No other guests had yet appeared in the garden. It was awfully early, still.

She cleared her throat.

"I should like to say, Colonel Brightwall . . . well, forgive me if you're terribly weary of . . . of . . . talk of shooting altogether, after the war," she ventured. "I wasn't certain if . . . well, say the word, and I promise I won't mention it again."

He paused.

"It's very considerate of you to think of me," Brightwall said gently. "But there's nothing to forgive. Early in my career, as a foot soldier and infantryman, I did a good deal more shooting. In the war we just won, my job was primarily to tell young men where to point their weapons, and at whom. The answer to both was typically 'at the French.'"

This, she thought, was carrying modesty a bit too far.

"My goodness. It sounds so easy, Colonel Brightwall. Perhaps *I* ought to go and be a colonel."

"I'm not convinced you wouldn't make a fine one. Diplomacy is half the job."

She fell quiet. On the one hand, it was refreshing to be appreciated for something she did indeed consider a bit of a skill, and which everyone else rather took for granted. On the other hand, she felt a little like a magician whose tricks have been exposed. A bit raw. A bit disgruntled.

She was beginning to understand that he saw her through a prism of life experiences entirely different from her own. Or from those of any of the young men among whom she'd been raised, for that matter.

"It's just that if you need to feed yourself, you'd rapidly learn how to become an expert with a fork," he added. "That is, provided you're fortunate enough to be possessed of at least one hand or tremendously dexterous feet. It's a bit like that, I suppose—my gun was the means by which I survived and thrived. I've always been reluctant to view my good aim as anything like a gift when I had quite a powerful motivation to get it right."

"If you insist. But I think you have refined self-deprecation into an art."

He paused in his knot picking and straightened slowly to his entire formidable height to study her, his eyes warm, yet also frankly assessing. His expression was undershot with something more somber and intent. A sort of uncertainty. Almost . . . a reluctance.

As if he could not, or did not quite want to, believe the wonder of her.

She found she could not look away from this expression. Even as she wanted to, because it confused her, and made her cheeks blaze with heat again.

"What do you do best, Miss Bellamy?" he asked softly.

Her mind blanked with surprise.

There was no reason she ought to feel ambushed by the question. But she did.

Survive. It was the answer that sprang at once through every one of her defenses, through the filters of charm and care and diplomacy. *Survive* throbbed at the core of everything she did and said.

And yet this seemed patently absurd. She would never dream of saying something like that aloud to this man, who had saved the Duke of Valkirk's life almost at the cost of his own. Wasn't she here, on a beautiful and ancient estate, wearing this year's fashions and a fine bonnet pinned too tightly to her head? Wasn't she the well-loved daughter of a viscount?

But she had fielded deaths and dramas and illnesses and fluctuations in fortunes that had beset their family. She was proud of it.

But it was as if the colonel's sudden question had held up a mirror. And for the first time, in it she beheld an exhausted girl.

Brightwall's expression evolved into a sort of gentle, rueful sympathy. As though he knew every thought in her head at the moment. As if he understood.

Almost as if he'd wanted her to reach the conclusion she'd reached.

She turned slightly away from him. She decided she didn't want to answer his question, and
stubbornly refused to introduce another topic.

"Perhaps you know this, but I'm off to Spain
in another month. The crown would like to make
a diplomat of me, and I suppose that will be the
end of shooting as a career altogether," he said
casually.

"Ah. Spain is warm," she said somewhat
inanely.

"It is indeed," he agreed politely. He stood back.
"Alas, I fear it's time to bring out the weapons."

"If we must. I'm certain I can repair it in some
fashion, regardless." Of course she could. Because
didn't she always repair what needed repairing?

"All right then. Put your hand on the top of
your bonnet and hold it fast."

From nowhere he produced a knife, and with a
winking flash of the blade he cut the ribbon.

The fine branches snapped violently back like
a slingshot, and took a scrap of her ribbon with
them. Leaving her with the rest, thankfully.

They stared up at that pink scrap clinging to
the twig, destined to wave in a breeze until a bird
or a squirrel collected it for a nest, she supposed.

"Free at last, Miss Bellamy."

She smiled at him. "Thank you, Colonel. I
suppose we can add my rescue to your lore."

"If you would be so kind as to lie about my
skill with knots, I should be obliged."

She laughed.

They regarded each other a moment longer. She had the strangest sense that he was memorizing her.

Perhaps because she was memorizing him, and how he looked in that moment. She would perhaps tell her grandchildren the story of the time the great Colonel Brightwall had freed her from the clutches of a tree.

"I'll bid you good morning now, shall I, and leave you to your sketching? I hope you find the red crayon you're seeking. I imagine it's useful for drawing soldiers. And blushes."

His eyes glinted wickedly again.

And without another word he continued his stroll across the grounds of the house her father might in fact be on the verge of losing. She noticed he favored one leg a very little, and her stomach tightened in sympathy.

After that, it had felt to her that they had become friends: often, she would catch his eye in a gathering, and his would shine like a coconspirator's.

A few days later he'd touched his ear during a large gathering in the sitting room.

She'd felt proud and mischievous, a heroine, swooping in to rescue the hero from Mr. Perriman.

But then the inevitable house party shooting competition had indeed been got up inside a week. It featured apples propped on posts of different heights and requirements to stand at various distances, and a few timed bouts, too.

Every man present insisted on having a go.

Brightwall won every single round.

She watched him with that rifle, that so-called utensil of his survival: the choreography of loading powder and shot, the lift to his shoulder, the minute adjustments in his stance, his deadly, efficient aim. The resulting destruction. He made it all look as innate as breathing.

But she knew that what she witnessed each time he fired a weapon was in fact a dozen decisions and calculations made in a matter of a couple of heartbeats. She understood that someone who could casually dismiss such a lethal skill was complicated and formidable in a way she might not ever be able to fully comprehend. It underscored completely that he was not of her world.

For the first time she paid particular attention to which of the young lords present were good-natured about their losses and which ones blustered a bit, or went quiet or moped. She supposed gentlemen—the sort raised with money and titles and university educations—were seldom given opportunities to thusly prove themselves. They were told who and what they were from birth. They did not necessarily need to *become* anything.

Brightwall had winked at her when she'd suggested bringing out brandy for all the losers that evening.

So he'd gone back for that scrap of ribbon clinging to the fine branches.

And he'd kept it all these years.

She stared at it now.

Grief swooped down upon her, and an old helpless fury pressed against her chest.

But through it all, something soft and bright seemed to be struggling to break free. Like a ribbon in a tree.

She had known her own heart in that moment.

Or so she'd thought.

She had given very little thought to the contents of Brightwall's heart. Why should she have?

How could she have possibly known how he'd felt?

He'd never said a word about that.

He'd merely politely bought her.

Five thousand pounds.

It had torn her breath away when her father told her.

It tore her breath away still.

And because she'd had a few years of loneliness and self-recrimination to reflect, she understood now why she'd done what she'd done on her wedding night.

Still. She'd never meant to hurt Magnus.

And because of that money—because of her—her family was at last thriving. Improbably her brother had put his restless energies and lust for a good argument to good use in America, where he was studying law. He loved the newness of everything there. He had been to visit Brightwall's New York estate and reported that it was enviable, an elegant home in a classic style, beautifully situated and well-kept by a staff paid from the account Brightwall kept at an American bank. Courtesy of Brightwall's money, her sister had been sent on a journey to sunny Italy, fully recovered her health, and returned to marry one of the titled boys who had once courted Alexandra. She was temporarily living with her husband in the now repaired and restored Bellamy family home while their own new home was built, but they were currently traveling through Italy together. Her father had gone to visit her brother in New York, and had stayed longer than expected: he'd met a woman, her brother had written to her. She seemed lovely.

But Brightwall had played her family like a chess master. The ruthless strategist, the man who could make a dozen swift decisions in the span of two heartbeats, had assessed the Bellamys and their circumstances and their relationships like the battlefield commander he was and knew he could not fail to get what he wanted.

What he'd wanted was her.

I do think we'll suit, Alexandra.

And because he'd known how she felt about her family, he must have known she'd have no choice in it at all.

She supposed it was this she could never forgive.

She closed the lid on that little silver box.

And she put the box back in his coat, like she was tucking her own heart away forever.

Chapter Six

⤬⤬⤬

IF HE had instead arrived during the gray light of dawn.

Or in the full dark of evening.

If his exquisitely tailored civilian clothes hadn't felt foreign against his skin after years lived in a scarlet uniform, as though he was an ill-rehearsed actor wearing a costume.

If he hadn't felt awkward and uncertain without a sword at his hip or a rifle in his hand, as though he had just lost a limb.

If he hadn't spent most of his life superbly negotiating that razor-thin line dividing the tedium and terror of warfare and had yet to discover who he was in a world that now required little more of him other than to let it fête him and put him on a pedestal.

If all of these things hadn't caused the usual chain mail of his defenses to slip.

But he'd arrived at the Bellamy house at noon that fateful day.

And if the white marble foyer hadn't been gleaming like the halls of heaven in the noonday sun, perhaps she wouldn't have looked to him like an angel gliding toward him. Perhaps the sun wouldn't have gilded the crown of her coppery hair, and her sheer muslin dress wouldn't have floated tantalizingly about her lovely body with her every light, quick step. Perhaps he wouldn't have noticed the little russet and gold flecks floating in her clear hazel eyes like leaves on the surface of a clear pond when she looked up at him for the first time. Perhaps he wouldn't have seen the flicker of shy uncertainty in them— he'd seen that expression many a time in the faces of women, sometimes tinged with pity, or wary solemnity, even fear—give way to warmth and a sort of dancing light.

He knew what she saw: a cool, fearsome edifice of a man.

But it seemed at once to him that her essence— crackling yet gentle, brave and singular—shone from her eyes.

Once when he lay bleeding on a battlefield, a hail of moments from his life had pelted his consciousness, each distinct as a portrait. The first time he saw The Honorable Alexandra Bellamy was a bit like that: a few thousand simultaneous convictions and desires assailed him.

He would kill for her.

Or die for her.

Whatever she required of him, he would do it.

He could very clearly imagine murmuring filthy endearments in her ear as he took her up against a wall, her eyes hazed with bliss as he moved in her body.

He wanted to curl an arm around her, draw her

gently into his chest, fold himself around her to protect her for the rest of his born days.

He wanted to give her things: Money. Jewelry. Flowers. His name. Babies.

He wanted to know what made her eyes dance.

He wanted to be the reason her eyes danced.

He felt simultaneously ancient, as primitive as the first man, brand-new, blank of mind and absolutely surging with base needs, and like the shy, homely hulk of a boy who'd always known he wasn't wanted, that he was, in fact, alive on sufferance, so he'd made bloody certain he was needed.

He knew in his bones there was no way a woman like her would want a man like him.

She was the sort who would marry a duke. He wasn't the kind of man who would haunt the dreams of a woman like Miss Bellamy, unless he took the form of a creature lurking in a maze, like a Minotaur. Which, coincidentally, was just one of the things the newspapers had called him over the years. He'd needed to look the word up. He'd been darkly amused but not dissatisfied to be compared to a mythical monster. He remembered vividly how it had felt to be at the mercy of others' charity. To have no defenses at all.

When he was a boy, he had silently wept the first time he'd been called a beast. He had long since recognized the power in the word. He had claimed it for his own.

He wasn't erudite, like General Blackmore, who was now the Duke of Valkirk. He hadn't a classical education, like so many army officers who had bought their commissions and subsequent promotions. The kind that aristocratic gents had, where one would say something about, oh, Aristotle, and they would all laugh and nod sagely. It was their shared language, a sort of password into their society.

But he was confident of his own unique brilliance.

And if "charming" was seldom the first word people used to describe him, perhaps it was just because there were so many better choices. All the "F"s, for instance: Fierce. Formidable. Forbidding. Frightening. "Bastard" was trotted out with relative frequency, used both literally and figuratively. All of this was true, so none of it bothered him. But he hadn't soared through the ranks of the army on skill alone. Those who mattered liked him for other reasons. He could be insightful, even sensitive, in a way that never compromised a man's dignity. He was frank. His sense of humor trended toward dry and black and his integrity was impregnable. The men under his command would walk through the fires of hell for him, because they knew he would do the same for them.

He didn't know how to court a woman. There had simply never been time for such grace notes in his life; he'd bought his commission with earnings from a shooting contest he'd won at age sixteen.

But one advantage he had over all of these aristocrats was that he knew how to revere even the smallest moments of beauty and pleasure. For all of his had been rare, fleeting, and hard-earned.

He knew he could make a woman laugh.

And he knew how to make a woman come.

When he laid eyes on her, he understood after sixteen years in the army, his soul was at last sore and weary from bearing the weight of grief and death and responsibility and the mantle of triumph and a nation's gratitude. In her presence he'd felt that weight lift and shift long enough to imagine what his future could look like.

No one knew better than he did that peace was an illusion. But he understood at once that the closest thing to personal peace was a sense of "rightness." And nothing had ever felt so right to his soul as her.

He knew nothing about love.

But he knew how to cherish.

And he bloody well knew how to win.

Within days of his arrival he'd decided she would be his before he left for Spain.

But today, when he'd seen those women gathered around Alexandra in that Newgate cell, their faces turned up to her as though she was the fire on a hearth, her own sweet face open and welcoming and drawn with fatigue, he understood that not a damn thing would have made a difference. No matter when, no matter how he'd first seen her, the result would have been the same.

Somehow, she was now embedded in him, like that shrapnel in his leg.

She hadn't wanted him then. He'd known that.

But he'd understood full well why she'd married him.

He'd counted on it, in fact.

And he knew she would have likely patiently and kindly endured her marriage to him, because she was patient and kind. She would perhaps always view him as something of a savior, and he would have been apportioned gratitude for that, too.

But he'd been convinced there was a spark between them.

As a man who had built many a fire with flint and steel, he knew even the tiniest of sparks could be fanned into a conflagration. In his hubris, he had thought himself perfectly capable of building that between them. All it required was time, and he would have had the rest of his life to do it. He would have, as the vows said, worshipped her with his body.

Well.

He'd presciently anticipated French troop movements during major battles.

But he had failed to consider that his twenty-two-year-old wife might already have a lover.

At least history was rife with formidable men who had proved to be fools when it came to one particular woman.

Since he'd needed to leave for Spain the day following his wedding, he'd had mere hours to decide upon the right and just thing to do.

Ultimately, he'd done what felt like the just thing.

But he'd had years to contemplate whether he'd done the right thing.

He still didn't know.

Even now, he couldn't quite forgive her. He simply was not made that way. Although sometimes he thought all this meant was that he couldn't quite forgive himself.

He'd gone to ask the staff of The Grand Palace on the Thames to prepare her a bath and bring her a little meal—there was an extra charge for both, the proprietresses had sweetly informed him, although breakfast and dinner were of course included with their board—and he would be going out again to order the town house servants to pack trunks for her.

They'd never spent a single night together.

And even though in the eyes of the law she was his, it seemed intrusive and wrong to watch her sleeping, while she was unaware and vulnerable.

But he lingered a moment anyway.

She remained the most beautiful woman he'd ever seen. And even now desire pulled his muscles taut.

It wasn't precisely about the arrangement of features, which were inarguably lovely when considered together and separately: her bold hair and her soft eyes; her full pink mouth and her long slender neck; her generous curves and her clean, sharp jaw. She was a mesmerizing study in contrasts.

From the first he'd felt her as much as, or more than, he'd seen her. Something happened to his insides when she was near. He'd come to think of it as his entire being pulled toward her, the way the moon relentlessly lures the tides to the shore.

But perhaps even this feeling hadn't any of the profundity he'd ascribed to it.

After all, he'd been shot because there was a war on. That had merely been a consequence of circumstance, with lifetime ramifications. Perhaps how he felt around her was only that. Perhaps because he'd no other experience of love, he'd built it into something grand in his head.

Perhaps a brute like him ought never to have aspired to a woman like her.

Even an imbecile knew that if you closed your fist around a little flame in an attempt to keep it, you extinguished it instead.

And, of course, you also got burned.

He gently laid her slippers on the braided rug next to the bed. As if by way of apology for being the cold bastard who had caused her to throw them.

He found no relief from his own pain by punishing her with coldness. Only a weariness, and a nice little smattering of self-loathing.

He *had* meant to take care of her for the whole of her life.

And even though she'd betrayed him, he still, somehow, felt like he'd failed her.

He'd never asked Mr. Lawler or anyone else to spy on her. But in his subtle, almost admonishing way, Mr. Lawler had included informative little sentences in his expense reports: "As Mrs. Brightwall never spends an entire evening away from home or entertains guests at night, I am confident the expense of a new gas lamp will be offset by the reduced need for firewood." That sort of thing.

But she was young. He had no doubt she was passionate. There would come a day when she *would* bring a lover home.

He did not think he could bear that.

Enough was enough. It was time to settle the thing between them, so they could move on with their separate lives.

And the day when he'd wanted to be alone was long past.

He settled the coverlet over her, making sure to cover her stockinged toes.

BY THE TIME she'd stepped out of the bath a pair of cheerful maids had hauled up the stairs for her, a small trunk of clothing had arrived—Magnus had arranged for the town house maids to pack and send over day and evening dresses and all the furbelows that went with them, including hairpins. She'd devoured two scones clearly baked in heaven's ovens and the accompanying slices of cheese, cold chicken, and soup. She drank half a pot of tea.

She was warm, clean, fragrant, and fetchingly outfitted in a bronze silk day dress when Magnus handed the newspaper to her.

BRIGHTWALL THE BEAST'S FERAL
BRIDE TAKES ON THE ARMY

Now we know why Brightwall keeps his bride hidden away: she runs amuck when let off her lead. It took an entire battalion to contain her when she took it into her head to help steal a carriage.

The illustration accompanying the little passage depicted her with arms and legs whirling. Her mouth was twisted in a snarl.

Her hair, however, looked wonderful. It was lusciously arranged. Not a lock out of place. Rowlandson, the infamously, caustically witty caricaturist, had outdone himself.

It was the most peculiar sensation. Half of her found it so transcendently funny she nearly elevated out of her body. The rest of her was so scorchingly embarrassed she wished the ground would open up beneath her and suck her under.

She lifted her eyes to her husband's. He sat across from her at the little table near the window in the room.

And for a vanishing instant, humor crackled and arced between them.

In other circumstances—or if they were different people—they might be able to laugh at this together now.

She cleared her throat.

"The little swirls in front of my nose . . ." She pointed. "I suppose I'm meant to be snorting?"

"Yes. I believe so. Like a bull. Because we're both meant to be beasts. You're snorting like a beast. Mrs. Beast."

One little drawing could hardly devastate her if all of the other vicissitudes of her life hadn't yet. Rowlandson was famously merciless to everyone.

If, however, it carried on . . . if the ton at large decided the Mr. and Mrs. Beast theme was great fun—and she could easily see how they would—it might *never* end. There might be endless variations of those images, the way there were apparently endless verses of "The Ballad of Colin Eversea."

The idea of this wasn't funny in the least.

It was odd. Somehow, sitting here in this pleasant suite, fresh from her bath, it seemed so easy not to do anything to besmirch her husband's good name. Let alone wind up in jail and become an indelible Rowlandson caricature. And yet the evidence that she had managed to do just that was undeniable.

"I expect you can imagine the potential ramifications of this." He said this almost dryly.

"Yes." Her voice was frayed. "I am imagining them now."

"I have a sense of humor, Alexandra. But it's quite another thing to be viewed as a public laughingstock. Another man might find the patience within him to stoically tolerate the . . . relentless illustrated campaign that might ensue." He paused. "I find that I am not that man."

She could feel her pulse ticking in her throat. She swallowed hard.

"No. You should never have to tolerate it."

"Your conduct is a reflection on me." He stated this evenly, as fact.

She nodded. She found she could no longer speak.

"I was called back to London in part because there have been talks to the effect that the king intends to create Letters Patent designating me the Earl of Montcroix. It will be a hereditary title. Should this come to pass, this of course means your title, for the rest of your life, will be the Countess Montcroix."

She blinked. She was stunned at what seemed a sudden and glorious change of topic.

Genuine joy suffused her. "Oh, my goodness. Congratulations, Magnus. That is quite extraordinary. Nobody deserves such an honor more."

He merely nodded. "But the warrant instructing the Lord High Chancellor to prepare the Letters Patent creating the title has not yet been delivered to him. As you are no doubt aware, His Majesty's popularity is a tenuous and fluctuating thing, a matter of much concern to him, as he wishes to be beloved."

He said this rather dryly: there really was no hope of King George becoming beloved. He'd made his own bed, as it were. And as it so happened, parliament refused to grant the king his divorce, which had been a process so thoroughly messy and degrading and public it ought to discourage anyone from attempting a divorce in England for decades to come.

"And he still might conceivably decide he'd look even more foolish if he elevated to the aristocracy a man whose wife had the poor judgment to consort with an alleged carriage thief, even if the thief was her hapless third cousin Lord Thackeray. Needless to say, even more attention will be called to the alleged carriage theft if I am indeed made a peer of the realm."

And now she was alarmed.

Oh God. Her poor cousin! Was he still in prison?

"In light of this recent event, and for other reasons, it is increasingly clear to me that, in order to live our lives with dignity and peace, it is best if we effect as permanent and complete a marital separation as possible within the limitations of the law."

Her breath left her. She stared at him as if he'd whipped out a broadsword.

Ice flooded her stomach again.

He'd made it clear to her on their wedding night that both divorce and annulment were out of the question, as it would be nearly impossible—even attempting one would be financially and socially annihilating for both of them, and particularly humiliating for him. The granting of a divorce required an actual act of parliament and public hearings. Her family's name would be tarnished forever, and she in particular would become a pariah. The one—the *only*—impulsive, foolish, brief indiscretion she'd ever committed would become not only national knowledge, but part of English history.

"He knew I was happiest here in England, among my family," was all she'd said when anyone she knew inquired about his absence. "We correspond regularly. He will return one day."

None of this was entirely untrue.

She always adroitly and firmly steered the topic of conversation to generalities when the subject arose.

And Brightwall had, as he'd promised the evening he'd outlined her fate, remained entirely silent on the subject. He'd merely nobly fallen on his sword.

Regardless of what she told him, her father had clearly been distressed for her. And he felt a little guilty. But his position was awkward, indeed: he was disinclined to suggest the man who had saved his entire family from penury had subsequently cruelly abandoned his daughter. Alexandra knew he felt he hadn't a right to confront the colonel. Alexandra had assured him that she was content with the conditions of her life, and wanted for nothing. And this, on the face of it, was true, too. At least as far as material comforts were concerned.

"This is what I propose," Brightwall continued calmly. "Over the next week, we will appear together at several functions—a ball, a banquet and reception, a statue dedication—to be held in my honor, and present ourselves as a united, committed, entirely civil and civilized couple, thereby putting paid to any malicious gossip and restoring, to the extent possible, dignity to the Brightwall name. At the end of this period, you will then travel as planned to the United States. You may recall that I own an estate near New York, near, in fact, where your brother now resides." He paused. "I've long thought someone should be in residence to look after the home and the lands. I have been considering going to stay for some time, when my duties allow it. Instead, I should like you to stay there."

Her breath was coming shallow now.

"For the duration of my visit to my brother?" Her mouth had gone dry.

The eloquent pause betrayed his answer before he said the words.

"For the rest of our lives."

He said it almost gently.

The world seemed to tilt; shock flickered her vision from brilliant to black and back again.

"I will deed the New York property to you, and settle upon you a single sum large enough to live for the rest of your life in a manner both comfortable and gracious, including the keeping of horses, if you choose. You will be at liberty to hire your own staff and make decisions about purchases. To the extent possible, you will thenceforth be entirely free of me."

Her breathing had gone shallow.

She couldn't feel her limbs.

Had she expected rapprochement?

Had she even wanted it?

"So I'm to be sent to Elba, is it?" Her ears were ringing. Her voice was pitched unnaturally high.

"New York is no longer the wilds, nor is it isolated, nor will you be alone. And unlike Napoleon, you did not preside over the slaughter of thousands of Englishmen."

"No. Just the one apparently," she said bitterly.

He didn't reply.

He did, however, look a little white about the mouth.

He clearly wasn't enjoying this, either. Just as he probably hadn't relished ordering deserters shot. It was simply something that had to be done.

"And if I do not want to stay there?"

Her dread swelled anew at his lengthy silence.

"Your income will be reduced to an amount required to purchase necessities. As for housing, I imagine you will be able to live with your sister and her husband or with your father, should he return to England."

He said it quietly.

He had clearly thought everything through. Naturally.

A fleeting, blindingly pure hatred for the man sitting in front of her flashed through her.

He had no obligation to be generous, of course. But until the end of her days or his, he would be required to financially support a woman who was his wife in name only. He could go on to have children with a mistress one day, if he chose. So many men did.

No such option remained to her. She could of course bear children, or take a lover. But that would mean living on the outskirts of respectable society for the rest of her life, and the taint of that would touch everyone in her family.

Her breath seemed to scrape her lungs on its way in and out.

It was hideously unfair how profoundly he excelled at not blinking.

"If you tell me you're happy with your life as it is . . . I will know you're lying, Alexandra." He said this almost gently. "It seems very clear that we are not a successful match. I have learned from warfare that life is short and that wallowing in regret is . . . such a waste of time."

Her eyes had begun to burn.

Do not weep do not weep do not weep.

She couldn't speak.

"I'm not happy, either." His words were scarcely audible. As if he was ashamed to reveal any kind of vulnerability.

His tone wasn't accusatory. It didn't need to be. Her own conscience flailed her.

"I think such a change will be beneficial to both of us. If you agree, you might find comfort in the fact that soon you need never see my face again."

Was this what she wanted? It wasn't the sight of him that tormented her. It never had been.

She forced herself to think about it. If she lived an ocean away, she could perhaps cease hearing about him so frequently, or reading about him in newspapers, and perhaps, as the years went on, even wondering overmuch about him. And perhaps the fact that she had inadvertently ruined this man's life would become a distant, dull echo in the background of hers. It would bother her the way the shrapnel in Brightwall's wounded leg bothered him.

Like little fissures of air in a sealed coffin, tendrils of possibility began to wind through the dark snarl around her heart.

The notion of an entirely new life, unfettered by obligation to a man, *any* man, did indeed seem like freedom. Nor would she be obligated to solve the problems of her family. They were all thriving, thanks in large part to Brightwall's money. God knows where they would all be now if she hadn't married him.

It would mean leaving everything she knew behind.

But suddenly this notion seemed almost exhilarating. And even though the decision would always be bound to a certain sadness and guilt, she had learned that one couldn't get through life unfettered by regret. She had loved and been loved by a young man once, briefly. Perhaps that was all one got in a lifetime. She wouldn't be the first human who had changed the course of her life with one fateful mistake.

All at once she realized Magnus had hit upon the right solution.

She swallowed hard.

She dragged in a breath and settled her shoulders on an exhale.

"Although I of course have no rights that you haven't bestowed upon me, I agree to your terms.

I will appear at your side for the events in your honor, and then I will go to live in New York."

There seemed a terrifying finality in even saying the words.

His shoulders rose and fell as he exhaled in what sounded like relief.

"But what if our performances as devoted spouses prove unconvincing to the ton?" she asked.

"As your own reputation and your family's reputation are also at stake, I have no doubt you will acquit yourself well."

In other words: *It's clear to me that I don't matter to you, but your family does, Alexandra.*

This wasn't true. But she wasn't going to belabor the point. She would do her duty, because that's what she'd always done, and then they would be as finished with each other as was possible.

"I'm afraid that doesn't entirely answer my question," she managed to say calmly.

He understood. "If at any point it becomes clear to us that we cannot convincingly portray a devoted couple, and if it appears we are in fact making things worse, rather than better, we'll end our arrangement at once. You may proceed to live with your sister. I will leave it up to you to explain to your family why you will not be occupying any of my properties."

He really was such a cool, unmitigatedly ruthless bastard. It was utterly impressive. She might even have been proud to witness it, if she hadn't been the one cornered. He knew full well she was too proud to go and live with her sister, let alone explain to her sister why her marriage had failed.

She recalled well what he'd said about there being no pleasure in stripping a man of his pride. His armor, he'd called it.

Magnus took his seriously.

And so did she. It went down jaggedly as she swallowed it now.

"I'm certain I can manage to be a credit to you long enough to fool the ton." She managed to say this with just a frisson of irony.

He nodded.

After a moment he said, "I always did think you would be a credit to me." He said it quietly. Again, no recrimination. Simple truth. He sounded almost puzzled.

She dug her fingernails into her palms to keep the tears from spilling from her burning eyes.

She cleared her throat. "Before we formalize our agreement, I have a request."

His eyebrows leaped.

She pulled in a long sustaining breath. And then she pulled in another one, because the first wasn't sufficient to fuel her nerves.

"I expect the habit of ordering people about dies hard. I understand that you are accustomed to getting soldiers to jump to do your bidding with sharp commands and to frightening subalterns with stony looks of displeasure or icy silences. In the context of war, I imagine these are very useful skills. I am . . . struggling to say this politely. I'm not a soldier, Magnus. I understand you have a grievance, but bullying is beneath you. I fear I simply will not respond to *orders*. I ask that for the duration of our agreement you treat me with the politeness and respect you would a partner. Because I have discovered that I am willing to throw things if that's my only recourse and I cannot promise I won't do it again, even if we're in the middle of a ballroom."

He had listened to most of this in absolute rigid stillness, apart from his eyebrows flicking with amazement.

Then his jaw had set.

But halfway through this recitation he'd propped his elbow on his knee and placed his chin on his hand, his expression absorbed. Listening to, and watching her.

And damned if his expression hadn't reflected something like rueful admiration.

When she'd finished, her heart was knocking so hard it seemed a miracle that neither of them could hear it.

They regarded each other intently.

And for an odd moment, a slippage in time, she saw him as if for the first time, outside of the context of all she knew of him. Almost as if another woman entirely was sitting beside her and asking: "Who is this man?" She noticed how beautifully his dark coat fitted across his shoulders. She noticed the noble set of his head, and his remarkable, weathered, singular face, and the burn of his pale gaze, and how his thick, hard-muscled thighs pushed against the nankeen of his trousers. His presence was so *weighty*, so thoroughly intimidating and compelling, it left her nearly airless. It was impossible to imagine a circumstance over which he wouldn't triumph.

But the shadows around his eyes looked less like fatigue, and more like grief.

He had meted justice to her, but she would warrant he had paid a cost in loneliness, too.

Finally Magnus straightened again, and pressed his lips together. He pushed a hand through his hair.

"Everything you've said is correct," he said simply. "I apologize sincerely for being a rude bastard. You have my word I shall endeavor to be respectful. And consider this the last time I say 'bastard' within your hearing."

She shakily released the breath she'd been holding. "Thank you." Her voice was scraped raw.

"But if you take a notion to throw things . . . you may have noticed my reflexes are excellent."

She made a soft sound. Not quite a laugh.

She ducked her head because she didn't want to dash tears away from her now-brimming eyes while he was watching.

She'd never wept easily, and almost never in front of anyone else; she supposed that was pride, too.

"Alexandra." He said it softly. But the word was taut with emotion.

She glanced up in surprise to find he was extending a handkerchief.

She could have sworn his hand was shaking a little.

She glanced from it to his face and discovered there was a peculiar tension around his eyes.

She stared at him, suddenly wondering if he'd ever wept over her while he was alone in Spain. Did he ever weep at all, or had war evaporated all of his tears forever? Perhaps he'd simply been born incapable of ever being thoroughly crushed.

But she thought of that ribbon scrap in the box.

She took the handkerchief from him. "Thank you." Her voice was thick.

"I expect you'll want to rest more before dinner. I'll return before then," he said abruptly.

The door of their suite closed behind him seconds later.

Chapter Seven

꩜

MONEY AND a musket: there wasn't much a man couldn't accomplish if he was good with both.

Magnus was. He'd applied everything he'd learned and observed by growing up in a squire's household and by rising through the ranks of the army. By the end of the war, clever, fortunate investments had made him a man of consequential wealth and property.

And what he'd told Alexandra the day he'd freed her bonnet ribbon was true: he never judged people. Judging limited one's tactical options.

But he noticed nearly every detail about them.

He'd met her father, Viscount Bellamy, at White's some years ago. A man of great charm and fine looks, his interests were far ranging, and he was amusing company when he got to talking. And while his penchant for impulsive, risky investments was at odds with his expensive proclivities—food, wine, horses, lavishly entertaining wealthy friends—Bellamy never postured, or tried to impress or challenge him when they met, unlike many aristocrats. He seemed entirely comfortable with who he was, and Brightwall always respected that sort of man. When he was invited to Bellamy's house party at his legendarily lovely country estate, he'd decided to make it his last stop in England before he left for a diplomatic assignment in Spain.

And there he'd met his daughter.

He noticed how the eyes of every man present at Bellamy's house party unconsciously tracked Alexandra when she was near, the way one would watch a bird, or a butterfly, for that fleeting feeling of weightlessness a beautiful, graceful thing brings.

He noted in particular the heat and yearning in the eyes of younger men, most of whom possessed pedigrees and fortunes.

He saw the fraying edges of the Bellamys' gentility in the unkempt far reaches of the garden, the worn edges of carpets and the odd bedraggled hem on a curtain, in an un-dusted windowsill. He knew staff was the first to be peeled away when financial disaster loomed.

He saw the purple shadows of sleeplessness, the drawn worry, beneath Lord Bellamy's eyes.

And because Magnus's very presence inspired both confidence and confidences, he learned of Bellamy's concerns about his recalcitrant son, and his sickly younger daughter, and he soon learned exactly how much money Bellamy owed creditors. The amount gave Brightwall pause.

And because many lavish dinners, outings, and gatherings were arranged during his visit, he'd had plenty of opportunities to witness both the affection and the tension between all the Bellamys, and how Alexandra was consistently the family balm. The fulcrum around which their family turned.

He was reasonably certain Alexandra would do just about anything for her family.

And even while those yearning, rich young men were constrained by the need for their fathers' approval before they married, there might be one in the pack capable of impulse.

Time was of the essence.

Above all, Magnus knew Bellamy was desperate.

Every brilliant wager carries a risk equal to the reward. And Brightwall had nothing if not nerve.

One afternoon, he'd requested a meeting with Bellamy. Sitting across from him in the man's cozy library, brandies in hand, the gilt titles of leather-bound books winking from the wall-high bookcases, Brightwall calmly explained to the viscount that he would pay the entirety of his debt at once, as well as settle a sum of five thousand pounds on him.

"With the stipulation that your daughter Alexandra and I wed before I leave for Spain."

The silence that greeted this seemed endless. He'd clearly shocked Bellamy nearly witless.

Magnus had simply waited, outwardly impassive. He remembered, however, how he could feel his own pulse rushing beneath the thumb he'd pressed to it.

Finally, Bellamy cleared his throat. "Well. Colonel . . . it is . . . this is a great and unexpected honor. Does she know that you would . . . how you . . . that you . . ." Bellamy's voice was frayed. His complexion stark white.

Magnus merely said, "I am confident we have developed a rapport during our admittedly short acquaintance, and I believe she will be a credit to me in my life as a diplomat."

Lord Bellamy stared at him. And Magnus saw what he'd seen before in the eyes of men: a stunned realization that he had failed to fully estimate the character of the man in front of him. The uncomfortable comprehension that so many things said about Colonel Brightwall were, in fact, true: He might possess a certain charm. But he was also, indeed, cold. And ruthless.

There passed over Bellamy's face a swift spasm of fury, no doubt at the realization that he, a viscount, had been played into a corner by a man who'd begun life in a potato sack. But it was likely more a reflex born of some ancient, hereditary sense of entitlement that flowed through his veins. Bellamy was, at heart, a decent man.

Magnus wasn't without sympathy. But Bellamy would recover. He was certain the viscount hadn't the fortitude or discipline required to hold a grudge, or to endure long stretches of unpleasantness. He was an intelligent, albeit currently a financially flailing, man who had just been handed a miraculous and quite respectable solution to all of his problems.

"The offer expires in one week," he told Bellamy calmly.

But some of the color was already beginning to return to Lord Bellamy's face.

And some of the tension had already left his shoulders.

"I'll talk to her," Bellamy finally said quietly.

But Magnus already knew he'd won.

A FEW DAYS after that, Bellamy told him, "I spoke to her. You may approach her privately at any time now."

So Magnus had taken Alexandra for a walk in the garden to propose.

He had known by her uncharacteristic, nervous silence that she'd been expecting it.

He regretted that his words were stilted and formal. He could not quite bring himself to articulate the intensity and specificity of any of the things he felt about her. If they unnerved even him, they would likely frighten her.

He would rather die than see pity or confusion in her eyes.

He tried to say with his eyes, with the warmth of his voice: *You may not want me yet, but I will live to make you happy, Alexandra.*

And though the conclusion was foregone, he exulted when she accepted him gravely, and with the graciousness that characterized everything she did.

"I should be honored to be your wife, Magnus," is what she said.

It marked the first time she'd used his Christian name.

Her hand was trembling when he raised it to his lips.

"I do think we'll suit, Alexandra."

He made it sound like a vow.

By virtue of a special license he'd been able to obtain from the Archbishop of Canterbury, who did indeed consider him a hero, they were wed one day before he was due to leave for Spain. Only her immediate family was in attendance.

And that night he'd felt like the most blessed man on earth.

Tonight they would share a bed for the first time.

His wife. The word "wife" seemed to him so very soft. Soft as a featherbed, soft as her eyes, as soft as the way he would draw his fingers over her skin.

He was accustomed to packing swiftly and lightly; anything he needed that he didn't already own he could acquire in Spain. But a half dozen servants had been packing for Alexandra all day, and she'd been supervising. A caravan of trunks would join them on their journey.

He leaned out the window of his bedroom.

The sky was filled with a gray-purple light, soft as a dove's wing. The moon, waxing toward fullness, silvered the edges of the leaves on the trees and the hedgerow. Everything was still, the air like a feather on his skin. He remembered this part well. The beauty and peace of it. He was too seasoned to ascribe portent to weather. Battlefields could run with blood on sweet, balmy spring days, too. Birds still sang in the trees when bodies were rotting below. But knowing this only made him mark beauty wherever he found it.

He went still when he heard voices.

The cadences were urgent. Their words a tumbling rush, in a volume just above a whisper.

One of them was Alexandra's.

And the other . . .

The other was a man's.

The little hairs on the back of his neck prickled to attention.

It wasn't a voice he'd ever heard before.

His heartbeats fell like hammer blows in his chest.

He swiftly descended the stairs and pushed open the door into the garden, moving stealthily toward the conversation. The grass muffled his footsteps.

Alexandra and the man stood with the garden gate between them. Their closeness and their postures suggested a familiarity that made the hackles rise on Brightwall's neck.

He could not see the man's features; he was a tall, slim, shadowy figure. Coltish. Clearly young.

His breath ceased flowing into his lungs when the man lunged across the gate for Alexandra and pulled her into his arms.

And he kissed her.

She went rigid.

Every muscle in Magnus's body tensed to lunge toward them, to hurl that man away from his wife. To tear him limb from limb.

But some instinct made him wait.

Because somehow he knew.

He watched her soften in the man's arms. Watched their two dark silhouettes blend into one as her arms went round his neck. Watched her give herself up passionately to a lingering kiss.

Brightwall felt as though his lungs were being ripped from his body.

Long moments—an eternity, it felt to him— later Alexandra pulled away.

The two of them tenderly, briefly held each other's faces.

Then she stepped away abruptly and ducked her head and shook it swiftly, roughly.

She uttered a single syllable. It sounded like "go."

The man backed away from the garden gate. For a long time, he walked backward, as if to savor every last sight of her.

And then he ran.

Magnus watched until he could no longer see the man's shadow darting through the trees. It occurred to him that he hadn't really drawn a breath in all that time.

He was reluctant to draw one now, in a world that had just changed forever.

Alexandra dashed a palm against her eyes, as if to brush away tears.

Magnus watched, heart lodged in his throat, as she straightened her spine resolutely and turned toward the house.

That's when she saw him.

Her face at once flashed stark white as the moon.

She swayed as shock poured violently through her.

And even then his muscles tensed to spring to catch her before she fell.

But she didn't faint.

Nor did she flee.

She stood before him, silently, like a rabbit caught before a wolf.

He knew a little about rank fear. Doubtless she couldn't move right now if she tried.

Oh, but he could move. He was accustomed to moving forward through unbearable circumstances. To making wounded limbs do things against which sense and sanity balked.

And so, slowly, as if through a dream, he paced to her.

In that low purple light, they stared at each other in silence.

Now that he was close, he could see that she was trembling. Despite everything, he knew an impulse to wrap her in his coat. He cursed the traitorous reflex to protect her; it seemed innate, not a thing he could help.

"Magnus . . ." His name was a choked plea.

"Who is he?" His voice was calm. If perhaps a little loud. There was an odd ringing sound in his ears.

For a time, all he could hear was her breath shuddering in and out.

In and out.

He waited.

She swallowed. She pulled in a longer breath.

"The person at whom you are angry is me." Her voice shook. "If you wish to throttle me, I will not stop you. You are entitled. But I will not give you his name."

"Oh, no, Alexandra," he explained, with gentle menace. "I'm angry at you *and* the foolhardy bastard who kissed my wife on my wedding day. Give me his *name.*"

The last four words were hard and dangerous as bullets.

But she didn't flinch. She stood before him demonstrating, maddeningly, nearly every quality that made him admire and want her so: her poise, her pride, her grace, spirit, her gentleness, her beauty.

Her loyalty.

Even if it was to some man he somehow had failed to anticipate at all.

This stubbornness he'd only recently come to suspect.

Her voice shook only a very little. "I am not a soldier under your command. I am a woman, the daughter of a viscount, and now your lawful wife. I will not respond to orders as though I'm a subaltern. You've every right to be angry. So shout if you must, or make threats. But nothing you do will persuade me to tell you a name you do not need to know, because that man is—and I swear this on my life and the lives of all I hold dear—irrelevant to our future. He is my past. Nor could I bear any harm or scandal to come to *you* as a result of harming him. For your reputation for mercy does not precede you and you deserve to live a peaceful life."

It took either extraordinary nerve or insanity to issue any part of that little speech acerbically.

And yet she had.

Pride died hard.

He knew that too, too well.

"Harm?" he said almost offhandedly. "No one would blame me, Alexandra, if I surgically removed his cock with a rapier. I suspect I could, in fact, gather a cheering audience for the deed."

She visibly jerked, as if he'd pricked her skin with said rapier.

No, she had not married a born gentleman. But she knew that.

"I need his name." The words were slow, measured, and shot through with ultimatum.

He felt, somehow, as though he were floating above the proceedings. Because even as he said the words, he knew she was right: What would knowing the man's name change? He realized then he was just saying words, any words, because he had no idea know how to articulate the furious tangle of things he felt. Knowing the man's name wouldn't give him what he needed, which was for all of this to never have happened. For her not to have kissed that man.

And for him not to have witnessed that kiss.

When the moonlight illuminated tear tracks on her face a vise clamped over his heart.

"You don't need his name." Her entire body was visibly trembling now. "You will never meet him. I will never see him again. He is leaving the country, and so are we. I wanted to visit the gate tonight, as this part of the garden has been my favorite, and I did not know he would come here tonight, I did not know he meant to . . . to . . . kiss me, I certainly did not mean for you to witness it. I am . . . horrified . . . if I have caused you pain. And I am . . . I am more sorry than I can express."

If I have caused you pain.

And he thought, with a scalding epiphany: this was a fair statement. What did he truly know of love, or being loved? What woman had wept for him, or missed him, or suffered for him?

Why should she assume he suffered from anything more than wounded pride? He had essentially bought her.

He only knew that he did suffer. And though the church, the law, and his vows said she was his, he realized he hardly felt he had the right to his own suffering.

His pride had stopped him from telling her how thoroughly, swiftly, unreasonably she had conquered him because he'd never wanted to see anything like pity in her eyes.

And now he was glad he'd never told her. Because that left him a shred of pride.

"I would caution you against attempting to tell me that man is nothing to you."

"No." Her voice was frayed. "I can't say that. But I ended it with him the moment I accepted your proposal. He is my past. I *swear* to you."

"He knows you are married?"

She hesitated.

"Yes." It was a whisper.

He could see the pulse beating in her creamy throat. He'd imagined laying his lips there tonight, in bed, as he made love to her for the first time. As he showed her the pleasures that could be had from the joining of their bodies.

Would she have been imagining this man instead?

He could not believe this woman he'd so admired—whom, despite all his wisdom to the contrary, he'd elevated to a sort of pedestal—had stood up in church next to him and taken a vow this afternoon, only to break it hours later.

"How long has this affair been—"

"Half a year. It was over before we were wed, I swear it. I made certain of it. I do not think . . . I do not even think I would call it an affair. We never made plans of any kind. We never intended to . . . I never intended to . . ."

"Perhaps you have a different definition of 'over' than I do. Is it your first affair, or do you make a habit of kissing men in the garden?" he said relentlessly.

She jerked as though he'd slapped her.

"First," she said hoarsely. Giving up.

"Has he done more than kiss you? Has he made love to you?"

Scarlet rushed her cheeks. "No. *Never.*" She sounded hoarsely horrified. "He has never before even kissed me. I swear on my life. How can you think . . . No! He has never kissed me

before tonight. I have never kissed anyone before tonight."

He stared at her in rank amazement. He'd just
caught her in a clinch in which she'd participated
enthusiastically. *That's* how he could "think."

But he believed her. He knew exactly what he'd
seen: her shock.

Followed by her ardent capitulation.

And then . . .

And then her grief.

He would never have known he'd married a
woman who was grieving another man.

How well, how stoically, she had hidden this.

He understood he was being hateful simply
to punish her. He was tormenting her because
there was no other place to put his fury or pain.
He hadn't known himself capable of it. He despised the sort of man who lashed out rather than
planned or resolved.

He pulled in an involuntary breath as he recalled her fingers touching that man's face so
tenderly. He didn't think he would ever forget it.

Another heartbroken man was out there in
the dark.

"Magnus . . ."

Her voice was so soft. So gentle. How he wanted
to move toward that gentleness.

This weakness in him for her infuriated him.

"I regret more than I can ever adequately say
the . . . the injury done you. What you witnessed
was the end of something I never expected even
to begin, and which has been a source of solace

before I met you. I have entered into our marriage in good faith and I am resolved to be a good wife to you. I honestly did not know that he would be there at the gate, or that he would . . . he would kiss . . . I did not know that *I* would . . . I've no experience at all of . . ."

Her eyes on his face were bewildered and tormented. Beseeching.

Oh Christ.

He briefly hovered a palm across his eyes.

He wanted to hear that she regretted it. But he didn't dare ask, because he knew she didn't, and he knew she wouldn't lie.

If he hadn't witnessed it with his own eyes, Magnus would never, ever have known that his new wife had kissed her allegedly erstwhile lover on their wedding day. *She* would have known, and her lover would have known, and he would have gone on, a blissfully ignorant fool, for the rest of his life.

To date, no one had made a fool of Brightwall without paying a price.

And now he was flailing. Here he stood, closer to forty years old than to thirty, infuriated and almost frightened that despite everything he'd survived and learned and lived, despite every sacrifice, every triumph—none of that had taught him how to reconcile or abide any of this: her white-faced terror, her perfidy, her loveliness, her beautiful mouth, her pleading, tormented eyes, his own madness for wanting this one, specific woman so badly that he'd engineered what he'd thought was a shrewd triumph.

Instead he was now confronted with a tragedy—a farce—he had somehow not foreseen. He had outsmarted himself. He had trapped both of them.

And he didn't want to admire her in this moment. If he was brutally honest with himself—he generally was—he did anyway.

He could not abide her suffering, because it made his own heart feel like shards in his chest.

He could not abide the fact that this very conversation made it so clear that they didn't know each other well enough to maneuver through it, and now likely never would.

Let alone well enough to ever touch each other's faces tenderly.

And yet they were legally bound to each other. Married strangers.

Forever.

He gave a soft, bitter, almost wondering laugh. "And I would have done anything for you."

He heard her breath snag in her throat.

She must have realized that whatever he decided to do next, mercy for either of them wouldn't be a part of it.

THE NEXT MORNING he left for Spain.

Alone.

Chapter Eight

❦

AFTER MAGNUS departed following their rather draining, future-deciding conversation, Alexandra had gone back to sleep. It had been a proper, deep sleep until she awoke with a start from a dream of being trapped in a thicket. She had heard Magnus's voice calling to her from far away. She had called out to him, too, until her voice was hoarse. But he'd been too far away to hear her, and his voice had grown ever fainter until it stopped.

She rubbed her palms against her eyes and slid from bed to part the curtains.

It had gone full dark; no doubt she had already missed dinner. She could not have guessed what time it was.

She smoothed her hair in the little face-sized mirror hanging over the writing desk, then opened the door a crack and peered out.

Magnus was sitting on the settee in front of the fire, a book in his hands. He'd shed his coat and cravat and rolled his sleeves up to his elbows. This was a bit startling, but certainly fair: they were married, and he was allowed to be comfortable.

It wasn't as though she'd never seen a man's forearms. She had a brother and a father, after all.

She'd never seen forearms quite like the ones currently on display.

Bronzed by both sun and burnished firelight, hard, sinewy, corded with muscle, and coated with golden-brown hair, like the hair on his head.

She stared, feeling a bit like a spy now.

He furrowed his brow when he read. As though he was responsible for the welfare of all the characters in the book, and was contemplating whether to order them about or to have them shot for desertion.

This, for some reason, made her smile, albeit somewhat ruefully. That man did absolutely nothing by halves, she had come to understand. When it came to reading, when it came to shooting, when it came to winning battles, when it came to getting the wife he wanted, when it came to disposing of said wife for faithlessness.

She supposed one couldn't equivocate in battle, and he'd never lost the habit.

She distinctly remembered a moment on that day when he'd worked to free her ribbon: he had not so much looked at her as *into* her, and she'd simultaneously felt imperiled in a way she hadn't fully understood, and protected in such a way that made her realize it had been years since she had felt safe, such had been the caprices of her life. But she supposed a castle on a hill might inspire similar feelings. Castles were meant to be a refuge. And they were meant to inspire fear.

She supposed his absolute certainty about

things contributed to that feeling. One got the sense there was nothing he couldn't manage.

She gave a start when he looked up and caught her still wearing that rueful smile.

He offered her a polite, tentative smile in return.

He held up his book. "It's *Robinson Crusoe*. Captain Hardy loaned it to me. He says it's very good, but he can never find the time to finish it. I read it some years ago."

She ventured out of the room and gingerly sat down on the long settee at a polite distance from his bronzed, hairy arms.

There was a somewhat weighty but almost elegiac peace between them now. They knew where they stood with each other. Paradoxically, deciding to be apart had made it easier to be together.

An undercurrent of tension remained, but it was less seething and fraught. Tension always took a little while to dissipate in the aftermath of a new truce.

She knew they would both do their best to get through the next few days of events, before she left for New York.

"My brother loves *Robinson Crusoe*," she told him. "Boys always seem to love it. All the fighting and adventure, I suppose. Perhaps I should read it as a sort of guide for surviving exile."

It was quite a dry, black little jest, as jests went. A little risky.

But she wasn't surprised when he quirked the corner of his mouth and nodded, ceding her a point.

"I think we all vicariously enjoy a story of survival. There's nothing more satisfying than thriving despite the odds. Than exercising our resourcefulness. And besides, Robinson Crusoe is not alone in exile. There are cannibals."

This surprised her into a short laugh.

He smiled, too. Then it faded. "Ah. I should have considered . . . well, forgive me. I hope you don't mind." He gestured to his casual torso.

"Of course not," she said, politely. "You're paying for the suite, after all."

This statement was light, too, but edged in challenge.

He eyed her steadily, and chose to ignore the edge.

And besides, "mind" wasn't precisely the word she would have used. She had just discovered that his shirt was open at the throat, too, revealing more firelight-burnished skin and a peek of curling dark hair. This suddenly seemed an unutterably fascinating, acutely intimate thing.

Her eyes may have lingered a little too long there.

When they returned to his, she discovered he'd been watching her. But his face was entirely unreadable.

She hoped the light was dim enough to disguise her blush.

"Well, I've been reading the novels of Miss Jane Austen lately," she told him. "The story called *Pride and Prejudice* is about the Bennett family, who are a bit poor and chaotic. But the hero, Mr. Darcy, is a clever, imperious, wealthy, bossy sort of man."

He shook his head and clucked. "Those are the worst kind of men."

They smiled at each other.

His smile vanished and he turned his head abruptly toward the fire, as though punishing himself or her. His expression had gone inscrutable.

"Thank you for having some of my clothes sent over."

He cleared his throat. "I instructed the maids at the town house to send over shades of yellow, green, and pink gowns, if you had any, along with day dresses. Enough for about a week. I recalled you wearing those colors, and I thought perhaps you liked them best. I hope they'll suit for now." He still hadn't turned back to her.

A lump moved into her throat. She was moved that he'd remembered.

"Yes, I found them. Those will do, thank you," she said, quietly.

"We've a ball to attend tomorrow night, hosted by the Earl and Countess of Chisholm."

"I'll wear my rose-colored silk."

She'd never danced with him. She had never, in fact, voluntarily touched him. And it had been some time since she'd attended a ball.

Proving that she wasn't entirely dead inside, part of her actually looked forward to it. Even if it was a duty arising from a rather tensely sad bargain.

"I'm having the needed repairs to the town house roof and windows done so it will be fully

ready for sale. Interested buyers will likely be
viewing it this week. I have a variety of meetings
and errands of the business or mandatory sort
this week. I imagine you'll have letters and mes-
sages you'd like to write. You'll have time to ar-
range for the packing or storage of the rest of your
possessions if you like before your ship sails."

"All right," she said quietly.

She was sorely tempted to say, *You mean* your
possessions, since your money bought them, but a truce
was a truce, and he'd apologized. Nevertheless,
she was still going to be thinking about that.

She was glad he'd already informed the staff.
It wasn't a task she'd have relished. Still, they'd
been in residence when she'd arrived; they were
his employees, and always had been. While they
were competent and respectful, she had formed
no special attachments to any of them.

He didn't return to his book. He held it open
in his lap.

They studied each other solemnly. She'd never
seen him this close, in low firelight. There were
a thousand versions of this man, her husband,
that she'd never had a chance to know and now
never would. She was reminded of how he'd
looked by leaf-dappled sunlight, the day he'd
attempted to untie her ribbons. Craggy, nearly
pagan. But if he was a "beast" at all, he was the
grand sort out of mythology, calm, dignified,
and when crossed, thoroughly, unapologetically
dangerous.

Suddenly something like reluctant wonder

flickered in his eyes. It was there and gone, but it made her breath catch.

She suspected he would prefer it if she had no power to move him at all. But it seemed she still did. It changed nothing.

In the silence, a strange, soft warmth settled over her skin, a sort of unnerving awareness of everything that was so very unequivocally male about him. Magnus was nothing like the sleek aristocratic youngbloods among whom she'd been raised. She remembered how it had felt to be briefly pressed against Paul's slim young body; she remembered imagining that Magnus would engulf her, by comparison.

If they, in truth, had been a typical husband and wife, she would know by now what every inch of Magnus's skin looked like. And felt like. Not just these intriguing little portions of him from which imagination unfurled.

And grief surprised her with a short, sharp jolt.

"What time is it?" she asked at once. "Are we in danger of breaking rules by not going downstairs? Did you have your dinner? I'm not hungry yet. The scones and soup were delicious and very filling."

He fished his watch from his trouser pocket. "If you like, we've still time to fulfill our duty to obey the house rules by mingling with the other guests in the sitting room. Everyone should still be gathered. I met some of them at dinner, and I'm already acquainted with Hardy and Bolt. Mr. Delacorte is one of their business partners, and I've never met anyone quite like him, and that's saying something. It's a decidedly unusual but quite pleasant crew. Their cook, by the way, is indeed gifted. Dinner was marvelous."

"I think I would like to go down."

She was at heart a social creature. And it would be better not to be alone with him, she thought. And not entirely for the reasons she would have cited yesterday.

ALEXANDRA AND MAGNUS hovered a moment in the doorway of the sitting room.

Their proprietresses, the golden-blonde Mrs. Durand and the dark-haired Mrs. Hardy, were knitting. Next to Mrs. Durand a lean and darkly gorgeous man sprawled with indolent grace in a chair. She suspected this was Lord Bolt. He was holding his wife's knitting, and wearing a teasing smile, as if she'd just said something amusing.

Near them, the maid named Dot was stabbing a needle into and out of an embroidery hoop, her brow furrowed with concentration.

The two men sitting at a game table with a chessboard between them must be Captain Hardy and Mr. Delacorte, Alexandra thought. A dewily young couple, a man and a woman, sat across from each other at another table, and two handsome women who appeared to be in their middle years were the balance of the guests.

Alexandra discovered again how interesting it was to enter a room alongside Brightwall and experience the hush that fell as a group of people adjusted to an influx of awe.

And then everyone shot to their feet.

Their proprietresses were smiling with genuine pleasure. "We're so delighted both of you could join us tonight," Mrs. Durand said. "Come, let us introduce you, Mrs. Brightwall. And I don't believe you've yet met all of our guests, Colonel Brightwall."

Alexandra had guessed correctly: both Mr. Delacorte, who was shaped a bit like the letter "D" on legs and had rather dreamy blue eyes and a merry expression, and Captain Hardy—chiseled, handsome, with close-cropped hair and silvery eyes—bowed when she was introduced to them.

The two older women were Mrs. Cuthbert and Mrs. Pariseau. Mrs. Cuthbert's lustrously gray hair was piled intricately up on her head. Around her throat a string of small, fine pearls glowed. She was a woman who took great pains with nearly everything, if Alexandra had to guess, and the grooves around her mouth suggested she was seldom satisfied with everyone else's efforts. They were told that Mrs. Cuthbert was visiting London specifically to visit with her old friend Mrs. Pariseau, who was a permanent resident of The Grand Palace on the Thames.

"It's a pleasure to meet such distinguished guests," she said to the Brightwalls with the slightest emphasis on "distinguished." As though she'd been at her wit's end tolerating the rest of the riffraff in the room.

Corporal and Mrs. Dawson were the young couple. Both had blanched at the very sight of the colonel, and were now staring at Magnus as if Moses had strolled into the sitting room.

"S-such an honor, sir." Corporal Dawson managed a bow, but his knees appeared to be about to give way.

"Thank you. Likewise. At ease, Corporal," Magnus said.

This was almost funny. Alexandra was fairly certain poor Corporal Dawson would never experience a moment's ease in Brightwall's presence.

Alexandra was just twenty-seven, but the Dawsons briefly made her feel both ancient and a trifle wistfully envious of their obvious devotion. They would have a lifetime to grow up together. It was so like the marriage Alexandra had imagined for herself.

Mrs. Pariseau was a handsome, compact, curvy widow who had crackling dark eyes and a dashing white stripe in her dark, upswept hair. "I cannot begin to tell you what an honor it is to meet you, Colonel Brightwall," she said on a fervent hush, after performing a graceful curtsy. "And you as well, Mrs. Brightwall. I hope you will soon discover that we do have a lovely time in this room! We sometimes read aloud—we've been enjoying *The Arabian Nights' Entertainments* lately—or play spillikins or chess. And sometimes—not lately—we just have an invigorating discussion."

The "not lately" amused Alexandra. It sounded ever so slightly admonishing. As though Mrs. Pariseau expected better from everyone in the room.

Magnus was right: the characters assembled had the makings of a promising evening.

"I adore spirited conversation," Alexandra confirmed. "Magnus and I had one earlier this afternoon."

Her husband shot her a wary sideways glance.

Everyone resumed their seats and Magnus and Alexandra were settled into comfortable chairs near each other. The room was bathed in a flattering light courtesy of a huge leaping fire and a little collection of lamps. None of the furniture quite matched, but this somehow seemed the very secret to the room's cozy appeal. The pianoforte pushed against one wall strewn with what looked like well-thumbed sheet music suggested occasional musical interludes were enjoyed. On the mantel a large jar occupied pride of place.

"Well! I understand you've just spent some time in jail, Mrs. Brightwall," Mrs. Pariseau began brightly.

Mrs. Hardy and Mrs. Durand froze.

Mrs. Cuthbert visibly recoiled. Her head swiveled toward Alexandra. Her eyes had widened to cue ball size.

Her wobbly smile indicated that she was hoping against hope it wasn't true.

Alexandra, a trifle taken aback, recovered quickly, and smiled sweetly at Mrs. Pariseau.

"Oh, it was nothing. It was a silly misunderstanding." Alexandra waved her hand airily. "Born of a lark gone amok."

Magnus stiffened, but Mrs. Pariseau's question

didn't strike Alexandra as malicious or censorious. Mrs. Pariseau clearly just thought jail might be *interesting*.

And, well, she wasn't wrong.

"My dear, no one considers jail a lark." Mrs. Cuthbert was aghast. She looked around hopefully for approbation.

"Oh, Prudence. How would you know?" Mrs. Pariseau sounded as though she was losing patience with Mrs. Cuthbert. "Jail could happen to anyone."

This sweeping statement probably wasn't at all true, but Alexandra appreciated the passionate defense.

And frankly, if spirited discourse was indeed permitted per the rules of The Grand Palace on the Thames, Alexandra decided she was going to have a little fun with Mrs. Cuthbert.

Though she wasn't going to outright admit to being in jail.

"Did you know"—she leaned forward to address the gathering at large on a confiding hush—"that *hairpins* are actually considered a weapon? I'd never before thought of them that way! But in jail, they are. But then, Magnus says anything can be a weapon. And he ought to know."

She directed a fond gaze at him.

Magnus was staring at her, astonished, but not, it seemed, unamused.

Thusly she wickedly roped her distinguished husband into the controversy.

"Surely not," Mrs. Cuthbert stammered. "Surely not *anything*."

But Mrs. Pariseau was positively luminous with the possibility of an invigorating exploration of weaponry and clasped her hands in delight.

"*What* an opportunity to discover how resourceful all of us would be in an emergency. Can anything indeed be a weapon? If, for instance, a scoundrel who might be armed with a pistol, an intruder, was to sneak up on you now right where you're sitting . . . how would you defend yourself with the objects closest to you? I think I would jab him with *my* hairpins."

Alexandra nodded approvingly. "Very good choice," she said, as though she was suddenly an expert.

"What about you, Mrs. Hardy? Mrs. Durand?" Mrs. Pariseau turned to them.

Delilah and Angelique regarded Mrs. Pariseau levelly. While undoubtedly enlivening, they were not at all certain that figurative violence was the best way to inject spirit into the room's discussion. A milder topic might have been a safer choice for reviving the conversational momentum after a week or so of inertia. A recovering invalid shouldn't spring out of bed and dance a jig straightaway, after all.

But Mrs. Pariseau looked so pleased to finally have a topic she could sink her teeth into that Delilah cautiously capitulated. She tentatively held up her knitting needle.

Angelique followed suit. Cautiously.

They were prepared to rein the conversation in, if it came to that.

"What about you, Dot?" Mrs. Pariseau asked. "Perhaps your embroidery needle?"

Dot looked up from her sampler and tipped her head in thought. "I would throw my fist right into his jaw," she finally said. "And he would fall to the ground, unconscious. And then I would kneel next to him and brush his hair out of his eyes and say, 'Oh, please, oh *please* don't die. I don't want to go to Newgate!'"

This was greeted by a moment of thoroughly nonplussed silence.

"Thank you, Dot," Mrs. Pariseau finally replied politely. "I'm certain the intruder would never return again if you did that."

Dot smiled, pleased.

Mrs. Cuthbert's wide-eyed gaze had been whipping from person to person as Mrs. Pariseau called on them, as if stunned to find herself in a room full of potential brigands.

"What would you use as a weapon, Mrs. Cuthbert?" Alexandra asked.

"I—I would *never* use a weapon." Her chin had hiked defiantly.

Somebody snorted rudely. It was difficult to tell who.

"If a thief were to creep up behind you now in the sitting room, you would passively allow him to take your pretty necklace even when you have a chance of fighting back?" Magnus sounded genuinely curious.

Mrs. Cuthbert absently touched her necklace, a flicker of uncertain, bashful pleasure in her eyes.

But she was not going to allow flattery to divert her from the deliciousness of exasperation and alarm. "Why are we discussing this? Has an intruder ever done this? Do we need to prepare for this eventuality? Is this a *test*?" The pitch of her voice escalated with every word.

No one in the history of The Grand Palace on the Thames had ever been more confused about the purpose of the sitting room conversations.

"You could always hurl your slippers at him, Mrs. Cuthbert," Magnus suggested.

Alexandra turned swiftly toward him. Her jaw dropped.

He didn't meet her eyes, but she could tell by the little creases at the corners of his that they were glinting.

"But slippers are *not* for hurling!" Mrs. Cuthbert was aghast.

Alexandra covered her mouth with her hands to keep her little gasp-laugh from escaping.

"Huh. I've needed to get out of scrapes before but I never thought of throwing a boot!" Mr. Delacorte mused. "Mine would level a bloke with the smell alone."

"I know what *else* Delacorte could use as a weapon," Lucien said.

"Ha ha!" Delacorte knew, too.

(As did everyone else who lived permanently at The Grand Palace on the Thames. They had all learned the hard way not to share close quarters with Mr. Delacorte immediately after he'd eaten a rich meal.)

"Captain Hardy?" Mrs. Pariseau turned to him.

Captain Hardy drummed his fingers thoughtfully. "Oh, I'd whip out my knife, use my cravat as a sort of garrote, knee him in the back, and slam his head on the table."

Everyone gave a start.

Except Delilah, who had once seen him do something very similar.

"How very specific, Captain Hardy," Mrs. Pariseau approved finally, sounding both a bit rattled and breathlessly impressed. "How about you, Lord Bolt?"

"Hmmm . . . let's see. I'd get my knife out, too. First, I'd bash him a good one with the chessboard to stun him, then knee him hard in the groin."

Every man in the room hissed in an involuntary breath.

Mrs. Cuthbert visibly flinched at the word "groin." "Is *every* man in the room carrying a knife right now?"

Every man in the room nodded.

"*Oh,*" she peeped in dismay. She touched two fingers to her lips.

"What about you, Mr. Delacorte? What would you do?" Mrs. Pariseau asked.

"I think I'd step aside so Hardy could be my weapon."

Captain Hardy nodded, agreeably accepting that he was, in fact, a weapon.

"Or . . . I'd jam the rook into his eye socket," Delacorte added gleefully. "Or the bishop. It's pointier."

Everyone hissed in a breath this time.

Delilah cleared her throat noisily, preparing to hurl herself verbally in front of the runaway carriage that was this conversation. But it seemed to have acquired momentum.

"Corporal Dawson, what would you use for a weapon?" Magnus asked.

The boy paled so completely at being addressed by Colonel Brightwall himself that his freckles stood out like inkblots.

"Sh-shoot," he stammered.

"'Shoot' is not a weapon, Corporal. And you don't have a gun to hand right now, do you?"

"S-s-sorry, sir."

He stared dumbly, his mind clearly erased by the strain of looking into the face of a legend.

"I'm just a soldier, same as you, Corporal Dawson," Magnus said quietly.

He looked appalled at this comparison. "Oh, no, sir," he said with some conviction. "You are not the same as *anyone*."

"I was. I was, in fact, an ensign, who became a corporal, just like you," he reiterated gently but firmly.

Alexandra doubted profoundly the "just like you" part, but it was very kind of him to say.

But as if this had never occurred to Corporal Dawson, his frozen awe thawed a bit, and he eyed Brightwall with abject gratitude. As if a veil had been ripped away and he could imagine different possibilities for his future.

Brightwall tried again. "If, say, a Viking marauder were to storm through the window here with the intent of snatching up Mrs. Dawson and carrying her off—"

"A *Viking!*" Mrs. Cuthbert yelped, and clapped a hand over her bosom. "Now it's *Vikings*?"

"I've never known anyone to be so frightened of the *hypothetical*," Mrs. Pariseau muttered.

"I would pick up this entire table and hurl it at the Viking, sir," Corporal Dawson said at once.

An impressed, total silence honored the unique and exceptional violence of this solution.

"There's a good lad," Brightwall said contentedly.

Mrs. Dawson beamed meltingly at her husband, who was scarlet with pleasure now.

"What about you, Colonel Brightwall?" Mrs. Pariseau asked.

"Oh . . ." He tipped his head back in thought. "I'd probably subdue him with a stony look of displeasure or an icy silence."

Alexandra stared at him. He was quoting *her*, from their earlier discussion.

It was fascinating, and just a little gratifying. Because it seemed clear that this had somehow gotten under his skin.

He didn't glance her way. But his eyes had a challenging gleam, and the corners of them were crinkled ever so slightly.

No one seemed to know how to respond to this. Tentative smiles were the default response.

Delilah leaped gratefully into the lull.

"Speaking of stone, I understand a statue is being erected in your honor in Holland Park,

Colonel Brightwall, and there will be a ceremony in honor of it. We read about it in the
newspaper."

Which is where, presumably, they'd read all
about Alexandra's alleged jail stay.

"Indeed, I am to be so honored," Magnus
told Delilah. "I'm given to understand it's me,
on a horse. Entirely made of cold, hard stone, of
course."

Alexandra pressed her lips together.

"The king sent Captain Hardy and Mrs. Hardy
a silver cup as a wedding present. It's about this
big," Dot volunteered. She held up her hands.

"A cup is nice, too," Brightwall said politely,
somewhat mischievously, to Captain Hardy. Who
nodded, amused.

"If a statue was going to be made commemorat-
ing you, what would it be?" Mrs. Pariseau asked
the group at large.

Delilah and Angelique exchanged glances.
They were a little winded from the unpredictable
nature of the discourse tonight, but this question
seemed a trifle safer.

Although one never knew, of course.

"Mrs. Dawson?" Mrs. Pariseau aimed her bright,
inquisitive gaze at the young woman.

Mrs. Dawson flushed furiously. "I don't know.
I'm just a girl." Her volume was scarcely more
than a squeak. "It would be a statue of a girl."

Alexandra was fairly certain Mrs. Pariseau was
suppressing a sigh.

"And I'm certain you would make a lovely

statue, dear," Mrs. Pariseau replied patiently, finally. "What about you, Mrs. Brightwall?"

Alexandra liked these sorts of questions. "Oh, I think I'd like to be a statue in the middle of a fountain, the kind of fountain with tiers. So every kind of creature could come and have a drink—birds and bees and butterflies and deer and squirrels, and the like—and I could greet everyone, and see all the visitors."

"Oh, *lovely*," Mrs. Pariseau approved, beaming at her.

Something—a shift in the *feel* of the room—made Alexandra glance at Magnus in time to see an expression of something like longing fleeing from his face.

Stunned, she stared at him.

He did not return his gaze to her.

"Oh, I'd want to be a fountain, too," Mr. Delacorte concluded. "One of those statues that everyone knows about and which gives them a right laugh. Squirting water in a funny way, perhaps. Leaning back and shooting it out my mouth. Or I'd be standing there, with my trousers down, you know, having a—"

"DON'T SAY HAVING A PISS," Mrs. Cuthbert implored.

A silence dropped like a dome.

Clearly Mr. Delacorte had slowly eroded Mrs. Cuthbert's being fibers over a period of days, and they had finally snapped.

The Epithet Jar seemed to pulse.

Everyone stared at Mrs. Cuthbert with varying

degrees of sympathy, suppressed glee, and smug satisfaction.

Mrs. Cuthbert's eyes grew and grew in size when she realized what she'd done.

"You . . . you were going to say having a p-piss," she said weakly to Mr. Delacorte and the company at large. "I know you were."

"I might have done," Mr. Delacorte agreed gently, "but *you* said it instead." He paused eloquently. "Twice."

No one spoke. The rules were clear. The Epithet Jar performed an important function in maintaining a civilized atmosphere, and everyone took it seriously. It was also often how The Grand Palace on the Thames paid for the morning newspapers.

"Here," Mr. Delacorte said kindly. He fished a penny from his pocket and brought it over to Mrs. Cuthbert. "I'll walk with you to the jar, if you like, so you won't feel alone. I know the way."

She stood, and, like an abbess escorting a novitiate nun to have her head shaved, Mr. Delacorte escorted Mrs. Cuthbert to the Epithet Jar.

She dropped her penny in.

"We've all had to do it," Mrs. Pariseau said more gently to her old friend. Whose lower lip was wobbling.

"Really?" Mrs. Cuthbert said tremulously.

Everyone nodded supportively, even though this wasn't true.

"Perhaps we should have some music? Would you like that, Mrs. Cuthbert?" Delilah shot a warning glance at Mr. Delacorte. He had a fondness for one particular song which was somewhat naughty and featured clapping, and he tended to advocate vigorously for it when they decided upon a musical evening. "Would you like to sing?"

"Yes, I would like that," Mrs. Cuthbert managed with dignity. "Do you know 'Black-Eyed Susan'?"

"We do!" Angelique and Delilah enthused in unison.

Angelique settled in at the pianoforte, and Delilah went to turn the pages of the score.

As it turned out Mrs. Cuthbert had a decent, and startlingly emotional, soprano singing voice.

People will always surprise you, Alexandra thought.

And as it soon became clear that the rest of the evening would be devoted to playing and singing sentimental ballads, Alexandra decided to take her leave. She played and sang passably well, but that pitiful sailor poetically pining for his black-eyed Susan made her feel jaded, and reminded her that she would be on the ocean soon and, unlike Susan, leaving behind a man who didn't want her.

"I'll just bid everyone good-night, shall I?" she whispered to Dot, who was nearest.

And when she rose, Magnus rose, too, to escort her out.

IN SILENCE, THEY traveled back to their suite in the annex. He had offered her his arm on the way into the sitting room, for appearance's sake.

He did not do that now.

"Surprisingly, I enjoyed every bit of that," she said finally, as they scaled the stairs. "I wouldn't mind having an evening like that every night."

"I did, rather, as well," he admitted, after a hesitation. "Except for the ballads. I would rather gouge out my eye with a rook or a bishop than listen to Mrs. Cuthbert sing about yearning."

She laughed, because she couldn't help it. And because she agreed.

But then she regretted laughing a little, as part of her remained resistant to feeling entertained by her husband.

He sighed with relief and shook himself out of his coat the moment the door closed behind the two of them, and then reached for his cravat.

For such a big man, his movements were always so graceful and purposeful. She was oddly captivated, as if she was witnessing some rare wild animal in the act of shedding its skin.

He paused in the process of practically clawing away his cravat. Suddenly aware that she was watching him with some blend of amusement and bemusement.

She'd caught him in the middle of a reflex, she suspected. The immediate coat and cravat removal. This was something else she would have known about him if their marriage was a more orthodox one.

"You're shedding all of that as though you feel like a cat stuffed into a coat," she said.

He laughed shortly. "My apologies. I suppose

it's a bit of a habit. They get to feeling a little confining after a while, cravats and coats."

"You ought to try wearing stays," she told him.

His smile evolved into a laugh. "Maybe I will, one day."

He finished slowly unwinding the cravat. It dangled from his hand.

"You're not going to fling that at me, are you?" She tried a risky joke.

He pretended to ponder this. "Fair's fair, Alexandra."

They regarded each other from across the room. His eyes were glinting.

She wanted to laugh again, so, perversely, she didn't.

She cleared her throat. "Well, I'll just say goodnight, shall I?"

"Good night. And remember . . ." he said, as she began to close her door, "slippers are *not* for hurling."

Damn him.

Because she laughed at that.

She sighed, and poked the fire to get it to blaze a little more, took off her projectile slippers and left them in the middle of the rug again.

And then she just lay quietly on the bed in her clothes for a time, and reflected.

The odd relief she felt was akin to being fed a meal after surviving on soldiers' rations. She'd been *starved* for companionship, and diverse entertainments, and lonely for people she genuinely liked. For *camaraderie*. It had been lovely to be surrounded by the determined if somewhat cockeyed warmth, and yes, familial atmosphere of the sitting room. She saw the brilliance in Mrs. Hardy and Mrs. Durand's mission for The Grand Palace on the Thames.

She considered how strange it was that both she and Magnus could laugh even after the emotional whipsaw of a fiery eruption of thrown objects followed by a quietly devastating, marriage-ending conversation. What did this say about her? About him?

Well, she'd always known she was resilient.

And he, above all, was a survivor.

She supposed they both were.

How odd that it was something he'd seemed to sense about her long ago, too.

And she reflected on the gentle but firm authority with which Magnus had engaged that shy, green Corporal Dawson in the conversation. What a good father he would be for a boy, she thought. He would teach him survival skills, like in *Robinson Crusoe*. How to make a fire and aim a gun and all that sort of thing.

Eventually, maybe how to become the sort of man who could freeze the gizzards of a Newgate warden with a mere glance, and magically spring his wife from jail.

The thing that made Magnus thrilling in a frightening way, and frightening in a thrilling way, was the ruthlessness that ran right down through the core of him. She'd always known he was much more than that; he was a complicated man. But it was an unavoidable part of him, the support beam around which his very spirit was constructed. She had come up against it, and it had nearly crushed her. It would behoove her to never forget this.

She pictured him as he likely was now, sitting in front of the fire in his shirtsleeves, staring fiercely at the pages of his book, lost in an adventure. It suddenly made her restlessly sad that she couldn't just sit beside him and talk to him of idle things, because she thought they both might enjoy it. But she also felt they both had forfeited the right to do that. She suspected she was, as Agnes of Newgate had said, safer where she was: behind a door, and not anywhere near the bare, bronzed skin of his arms.

Chapter Nine

✥

ANGELIQUE LAUGHED. "Look at us! We're like a cuckoo clock this morning."

Angelique was right: the four of them—Delilah and Tristan and Angelique and Lucien—had popped from their rooms at almost precisely the same moment, indeed like a cuckoo on a clock. They were up even earlier than the maids this morning, in part because Lucien and Tristan needed to inspect a new warehouse the Triton Group, their shipping partnership, hoped to lease.

While everyone was still singing about the pianoforte last night, Lucien and Tristan and Mr. Delacorte had lingered over papers and numbers regarding the Triton Group in the smoking room. Their wives had already been asleep by the time they'd gone up to their bedrooms.

"This will be the first time I've beaten Delacorte to breakfast, I reckon," Captain Hardy said.

They had all taken a few steps down the hall when Delilah stopped and laid her hand on Tristan's arm to stop him, too. "Do you all hear that? It sounds like . . . someone weeping."

They paused to listen.

The sound was faint but unmistakable . . . and chilling: a low, mournful keen that seemed to come from everywhere and nowhere.

The little hairs lifted on Delilah's arms.

Angelique swallowed. "Surely it's the wind. Though I thought we did manage to find and repair all the drafts after the last storm."

"Maybe we've just never been up early enough to hear the ghosts before." Lucien was whispering for some reason.

"Shhh." Angelique squeezed his arm.

The sound seemed to increase in volume as they moved down the hall.

. . . *ohhhhh* . . .

It had acquired a distinct note of anguish.

"Christ," Lucien breathed. Unnerved now.

"Where is it *coming* from?" Angelique's head tipped back toward the ceiling, as if this was the province of ghosts.

Captain Hardy gestured them forward, as if they were a landing party confronting a hostile army. As a group, they tentatively descended a few stairs.

Then stopped again to listen.

Seconds later they heard:

. . . *oohhhh* . . . *OHHHHH* . . .

Much louder now. And . . . hoarser.

"It's definitely someone in pain," Captain Hardy said grimly. "And it's a woman. I think she's saying 'no'?"

"Tristan!" Delilah gasped.

Tristan and Lucien swiftly produced pistols

from somewhere on their persons—neither Delilah nor Angelique asked questions anymore—just as a hoarse scream froze the blood in their veins.

. . . Ahhh Ahhhh AaaaAAAUUGGGGGH *Simon!*

En masse, they hurtled down the stairs.

The echoes of that scream were dying behind the door of Corporal Dawson's room.

"Oh God oh God oh God," Delilah fervently prayed.

"Stand back!" Captain Hardy hoisted a leg to kick the door down.

"Wait!" Lucien seized Captain Hardy's shoulder. "Listen."

Then they recognized it: A sound reminiscent of a goat kicking the slats of its stall.

A rhythm as old as time.

In other words: the legs of a bed against a wooden floor.

Thump. Thump. Thump. Thump. Thump.

Thumpthumpthumpthump*thumpthumpthump-THUMP!*

The last mighty thump had them scrambling backward as if the door were about to explode.

Too late, Delilah crossed her arms over her head in a futile attempt to prevent Corporal Dawson's gurgling cry of ecstasy from entering her ears.

And then all was blessed silence.

As this was not an experience any of them had ever anticipated or hoped to share with one another, no one knew quite where to aim their eyes, or what to do with their hands. Tristan and

Lucien were still holding pistols. They were all in fact crouched a little, as if the ceiling was caving in.

"Holy Mother of God," Lucien finally breathed, in awe.

He spoke for all of them.

They were all silent, winded from being buffeted between terror, mortification, relief, and maybe just a little envy, in a matter of seconds.

It was all cooing and murmurs behind the door now. And giggles.

"I say we shoot them anyway," Captain Hardy suggested darkly.

They stifled uneasy laughter.

This little tableau—the drawn pistols, the stupefied expressions, the cringing postures, as if they wished they could all change out of their old skins into new, unsullied skins—was what greeted Mrs. Pariseau when she exited the room adjacent, handsomely dressed in a maroon day dress.

They all gave a guilty start.

"Well, good morning, everyone." She turned the key in her lock.

"Good morning, Mrs. Pariseau," they replied in absurd unison.

She paused to study them, amused.

She gestured with a head tilt at Corporal and Mrs. Field Mouse's door and whispered, with an eyebrow wag, "Third time today!"

They stepped aside so she could pass down the stairs.

ONE OF THE things Delilah and Angelique loved about being proprietresses of a boardinghouse near the docks was the variety. And while the day-to-day was on the whole delightful, they had also contended with the British soldiers pouring into the building, a runaway French princess, a secret tunnel, smugglers, ravenous German musicians, a scandalous opera singer, several attempts by various aristocrats to steal their cook, a makeshift gambling den, financial fluctuations, Mr. Delacorte, and Dot. They had managed all of this more or less with aplomb.

Somehow confronting this newest challenge seemed to require more courage than all of those combined.

As the comfort of their guests was paramount, they intercepted Mrs. Pariseau in the foyer when she returned from her morning jaunt and invited her for a cup of tea in the kitchen.

The three of them sat at one end of their large worktable while Helga rolled dough for tarts at the other end.

"Mrs. Pariseau, we're so terribly sorry about the . . . the neighborly disruption. Would you like us to move them to another room? Would you like us to prepare another room for you temporarily?"

Mrs. Pariseau lifted a hand. "Oh, please don't trouble yourselves, ladies. I can pretend it's the sound of wild animals murdering each other on the savanna or some such. It's an inexpensive way to go on an educational little holiday in my mind. Last night I imagined it was a hyena taking down an antelope. I went to a lecture about those animals not too long ago, as you may recall. So interesting. And Corporal Dawson is only on leave for a fortnight, after all."

They were currently about five days into this fortnight.

"And, well, we're all only young once." Mrs. Pariseau shrugged one shoulder. "I can sleep whenever I like these days."

An awkward little silence ensued. Both Angelique and Delilah were just over thirty years old. Neither one of them was inclined to volunteer that their own youthful experiences had been significantly less abandoned.

"That's quite generous-spirited of you, Mrs. Pariseau," Angelique finally said. "But good heavens . . . that is . . . they're at it both day and night?" She lowered her voice to a hush, even though the maids were off performing their duties. She tried to keep that frisson of envy out of her tone.

"Whenever you don't see them in the sitting room, and they haven't gone out the front door, assume they're mounting each other," Mrs. Pariseau confirmed.

Delilah's shoulders flew up to her ears in a scrunch at the word "mounting."

"And you know . . . it's the same sequence of noises every time. It's absolutely fascinating," Mrs. Pariseau mused. "Like a mating call. Many animals have a unique one they use to attract a mate, were you aware?"

There was a silence, as Delilah, Angelique, and Helga all marveled at the store of arcane and occasionally uncomfortable knowledge that Mrs. Pariseau seemed to possess. As a relatively monied widow, she was able to liberally indulge her passion for learning.

They fervently hoped Mrs. Pariseau wouldn't be inspired to ask "If you had a mating call, what would it be?" in the sitting room.

"Funny thing, however. They were in residence for a few days before it started up," Mrs. Pariseau added.

They all reflected on this.

"Maybe Corporal Dawson finally found . . . er, her, you know . . . ah, *it*," Helga whispered.

Delilah nearly choked on her tea.

When Dot entered the kitchen seconds later, she found them all scarlet-faced and muffling snorting laughter in their palms.

"What did Corporal Dawson finally find?" Dot asked.

"Love," Delilah said firmly at once, wiping tears from her eyes. "Isn't it lovely that he's found love with Mrs. Dawson?"

"I suppose it must be," Dot allowed, somewhat wistfully.

ALEXANDRA COULD SCARCELY even hear the cobblestones pass beneath them, so well-sprung, sturdy, and smooth was the carriage. Outside the window, the London streets unfurled as the four matched bays and the skillful driver took them to the first of the events during which they would attempt to convincingly portray a devoted married couple, the Earl and Countess of Chisholm's ball.

Magnus had been out all day, but he'd returned to The Grand Palace on the Thames in time for the cheery ruckus that was dinner.

"You hardly look like a feral beast at all," was what he'd said when she'd emerged from her room wearing the rose-colored silk about a half hour earlier.

But his pupils had flared to the size of farthings. At least four heartbeats' worth of utter silence had elapsed before he'd gotten the words out.

She'd almost forgotten the piercing rush of delight that came from experiencing herself as beautiful in a man's eyes.

Nothing apart from that stillness and pupil flare, however, seemed to interrupt his usual cast-iron composure.

"Thank you, Magnus. No one would mistake you for a beast, either. We're already winning, I think."

This exchange had mordantly amused Alexandra. What were the rules when it came to estranged spouses offering each other compliments? They were very careful not to tread over some tacitly understood line of effusiveness.

Whoever was tasked with dressing him understood how to tailor for his body. The fit of his black coat lovingly emphasized his imposing frame and tapered from his vast shoulders to his hips. His shave was fresh and his tawny hair was brushed back off his forehead and some of it was tucked behind his ears. His crisply trimmed side whiskers emphasized his strong jaw and hard, high cheekbones. Silver buttons glinted on his dove-gray waistcoat.

He looked stern and polished and regal and, if she was being honest, scary, in an intriguing way. It made her feel strangely a bit shy. As if this dashing man in this dimly lit carriage was yet another version of Magnus she hadn't yet met.

He took up most of the carriage seat opposite; he seemed to create his own atmosphere, like incoming weather.

He gazed across at her thoughtfully.

And unswervingly.

Rather the way one would keep something lethal or something miraculous in one's sights. A dragon, or a holy grail, she thought.

A warmth akin to a low and not unpleasant fever again flushed her skin. As if she had been set aglow by the fixed quality of his attention.

It was impossible to know what he was thinking. It seemed rude to look away. Moreover, she didn't want to, not at all, and this was what finally made her force herself to turn her head to gaze out the window.

She had spent most of her day making lists of the additional things she wished to bring with her to New York. The packet ship she would take from Liverpool required two copies of the list of the possessions each of the twenty-eight or so passengers were bringing on their journeys, and she needed to redo the chore in light of the fact that she would not be returning to England. So she fought back resentment and a thousand other conflicting feelings, and did it.

Rummaging through her head for things she could not live without gave her a reason to reminisce, and then she became reflective. She would be bringing a little more than she'd originally planned, of course, but far less than she'd anticipated. It was a revelation to discover what she truly valued: a few little mementos from her childhood, a miniature of her mother, her art supplies. And to find that even as her heart felt somewhat heavy at the reason for doing it, as though she were sorting through a dead loved one's possessions, she gradually began to feel oddly lighter. And to even dare to begin to look forward to a new life, given how thoroughly she had inadvertently botched the one she had.

"This carriage is new, isn't it? It's very beautiful." She aimed her words out the window. They were nearly to St. James Square.

"Yes, I commissioned it last year. For now, I keep it in a livery nearby. Eventually I will keep it in the mews of a town house on Grosvenor Square I'm in the process of purchasing."

Her heart jolted. She turned to him. "You're purchasing a home on Grosvenor Square?"

"Yes," he told her quietly. "I thought a new home would be the best way to make a fresh start. It's why I'm selling the town house."

She nearly swallowed, but she was afraid he might notice. Her eyes burned.

"Of course," she said politely, finally. "I hope it's all you want it to be."

THE FOOTMAN'S ANNOUNCEMENT—"COLONEL and Mrs. Magnus Brightwall"—was greeted by the swirl of bright dresses and flash of tiaras and jewels in the chandelier glow as everyone turned toward them.

Magnus was about as physically conspicuous as a man could be and a notable personage on the threshold of becoming even more notable. And Alexandra was somewhat new to the people of the ton, who were accustomed to seeing the same people over and over at all their balls and parties.

And she was beautiful. Beauty conferred a different sort of royalty on a woman.

The dramatic contrast between them essentially ensured that all eyes would be glued to them.

Magnus had known they would be.

He was accustomed to negotiating crowds and to the feel of hundreds of eyes upon him. But he'd never entered a room with a woman like Alexandra on his arm.

Her gown was the same shade as her lips and her blushes, and, he could not help surmising, her nipples. It was overlaid with a sort of gossamer net dusted with tiny gold flowers, and her skin and coppery hair were luminous.

She stunned, in every sense of that word. His senses were consumed with the fact of her. He was quietly furious that he'd briefly lost his ability to speak when she'd stepped out of her room this evening. As surely as if he'd been physically smote.

But he had grown adept at metaphorically locking inconvenient feelings away into little cells, as if they were criminals who oughtn't mix with the civilized population, and a particularly inconvenient feeling was desire for the wife who had betrayed him.

It was best to view her tactically, as though she were a fine rifle. The best tool to accomplish a job needing done, which was restoring a measure of dignity to the Brightwall name in the eyes of the ton before he officially became an earl.

But bloody hell, he loved the way her face lit each time she was introduced to someone new, as if she was opening her whole self to this person, inviting them into her warmth. Of all the tasks he'd been given when he was a little boy in the Coopersmith house, where he'd grown up—so many of them vile, so many of them only tasks the other servants didn't want to do—he'd loved best carrying a candle with him through the halls to light the sconces. It had always felt like magic to him that one little flame could create so many others. And that's how he felt with Alexandra on his arm as he made introductions and greeted every titled, distinguished person in the ton—as though he were bringing her light to them.

He noticed, too, how all the men looked from her to him and back again, with envy, or wonder,

160   Julie Anne Long

as if he was some sort of mad genius for marrying such a beautiful woman.

And sometimes they looked at him with sympathy.

Most unlovely husbands of beautiful women eventually learn the perils involved, as well, he suspected.

"WHY, YOU DON'T look feral at all, Mrs. Brightwall," Lady Chisholm purred. "I'm almost disappointed."

Alexandra understood her mission—to enchant everyone to whom she was introduced, to make Magnus look like a genius for marrying her, to restore gloss and dignity to the Brightwall name by appearing to be half of an exemplary, perhaps even slightly dull, and devoted couple—and she'd had enough experience as a hostess to know how to tailor her approach to each new person.

Lady Chisholm was a bit of a doyenne: socially powerful, older, beautiful, and not, on the whole, a nice person, though she was known to never be dull. Her striking green eyes had taken Alexandra's measure swiftly and her expression suggested a piquant blend of guarded approval and acute and not entirely charitable curiosity.

The Earl of Chisholm had pulled aside Magnus, and the two of them were talking in low voices a little to the left of their wives. Perhaps there was a special club for earls he was being invited to join once the Letters Patent creating his title were officially filed by the king.

"'Feral'! My goodness! What a powerful word.

It's so fun to use, isn't it?" Alexandra replied cheerfully. "But please forgive me if I sound provincial when I confess to you that I'm not certain I understand the reference. Is 'feral' something the fashionable set is saying this year?"

Lady Chisholm's eyebrows launched. Uncertainty flickered across her features.

"It was the word they used to describe you in the gossip sheets," Lady Chisholm finally admitted. "Forgive my little jest. But it's part of the reason everyone is so eager to meet you this evening."

"Ohhhh." Alexandra gave a merry laugh and laid a gentle, friendly hand briefly on her arm. "I'm so sorry. I used to enjoy reading them, but suppose I got out of the habit after I married. Because when I think of how Magnus nearly died in battle . . ." She sucked in a sharp breath and squared her shoulders. "Well, the world is dangerous enough as it is, and after he nearly died all I wanted to read was kind and gentle things. The gossip pages are often witty, but they're so seldom kind. Was it at least amusing, what they wrote, if it wasn't kind?"

She gazed at Lady Chisholm hopefully.

Lady Chisholm pressed her lips together, nonplussed, and a trifle suspicious.

Alexandra radiated innocence at her.

"It was a drawing." Lady Chisholm's voice was rather subdued. "A Rowlandson drawing." As if that answered the "was it kind?" question, which, frankly, it did, and they both knew the answer was "no." She cleared her throat. "The article mentioned there was a bit of a to-do with a carriage, and . . ." She cleared her throat again, and added, somewhat hopefully, "Jail?"

Alexandra frowned. "Oh, *Rowlandson. That* rascal. I'm not certain what's meant by a to-do with a carriage, but it's almost an honor if Rowlandson chooses to draw a person, regardless of the circumstances, don't you think? But if I may share something with you, Lady Chisholm, entirely in confidence?" She leaned forward. "I know that Magnus looks like a fortress, and it's true he's very protective of me. I can bear just about anything on his behalf, but do think any sort of unkindness toward me would hurt him, and that troubles me so. Doesn't it seem like such a shame to cause pain for a hero who has already been so gravely injured?"

She gazed earnestly up at the countess.

Who stared back at her, speechless and clearly officially disarmed.

"You are right of course." Lady Chisholm sounded thoroughly chastised. "A shame, indeed."

"And I wonder if the newspapers are making things up out of whole cloth because Magnus has been away for so long, and I have been in England with my family, and no one has had a chance to see us together. But he's back now. I think they will discover the reality is much better, if also much less exciting." Alexandra smiled sweetly.

"I understand completely." Lady Chisholm was briskly earnest now. "Leave it to me, Mrs. Brightwall, to make certain no one brings up the topic to you again while you're our guest. They will need to answer to me."

"Thank you so much. Oh, I *knew* you would be thoughtful. You have that look about you."

"Have I?" Lady Chisholm, about whom such a thing had never before been said, was enchanted.

And then suddenly Lady Chisholm's head tilted way back to look up, which was how Alexandra knew Magnus had appeared behind her.

A light warmth hovered briefly at her back. Magnus's hand.

Ridiculously, her breath hitched in surprise. Of course he could touch her. He was her husband.

But his hand didn't linger against her. Unless one counted the tingle left behind. She found herself focusing on it, in order to make it last longer.

Lady Chisholm beamed at him.

"You must be so proud of your husband, Mrs. Brightwall."

"Oh, indeed. It's almost too much pride to bear," she agreed.

Out of the corner of her eye she saw the corner of Magnus's mouth twitch toward a smile.

"And how fortunate you are to have a wife who is such a credit to you, Colonel Brightwall," Lady Chisholm added generously. "How proud you must be of her."

And a little shadow moved over Alexandra's heart at the notion that Magnus might be forced to lie right in front of her. Of a certainty he could not truly be proud of her.

"I overheard her extolling my virtues to you a moment ago, Lady Chisholm, and I likewise cannot take credit for her charm. Only for recognizing it immediately."

Thusly he adroitly avoided answering that question.

The orchestra had begun playing the Sussex Waltz, and couples were moving out onto the floor.

He turned to her. "Mrs. Brightwall, I wondered if I may have the pleasure of this dance?"

Her heart accelerated oddly. She had never danced with him. "Of course, sir." She curtsied whimsically.

Magnus extended his arm, and he led her to the floor.

There was a reason the waltz had once been—still was, he supposed—considered scandalous. A man and a woman opened their arms to receive each other, in full view of the public. Unlike a reel, or a quadrille, they spent most of the music face-to-face. Which meant for the duration the man was treated to a long, uninterrupted view of the tantalizing tops of a woman's breasts pushed up by her stays, should he drop his eyes from hers.

It was not much of a stretch from there for a man to imagine his dancing partner pinned to a mattress, urging him to go faster and harder.

The minute leap of Alexandra's rib cage when he settled his hand against her waist made him feel both tender and nearly savage with possessiveness. Her small gloved hand disappearing into his made him feel almost violently protective. None of these feelings were rational. His feelings regarding her had never belonged to the realm of reason.

Simultaneously, as he reached for her, he recalled that a young man somewhere in the world knew the feel of Alexandra pressed against his body, and her lips against his, and the memory of her in that man's arms applied ice to the low burn of Magnus's longing.

But even before he touched her tonight, he knew their bodies had already started a silent dialogue. He had sensed it in their suite, as she'd sat near him on the settee the other night. In the dark of the carriage. He could feel it on his skin the way he could the promise of a thunderstorm. That crackle of portent.

He wasn't imagining it now, and he hadn't imagined it five years ago, when he'd sensed a spark. The male of every species was exquisitely attuned to this sort of thing, he supposed.

Then again, it wasn't something one could really control. It was the sort of thing that could still roil beneath the surface, even if they despised each other.

Through some miracle, he was certain she didn't despise him.

And they moved together, nearly oblivious to the other couples on the floor, many if not most of whom were watching them. His heart turned over to see himself reflected in her eyes, which were solemn, and searching. What did she see? A hard man, of a certainty. He was unequivocally that. He'd earned it. Not a handsome one. But the days when he'd longed to look like Hardy or Bolt were behind him; he did not see the point in longing for what could not be. He was seasoned enough now to appreciate about himself the things he had once rued, or suffered over.

He was perhaps foolish enough now to want to be wanted because of these things, not in spite of them. Wanted for everything that he was, the way he had never been wanted as a boy.

"I overheard you laying waste to Lady Chisholm's attempts to perpetuate the Newgate gossip. Nicely done. You might recall I told you once you'd make a good diplomat."

"I'm not certain how admirable it is to admit this, but I found it rather invigorating," she told him. "Like a badminton match. Perhaps I haven't been challenged enough recently."

"I can't imagine stealing a carriage makes the best use of your talents. Perhaps you ought to diversify your pastimes."

She looked both uncertain and tempted to laugh. "You're teasing me," she hazarded.

"Yes. A little."

Neither one of them seemed very inclined to give each other leeway when it came to being charmed. Both were stubborn.

A slightly weighty little silence followed. If things had been different, they might have had a family of their own by now. She would have, of a certainty, been occupied.

And he knew that despite the occasional speculative appearance in the gossip sheets, she had, in fact, been conservative about her entertainments over the past five years. He appreciated this. But he also felt a little twinge of guilt about it.

"The spirited discourse at The Grand Palace on the Thames ought to keep you on your toes," he said.

She did laugh then.

He'd forgotten her laugh was better than champagne.

"Do . . . do you like operas?" she asked suddenly.

He considered this. "I'm not really sure," he admitted. "I haven't decided."

Her eyes lit with amusement and curiosity. "Some are easier to like than others," she agreed.

"It's just . . . I'm still trying to learn what leisure pastimes I enjoy." He was a little embarrassed to admit it. "I've been a soldier for so long, and I've had little time for leisure pursuits since I was sixteen years old. Apart from the sort of leisure pursuits boys get up to. Shooting targets, five-card loo. Curse words. Fistfights. And I've been trying this and that."

She studied him with soft, intrigued sympathy. He felt a trifle abashed.

"Let's see. You like horses . . ."

So she was going to help him discover his pleasures and pursuits, and damned if he wasn't touched.

"All animals."

This made her smile. She thought a little more.

He looked forward to what she would come out with. "Gardens?"

"Yes. Trees, flowers, and gardens, both the very tidy kind, because it appeals to the soldier in me who likes to see things in formation, and the wild kind, because I rather admire the tenacity of anything that tries to be fully itself."

She looked rapt. "The ocean?"

"Yes, very much," he said quietly.

He suspected she was offering a list of things *she* loved.

"Ocean voyages?" She was tentative.

"Yes," he said gently, after a moment. Knowing she would be embarking on her first in a few days.

"And you like reading . . ."

"I do."

Suddenly her eyes were dancing. "If you were a fountain, what sort of fountain would you be?"

He gave a little shout of laughter. Then he sighed. "Mrs. Pariseau is invigorating."

"I thought so. And I rather like her prickly friend, too. Mrs. Cuthbert. She's like a dash of pepper in the stew. Or that one ingredient you're not certain you like, but which makes things interesting."

"Mrs. Cuthbert is likely just a bit too stimulated. Frightened creatures use whatever defenses they have at their disposal, and hers is disapproval. Other people throw gloves and slippers."

Her eyes flared in surprise, and a flush moved into her cheeks. But she didn't relinquish his gaze; she in fact inspected his face rather fiercely. Whatever she saw there made her eyes shine.

"And I would be an indestructible fountain, and I would never run dry, so that any thirsty creature who wants a drink can come and have one. How it looks matters not a bit, as long as those things are true. Perhaps it's a great block."

Her eyes were shining with delight now. "I'm certain people would come from miles around for the honor of drinking from the great block."

He laughed.

"Speaking of frightened creatures, I wonder how Lord Thackeray is faring in Newgate," she ventured.

Bloody hell.

Perhaps she liked her chances of persuading him while she was wearing that dress, and after she had just charmed him. He had to admire the tactic.

"Oh, he might be sharpening a stool leg into a shiv as we speak. Or bartering his shoes for food."

Charming men who were a bit feckless had a place in the world. But Thackeray had endangered her and Magnus remained quietly, implacably furious about it. Thackeray's crime—his *mistake*, as it were—was ridiculous. A grown man had no business being such a fool.

"There was a time when you told me you were disinclined to judge people," she ventured.

"It isn't judgment to allow people to experience the consequences of their actions," he explained, tersely.

And that's when he saw her jaw set.

"Of course not," she said, with great irony.

"And I suppose people also tell you what punishment they deserve with their actions."

And just like that, tension simmered. Because now they were talking about her, and him, and their wedding night.

"In my experience, unfailingly," he said simply, which he knew would madden her.

He didn't know why he liked the fact that she had a temper. It wasn't the spoiled or capricious sort; it arose from a defense of her rights and convictions, and he wholly respected it, even when he disagreed with her.

A silence fell for a bar's worth of the music.

"It's just . . . Thackeray is my family." She said this somewhat resignedly. Sadly. With the faintest hint of despair. "Maybe you don't . . ."

She pressed her lips together. He thought she might have intended her next word to be "understand."

They both knew he had essentially rescued her family once before, in exchange for a wife who had immediately proved faithless. And not once had he complained about his bad bargain.

"I do understand why you are concerned for your cousin's welfare," he said with a certain strained patience. "And I appreciate your sense of responsibility. I never knew my own family. But I look after Mrs. Scofield, the housekeeper from the home where I was raised. She's the one who found me as an infant."

He wasn't certain why he'd told her about Mrs. Scofield. His reasons for paying for her keep during her retirement were, in fact, a bit complicated. And he wasn't certain he understood all of them, himself.

"It's good of you to care for her," she said politely. "I imagine Mr. Lawler has been paying her bills, as well?"

"He has been, yes. Her lodgings are in fact near the park. Before the statue unveiling ceremony, I'd like to pay a short visit to her to ascertain everything is well."

"Very well." She paused. "I should like to meet her."

They didn't speak for a time; they merely moved in the dance. Embers of rancor still smoldered. But their eyes remained fixed upon each other's faces. He could not seem to think of a reason to look away, when she was the only thing he currently wanted to see.

Finally he said, "I apologize if you should like to dance a reel this evening. I'm not certain my leg is currently equal to it."

It was both a tactic to break the tension and, alas, the truth.

Her face suffused with softness at once and everything in him yearned toward it as though it was one of those cloudlike pillows at The Grand Palace on the Thames. But then, he knew she was just naturally kind. He needn't read a thing into it.

"Oh, my goodness, please don't apologize, Magnus. I have danced countless reels in my life, and I find social badminton invigorating enough."

He nodded.

"And besides," she added. "We have a curfew."

"Good God, I nearly forgot."

This made her smile again. Her smile faded. "Does it bother you often? Your leg."

"If I spend too much time on my feet without resting a bit, or if the weather is turning . . . it will remind me," he said ruefully. "But mostly it reminds me of how lucky I am to survive the war long enough to dance with you while you're wearing that pink dress."

He'd said this aloud despite every instinct to the contrary.

Perhaps because he was so painfully full of unsaid things, he craved the release of just one of them. Perhaps it was because touching her, and being close enough to her to smell the fine soap she'd used and the lavender in which her gowns were stored, would erode his control a bit at a time if he let it.

Perhaps because she still had so much power over him, he'd wanted to know whether he could move her.

He was rewarded when he felt that precious little jump of her rib cage as her breath hitched.

Her cheeks were blooming pink.

"We're all lucky you survived the war," she said softly. And, it seemed, carefully.

His smile was somewhat ironic. If he'd died on the battlefield, they never would have married at all. He wondered if she'd ever entertained that possibility. He wouldn't have blamed her one bit.

Chapter Ten

∾◦◦◦◦∾

As was their habit at the end of every day, Angelique and Delilah sank gratefully down on the settee in their little room at the top of the stairs to do a little mending and review the daily affairs of The Grand Palace on the Thames—menus and budgets and repairs and guests and the like.

They usually left the door of their little sitting room open, but tonight they closed it hurriedly just as the faintest strains of a moan began to waft through the halls. Since they had discovered the Dawsons' favorite pastime, the Hardys and Durands had gotten a little flinchy about going up to their rooms. They did not think they would ever reach Mrs. Pariseau levels of sanguinity about the noises. They didn't want to walk through a moan any more than they wished to be confined in a small room with Mr. Delacorte after he'd devoured a rich meal.

Angelique pulled a stocking needing darning from their basket, and she gave a little laugh. "Lately Lucien has taken to imitating Mrs. Cuthbert. Yesterday I dropped my stockings as I was tucking a bundle of clothes away into the press and I said to him, 'Darling, will you get those stockings for me?'

And he turned to me and said '*Stockings?* Now it's *stockings?*' with bristling outrage. We both fell about laughing. And yes, I know it's unworthy of us."

Delilah laughed, then sighed. "Now I feel guilty for laughing."

"I do suffer a bit, knowing that she's uncomfortable," she added.

"Mrs. Cuthbert not physically uncomfortable," Angelique said firmly. "We take good care of her, and we personally placed a copy of the house rules into her hands before we took her money, so the sitting room ought not to have been a surprise. Then again, there's no easy way to prepare anyone for Mr. Delacorte."

Angelique was always a little stricter and more pragmatic than Delilah, and Delilah knew in this instance she was right. But they both worried a little when one of their guests was less than enchanted with their experience in the sitting room.

"You call Lucien 'darling'?" Delilah asked a moment later.

Angelique nodded. Her cheeks colored a little. "We call each other that, and . . . other things."

"Tristan likes to say 'sweetheart,'" Delilah confessed on a whisper.

They were both a little rosy now and they exchanged swift smiles.

They knew how lucky they were.

"Have you noticed the Brightwalls don't seem to use endearments?" Angelique said. "They don't really address each other directly at all. But they seem to be enjoying the company of everyone else in the sitting room, and at the dinner table," Delilah said. "Individually . . . they fit right in."

"But Mrs. Brightwall was so pretty this evening in that pink dress. And Colonel Brightwall was dashing."

"They did look handsome. I wish either one of them also looked happy."

Both had seemed trepidatious for two people about to attend a ball in honor of one of them.

Delilah fished in the basket for one of Mr. Delacorte's waistcoats. His love affair with Helga's cooking meant his waistcoats frequently shed buttons due to enormous strain. He was always so touchingly grateful to have them restored. It really was a pleasure to make him happy.

"Well, we know for certain we have at least one happy couple lodged at The Grand Palace on the Thames, currently," Angelique said somewhat grimly.

"That must be why the Dawsons have been so quiet in the sitting room at night," Delilah reflected. "They're conserving their energies."

Angelique laughed. "Or they're too exhausted for conversation."

"Isn't it funny . . . I suspect we were all guilty of thinking the Dawsons were a bit meek and unexceptional, which was unfair. People will surprise you," Angelique mused.

"They will, indeed. I suppose it's only a surprise that something like this hasn't happened sooner. But we already have a rule about being quietly considerate of other guests. I sincerely hope we won't have to get any more specific than that. We just had new rule cards printed. And I wouldn't know how to begin to spell the sounds Mrs. Dawson makes in order to forbid them."

Angelique laughed.

"And I am not looking forward to having a word with them, if it comes to that," Delilah added.

"Well, I expect something like that probably happened every day, back in its Palace of Rogues incarnation," Angelique pointed out.

"True enough."

Gordon, their fat striped cat, stretched in his basket and trilled in his sleep. Delilah bent over to give him some strokes. He pointed his toes like a ballerina.

"Do you feel a little wistful that neither of us were able to spend that kind of time with our husbands when we were first married?" Angelique ventured.

Delilah considered this. "Perhaps?" she confessed on a hush. "Just a little?"

"Me, too. A little."

In truth, they were both skirting around the fact they missed Lucien and Tristan lately, as their schedules had been at cross-purposes. And all the sounds emanating from the Dawsons' room only reminded them of what wasn't happening behind the doors of *their* rooms. It was unnerving to discover how easy it was to begin to feel just a very little less close to the men they loved when they couldn't love them with their hearts *and* their bodies, and the palpable reserve between the Brightwalls seemed evidence of what could happen when couples spent too much time apart.

"I'm just hoping desperately Mrs. Cuthbert hasn't heard those noises yet. She already thinks we're libertines."

Angelique laughed. "We were prescient when we put her on the floor below, in the corner."

"*Are* we libertines?" Delilah wondered, gingerly, only half jesting. "Our conversations do tend to career a bit. Perhaps we've created quite a daring salon in the sitting room without realizing it."

Angelique snorted. "We are a delightful, cozy, genteel, exclusive boardinghouse by the docks. I'm comfortable that Mrs. Cuthbert is a stick-in-the-mud, but she's *our* stick while she's staying with us, and we will do our best to cherish her while she's here. And I'm fairly confident she, at least, will never surprise us."

"I WASN'T CERTAIN what to wear for the unveiling of a statue." Alexandra smoothed the skirts of her butter-gold silk day dress.

Magnus regarded her in silence so eloquent he might as well have been a speech before the House of Lords.

"You look like the very opposite of something made of stone," he said finally. Quietly.

Last night, after he'd stunned her with a compliment, they hadn't exchanged another word during their waltz. Nor had they danced again.

The ride back to the boardinghouse had been quiet and civil.

But every polite word they'd exchanged after that seemed to echo with nuance. It was now clear that a new tension was gradually building alongside the old rancor. Like the warmth of his hand hovering lightly at her waist, like the feel of his fingers delicately folded around hers, she called up the words again and again for the pleasure of stealing her own breath. For the mildly delicious torment of wondering what those words might mean to her or to him, if anything.

For another hour they had circulated through guests, so that as many people as possible who wished to say a few words to Magnus would have an opportunity to do it. He was, as usual, grave, gracious, and succinct, sometimes a bit brisk; alongside him, Alexandra did her best to sparkle and charm and make the people to whom they were introduced feel, momentarily, like the center of their universe. Together, they enchanted. At least this was the surprised consensus murmured among guests.

With people he'd long known and liked, Magnus's demeanor eased and his dry wit would flash, and she'd found it as exhilarating to witness as a shooting star.

Once she'd found herself reflexively, gently touching his elbow when he was a little *too* brisk with someone, a bit like an orchestra conductor telling the violins to ease back on the volume. He'd softened his tone immediately.

It was as though they'd done this a thousand times before.

If another man had said to her *But mostly it reminds me of how lucky I am to survive the war long enough to dance with you while you're wearing that pink dress*, she would have ascribed it to flirting. But he wasn't a flirt. He'd said it with the same definitive gravity with which he'd told her she was a kind person at that house party five years ago. In the same tone with which he'd told her he'd fought that war so that Mr. Perriman could natter on about pigeons, and so that he could stand in the shrubbery, helping to untangle her ribbon. He was not a frivolous person.

His silence after he'd said that during the waltz merely felt like a punctuation mark.

To her, the words seemed to reverberate in the room even now.

"Then again, you'll doubtless look a bit blurry to Mrs. Scofield," he said somewhat dryly.

TWENTY MINUTES LATER they stood in his former housekeeper's comfortable rooms in a respectable, working-class neighborhood a few minutes' carriage ride from the park. Mr. Lawler had sent word to Mrs. Scofield ahead of time that Magnus would be paying her a visit.

"This is your wife, Magnus?" Mrs. Scofield squinted up at her when they were introduced. "Me eyes are not the same as they once was but you looks to be a pretty one." She sounded skeptical.

"Oh, you guessed correctly, Mrs. Scofield. I am pretty." Alexandra said it mischievously.

The corner of Magnus's mouth twitched.

Mrs. Scofield's face was mapped with fine wrinkles and her soft, round body spilled over the seat of her rocking chair. Her pewter-gray hair was scraped up into a tight knot on the top of her capless head. Her brown wool dress and her visible furniture—a settee, a table and chairs, a rocking chair, in which she currently sat—she was unable to stand for very long now, due to rheumatism—were serviceable and clean.

"Hmmph. You nivver thought a pretty girl would even look at ye, isn't that so, Magnus? D'yer remember what Molly use ter do when she saw ye?"

Alexandra wondered immediately who Molly was.

But Magnus appeared not to be listening. He turned abruptly and paced to the window, apparently inspecting its frame. "Are you comfortable, Mrs. Scofield? Are the flues kept clean? Does the housekeeper visit regularly?"

Perhaps her hearing wasn't what it was, either, because she didn't reply to Magnus's questions. "Must be the money," Mrs. Scofield decided. "'e's got money now, and the blokes with the money always get the pretty wives, am I right, Mrs. Brightwall, no matter what them blokes look like?" She cackled.

This was when Alexandra went warily still.

She hadn't known what to expect—one of

those cuddly, heart-of-gold, salt-of-the-earth family retainers? Perhaps Mrs. Scofield and Magnus shared a sort of jesting relationship?

"Indeed, it's better when a bloke has money than when he doesn't," Alexandra agreed somberly, somewhat wickedly.

Magnus's back was to her, but she could almost feel sardonic amusement raying from him.

"Oh, but ye oughter 'ave seen 'im in those days, Mrs. Brightwall." Mrs. Scofield shook her head. "Nivver would have guessed such a homely, skinny baby would grow into such a great lout, all hands and feet. We found 'im girning in a potato sack next to a delivery of turnips. 'e was lucky we kept 'im and didna throw 'im to the workhouse or for the rats to nibble on. Ha ha ha! 'e wouldna be standin' 'ere today."

Alexandra tensed. Her heart began to race, as though someone had come at her with fists.

"All of England is lucky you brought him in," Alexandra managed evenly, carefully. "Which means you are lucky you brought him in."

"Oh, I suppose, certainly." Mrs. Scofield was airily dismissive. "We didna feel that way at the time, ye see. Such a burden 'e was at first! Ye'd nivver think 'e'd marry anyone. What was the name of the lady's maid who would cross herself when she saw ye in the 'all, Magnus? You would have thought she was a *princess*, way 'e looked at her. She was no better than she should be, that girl. And *did* she laugh at him! Said 'e looked like a—what was that word, Magnus? Fancy word."

"Satyr," Magnus said absently, as he peered up the flue.

The word squeezed Alexandra's breath right out of her.

"That was it! Too fancy by far, for him, that word. We called 'im Beast even then. Molly would cross 'erself and give a shiver like she was afeared of him and we'd all have ourselves a little laugh. And didn't 'e leave 'er a flower one day on her bureau? She thought it was from the footman she was sweet on and she tossed it right away, angry like, when she found out it was Magnus. 'ow we laughed at the boy."

Alexandra decided quite calmly then that she hated Mrs. Scofield.

She could feel the heat of antipathy wash over her skin. It filled her lungs, so that every breath she drew scorched her.

"But 'e made 'imself right useful every day, didn't 'e, though. Still does. Always watching to see what needed to be done. So needful and eager to help. And so we kept 'im, like. 'e could do everything from sew to lifting great kettles and mucking out stables and emptying slops. Did ye ever believe ye'd get yerself a pretty wife, now, when you was emptying slops?"

Magnus said, "Yes."

He moved away to the window.

This apparently gave Mrs. Scofield pause.

As if she'd never dreamed that the quiet, awkward, orphan child had in fact been *seething* with ambition.

"Mr. Coopersmith taught him to shoot and 'e won that contest and 'e nivver looked back. Was I surprised! We nivver did think 'e'd amount to much."

Alexandra stared at Magnus. Her heart still slammed in her chest sickeningly.

But he was looking at Mrs. Scofield.

"Everything in your flat looks to be in excellent order," Magnus said mildly. "I'm glad to see you're still comfortable. We ought to leave now, Alexandra, or we'll be late for the ceremony. They're unveiling a statue in my honor today, Mrs. Scofield."

He said this conversationally. As if this was something that could happen to anybody. As if in his lifetime he'd endured everything there was to endure, and nothing Mrs. Scofield could say or do to him now would stir him to anything other than ironic amusement.

"A statue! That ought to scare all the pigeons right out of the park! Ha ha!" Mrs. Scofield slapped her knee. "Goodbye, then, Magnus, and thank you. Goodbye, Mrs. Brightwall."

Alexandra deferentially knelt next to Mrs. Scofield and gently reached for her hand. She clasped it gently and gazed at her intently.

The woman gawked at her in bald astonishment.

Magnus went still.

"It's been an honor to meet the person who kept him alive even though he was allegedly not a pretty baby, Mrs. Scofield."

"Thank you," Mrs. Scofield said warily.

"And Mrs. Scofield?" Alexandra continued

gently. "Do not ever speak that way *of* him or to him again."

Alexandra's voice was so light, respectful, and kind that it was apparently a moment before her words registered on Mrs. Scofield. But then again, one scarcely feels the wasp land before it stings.

She knew when they registered because Mrs. Scofield jerked her hand back a little with surprise.

Alexandra refused to relinquish it. She gripped it *just* a little harder.

Mrs. Scofield swiveled her head toward Magnus, then back to Alexandra. Dumbfounded and alarmed.

Magnus seemed to have found something interesting to gaze at through the window.

"Magnus doesn't owe you a thing," Alexandra said calmly. "While I am grateful indeed that you and the rest of the staff kept him alive, it is only what decent humans would do, when presented with a helpless, hungry baby fussing in a sack. Henceforth—"

"'*Henceforth*'?"—Mrs. Scofield quoted, startled.

"—if you are ever fortunate enough to speak to him again, you will address him with the respect and deference appropriate to the differences between his rank and stature and yours, or you will not speak to him at all. You will not use his Christian name. You will use his title. You will thank him any time he deigns to grace you with his presence. You will not mention mucking or slops to him again. You will rise from your chair and curtsy when you see him. Do you understand me?"

Her voice remained polite.

Mrs. Scofield gaped at her.

"Magnus?" Mrs. Scofield was querulous and indignant.

Magnus had turned his head toward the door now, and was idly tapping the brim of his hat against his palm, as if his thoughts were entirely elsewhere. His lips seemed to be pursed in a silent whistle.

He said not a word.

"Do you understand me, Mrs. Scofield?"

Alexandra didn't raise her voice. But she somehow managed to imbue all of her words with the threatening tension of a drawn bowstring.

Mrs. Scofield's head finally bobbed rapidly in agreement.

Alexandra released her hand.

"We'll bid you good day, then."

IN THE CARRIAGE Alexandra pressed herself against the far corner, as if she wished she could curl up in a burrow. She was pale with anger. Positively suffering with it.

Fury always took a little time to ebb. Magnus knew, because he had a temper, too. His was icy. Downright biblical, when truly aroused.

Hers fascinated him.

Hers continued to be a revelation.

In more ways than one.

"Alexandra?" he finally said gently.

She merely shook her head. As if she couldn't yet speak.

Finally she said, "I overstepped. I was awful. I apologize."

"You didn't overstep. You weren't."

"Oh, I think I did." She sighed. "I suppose," she said slowly, "that mean people upset me."

"You don't say."

She made a sound that was as much a sigh as it was a laugh. "I'm sorry if you consider her a beloved family member. But she's a mean person, Magnus."

"She's not a beloved family member. I haven't any family members. And I know she's not a nice person. She *has* had a hard life. And she's elderly."

"You've had a harder life and you're not a mean person."

His slow smile evolved into a short laugh. "That's certainly a point of view. I could name a few dozen subalterns who would *definitely* beg to differ."

Her smile was wan. "Mean for the pleasure of it. The kind of mean that someone inflicts upon someone else because it makes them feel bigger. She knew the things she said were hurtful—how could she not?—and she said them anyway. That's the kind of mean she is. I found it . . . I found it intolerable."

Her voice was thick.

Neither one of them took up the reason she might find it intolerable.

Or that her reaction might be a trifle outsized.

But Magnus could not ignore what felt something like a glow in the center of his chest.

She refused to look at him yet.

"I would have intervened if I'd objected to the direction of your conversation," he assured quietly, after a moment.

She exhaled. "All right."

They rolled along in silence for a time.

He cleared his throat. "I'm grateful that Mrs. Scofield took me in from the potato sack. I get enormous satisfaction from knowing that I have the means to look after her. I would take no pleasure in knowing she was suffering any sort of penury in her retirement. And I did it because I liked knowing that I had an anchor in the world, after a fashion—a place I could point to and say, 'I started there.' Having someone to look after is sort of an anchor, too. And for what it's worth, my sense of duty is, I'm afraid, rather cast-iron."

She turned to study him.

Her eyes were somber, soft, and a little too searching. And as lovely as they were, he found he needed to turn away.

She was dutiful, too.

"I see how far I've come when I visit her," he said shortly. "And I like the reminder."

"So that's why you learned to shoot. I should say she was a marvelous incentive to improve your aim to get out of there."

He gave a short, not entirely amused laugh at her astuteness.

"She mentioned that you won a competition?" she prompted.

He nodded. "The master of the house, The Honorable John Coopersmith, began taking me out with him to the country on grouse hunts to carry things for him. I think he viewed me as a sort of useful pack animal. But he discovered I wasn't a dolt. Taught me to shoot both pistols and muskets. And . . ." He smiled slightly. "I became very good at it. And then he taught me to read, because it amused him and he thought I would be useful to him that way, too. I was about twelve years old, then. Once I was able to read and write I assisted him with some of his correspondence. I had a sleeping mat in the scullery and I was fed, but I learned to forage, too, and I did odd jobs in exchange for more food. I owe Coopersmith a good deal. He died during my second year in the army."

"I wish he could have lived to see the city erect a statue of you on a horse."

"So do I."

She was quiet a moment.

"They could have at least given you a bed."

He smiled slightly. "I was a superfluous household expense. A big, hungry one."

Alexandra shook her head again, roughly, shaking off this rationale. But she knew that was the lot of many servants, especially children. And that's what he'd been.

A decade ago, she might have been outraged if anyone had suggested she would ever marry a former servant.

Her fingers curled into involuntary fists when she thought of Molly the servant girl's cruelty. "Satyr" wasn't at all the right word for him. But comparing him to a demigod was, surprisingly, not outlandish at all. Mrs. Scofield had no idea, no idea at all, what she'd helped wrought. Perhaps she did bear some responsibility for the extraordinary person he became.

"How did the shooting contest come about?"

"Every year a local squire—not Coopersmith—who had more money than sense would hold a shooting competition. Men would come from miles around to participate. Hundreds of them. I didn't have my own gun, so it took all of my nerve to ask whether I could borrow Coopersmith's musket. He loaned me the shot, too." He paused. "And I won." He smiled faintly. "And I don't mind telling you, Alexandra, that sometimes I wonder if there wasn't more satisfaction in that win than in beating the French."

She smiled softly at that.

"That was the day I vowed that never again would a rich, indolent man compel me to perform tricks for money. And from that moment I determined I would be wealthier by far than he was. And I am. I bought an ensign's commission with my prize winnings."

She knew that the price of a military commission was entirely out of reach for the average servant, let alone one who slept in the scullery.

"I have always done my best to recommend men for promotions through the ranks based on talent and performance, because I know how much men who come from circumstances like my own have to prove, and how hard they're willing to work. I think some of my best strategic choices had to do with promoting some men and demoting others for this reason."

She didn't ask him why he'd taken her to meet Mrs. Scofield. She wasn't entirely certain. But she thought perhaps she knew.

Because he wasn't a man who did things on a whim.

Perhaps it was as simple as this: he wanted that harridan to see that he had indeed gotten himself a pretty wife. Even if that wife had promptly been faithless.

Even if he was sending that wife away.

But it also afforded Alexandra a glimpse into the crucible in which Brightwall the Beast was forged. Those circumstances—the labor, the humiliation, the resilience required to survive—had taught him control, endurance, determination. All had begun when Mrs. Scofield brought him into the house.

Some men might be ashamed for anyone to know they'd begun life as an orphan who had emptied chamber pots and slept on the scullery floor.

He probably knew it only made him seem more extraordinary.

His safety and survival had depended on observing people, on making himself useful, on learning everything he possibly could, on listening. And those were the skills that had helped him soar through the army ranks. That was how the boy who'd slept in the scullery had found a way to maneuver to checkmate.

This was how he'd become a military legend.

And this was how he'd strategized his way into getting himself a pretty wife.

She recalled that scrap of ribbon in a box.

And then she thought of a shy little boy leaving a flower on the bureau of a cruel girl.

She closed her eyes briefly as a stab of grief crushed the breath from her.

A GREAT TARP had been whipped from the statue, which was spectacular: immense, gleaming, and graceful. Both Colonel Brightwall's hair and the horse's mane and tail were, for infinity, wind-blown. His carved visage was stern enough to put the fear of God into any pigeons who might take a notion to dribble shite upon it.

Magnus stood on the dais before the crowd.

Flanking him were the Lord Mayor of London, Mr. Thorp, and Alexandra, who was smiling proudly and fondly. It was thrilling and humbling to realize that all those faces down below had come to see her husband immortalized in marble.

Magnus's voice boomed over the crowd. "Thank you for joining me on this auspicious occasion, ladies and gentlemen. I cannot begin to express how grateful I am to have given London an excuse to erect a statue of a man on a horse, since we have a dearth of them," Magnus began.

This was greeted by a roar of laughter, cheers, and applause.

"In truth, this one flatters both me *and* the horse. It's an exquisite work of art, rather unlike its inspiration." A scattering of laughter here, too. "I am proud to have been found worthy of the skills of Signor Almondo, whose artistic gifts grace our parks and buildings. To know I have been of any service to a country and people I love . . ."

His voice graveled. Alexandra sucked in a breath.

". . . well, the true honor is all mine. I thank His Majesty the king, Lord Mayor Thorp, my beautiful wife, and all of you for sharing this moment with me, for this extraordinary tribute, and for allowing me to serve you and Britain. God save the king."

"GOD SAVE THE KING!" the crowd echoed.

Magnus bowed to a cacophony of cheers and applause. A sea of hats waved.

Alexandra swallowed the lump in her throat.

"Mrs. Brightwall, if I may have a word?"

As Magnus shook the hands of various dignitaries and well-wishers, Alexandra turned to find before her a wiry man whose bright little eyes were about level with hers. His features were button-neat.

"My name is Mr. Gelhorn, and I'm a writer for *The Times.* How do you do, soon-to-be Lady Montcroix?" He swept his hat from his head and bowed. "I hope you will forgive the presumption, but London readers are hungry for more information about you."

Well, then. The man *was* presumptuous, but this was the opportunity she and Magnus had been waiting for. She'd best make the most of it.

"How do you do, Mr. Gelhorn? It seems you've heard something about Colonel Brightwall's elevation to the peerage."

"Indeed, it is my business to remain apprised of momentous political developments, and my sources inform me that a warrant has been delivered to the lord chancellor's office ordering the preparation of Letters Patent. It seems as good as done."

Her breath hitched. She wondered if Magnus knew.

"I wondered if you might be willing to share a statement with us on this auspicious occasion. Are you proud of your husband?"

She beamed. "I couldn't be more proud of him. Who wouldn't be? Don't you think he's magnificent? How intriguing it is that you seem to already know he's to be styled the Earl of Montcroix. The Magnificent Montcroix. That's what I'll call him from now on," she said mistily.

Mr. Gelhorn's eyes lit.

The newspapers and gossip sheets did adore their alliteration. She'd just given a gift to them.

"This might be a delicate subject, Lady Montcroix—shall I call you Lady Montcroix now, or do you consider it premature?"

"If you choose to do it, I shan't object," she allowed sweetly.

"—but I wondered if you'd like to comment on your recent incarceration in Newgate."

His eyes gleamed. He clearly thought he'd effected an ambush out of earshot of her big husband.

She didn't blink. "Oh, I saw that article. How silly, don't you think, that anyone would *write* such a thing?" She sounded puzzled. "You seem like such a nice person. I hope you didn't write that article, sir."

After a moment, Mr. Gelhorn's cheeks stained pink. Which answered the question.

"I did see the illustration, too. I can't imagine what the talented Mr. Rowlandson was thinking. But doesn't he have a gift for satire and for capturing the tenor of our times? It's always healthy to laugh at ourselves a little. I thought it was rather amusing, but I was also a little puzzled. Do I look like the sort of person who would ever spend a moment in prison? Or do combat with English soldiers, especially considering my husband is one of the most greatest soldiers of all?"

She gazed shamelessly and limpidly into his eyes.

"Dear *God*, no," he replied faintly. Dazzled.

"Silly, then, wasn't it?" She laughed merrily.

"Silly," he repeated dazedly.

"And I imagine you've such a challenging job and it's so difficult to get facts correct all of the time, but my goodness, one would think a man of my husband's caliber should be allowed a moment's peace after all he's given to our country.

Perhaps you'd consider writing an article lauding him? As a favor to me? It would mean so much and he deserves all of that and more." She said it softly, almost wistfully.

Mr. Gelhorn was visibly shrinking with remorse.

The shadow that fell across the two of them signaled the arrival of her husband at her side.

"Colonel Brightwall, ah, Lord Montcroix. Congratulations, sir." Mr. Gelhorn bowed. "I understand the Letters Patent have been prepared. I wonder if you might share with the readers of *The Times* your thoughts on that, and your return to England."

If Magnus was surprised to hear this, not a twitch betrayed it.

He fixed the man with his patented stern gaze long enough for Mr. Gelhorn to shift his feet guiltily. The writer knew ambushing Brightwall's wife hadn't precisely been cricket, and Magnus wanted him to know that he knew. "I am more honored than I can adequately express to be styled the Earl of Montcroix, and tremendously happy indeed to be back in my beloved England, for many reasons." He gazed down at Alexandra meaningfully. "I fear we must now take our leave of you. Shall we?"

From his vantage point of superior height, Magnus could see the pages of the little journal Gelhorn carried with him. The man had written:

". . . Newgate stay was nonsense."

". . . wife blushed."

Chapter Eleven

❦

THE CROWD hadn't yet dispersed, but Magnus looped his arm through Alexandra's and steered her deftly through a pair of tall, scrupulously groomed hedges onto a path, whereupon they undertook a somewhat circuitous route toward where the carriage waited for them.

Alexandra assumed the point was to evade any straggling well-wishers. Presently the hubbub of voices gave way to the songs of birds and the wind rushing through the trees.

He hadn't dropped his arm. Her hand didn't seem to want to relinquish its light grip upon it, either.

"Were you surprised to hear about the Letters Patent?" she asked.

"Yes, damn the man for springing it upon me," Magnus said good-naturedly enough.

Alexandra laughed.

"I'm so pleased for you, Magnus," she said gently. Almost shyly.

He nodded. His expression was abstracted, somber.

"Congratulations, Countess," he said quietly.

And in that moment, regardless of all that had

transpired between them: she was moved, suffused with his awe and triumph as surely as if it was her own. This boy who had once emptied slops was now a peer of the realm, outranking her own father. It was tempting to call it miraculous, but Magnus had earned every single honor along the way with sweat and blood, and in so doing he had conferred this honor upon her, too, though she felt she patently didn't deserve it. In that moment she fervently wished for him that he had never laid eyes on her, so that she would not have devastated him, so that nothing would taint the glory of this moment for him.

What's done was done. She wondered if he currently entertained similar thoughts—wishing he'd never laid eyes on her—but then thought, perhaps not. He was the one who claimed life was too short to waste a moment on regrets. He wanted to move on with his life, and he'd decided to do it without her.

"Mr. Lawler will send by messenger documents for you to review regarding the New York property, so you should receive them this afternoon. I'll have the carriage take you back to The Grand Palace on the Thames, and I'll get a hack to White's. I've a meeting with a number of gentlemen there. Earl or no, I'm a respecter of rules. So of course I'll endeavor to return in time for dinner, as the rules, and my admiration for the food at The Grand Palace at the Thames, demand."

"Very well. Thank you."

Her answer was a bit delayed. She realized

her head had gone slowly, increasingly muzzy
from the delicious feel of his big arm looped
through hers.

The gold top of his walking stick winked in the
sun as they strolled in silence for some time, just
like this, the wind rushing through the trees like
a crowd cheering the new Earl and Countess of
Montcroix.

They were both wordless for a long stretch,
as if strolling arm in arm was something illicit.
Or perhaps because, oddly, strolling with him
seemed as wholly satisfying as conversation. A
complete activity. She found she did not want
to forego this homely pleasure, regardless of its
transience. Regardless of whether it had begun
for the sake of appearances. It might never happen again.

Suddenly he gave a short laugh. "I was just
nearly lashed by one of your bonnet ribbons.
Such an unjust punishment for a national hero."

She hadn't realized they'd come entirely undone
again. "My apologies. But I'm afraid I had no choice.
My reputation for mercilessness precedes me."

He laughed again. "Stop a moment," he suggested amiably.

She obligingly came to a halt.

He pivoted to stand before her, snatching the
ends of her fluttering ribbons from the air.

She stood patiently still.

He was leisurely about tying them. So oddly
peaceful to be tended by such a large man.

He was doing it, she understood in a flash, because he wanted to render service. Specifically to her. He wanted to care. It was his nature.

She didn't know why watching him, his face absorbed, somberly go about tying her ribbon should make her heart contract with a bittersweet sort of pain.

He ought to have had a family to care for.

"I don't know how I manage to do it," she faltered. "I'm forever turning my head to look at things, I suppose, and in all that vigorous motion they just gradually undo themselves."

"There's so much to see," he commiserated absently as he pulled the satin into a bow. "Who could blame you?"

This was both true and a little silly, and suddenly they were smiling at each other.

There's so much to see.

That was precisely it. Figuratively and literally.

Because a realization had been settling slowly into place. The faint lines at the corners of his eyes, the scars, the hard chiseled edges and the soft sensual ones, the thick, stern brows—none of his features were precisely traditionally beautiful, but everything was exactly right. And this, paradoxically, seemed like the very definition of beauty. She could not look away.

She didn't know how this had come to pass, and it unnerved her utterly.

"There." His fingertips lightly, momentarily rested on the bow he'd just tied.

"Thank you. You *are* better at tying than untying."

He gave a short laugh, then, as a seeming af-
terthought, he gently grasped either side of her
bonnet and tugged it gently to adjust it.

And as he dropped his arms to his sides again,
his fingertips slowly feathered over the downy
hairs at her nape.

Such a remarkably subtle thing.

So very deliberate.

So absolutely devastating.

A quicksilver rush of heat poured from the
nape of her neck right down through the center
of her and pooled between her legs in a shocking,
sharp pulse of lust.

She was fairly certain her nipples were erect.

She stared at him, stunned.

Her skin seemed to be humming softly, as
though he'd called it to life like a choir director.

And that's when she realized that he must have
been noticing those minute changes in her sensual awareness of him, too, blooming in her like
her own secret spring.

And now . . .

Was he testing her?

Or testing himself?

His eyes were so dark now: all pupil. His face
was somber and taut.

Her mind flashed to the first moment he'd seen
her. That remarkable stillness, as if he needed to
brace himself to accommodate the fact of her. His
stillness last night, when she'd emerged from her
room. That compliment.

Looking at him now, she had a sense for the

first time of the sheer force of everything he kept leashed. It waited there, just below his surface.

And all at once she was suspended between exhilaration and fear.

"Did you love him?" His voice was low. A little gruff.

The question shocked her so thoroughly her mind went momentarily blank.

He asked it as though this was a continuation of that conversation they'd held in the semi-dark garden years ago.

Then again, in many ways, that conversation had never ended. It was the undertone of every word they said, in every single moment they'd spent together since then.

It had been, in many ways, the thread which had wound through her entire life since her wedding night.

And now her heart was rabbit-kicking away in her chest.

She stared at him. Stunned at the astonishing quality and timing of the ambush. Then of course, he was the strategist.

She could have sworn his breath was held.

There was so much she hadn't known or even anticipated about this man. But of the things she felt she instinctively knew about him, none astonished her more than the conviction that, in some ways, he was more vulnerable than she was. Hence her instinct to protect him from pain.

Another thing she knew for certain was that,

whether or not he believed her, she could not and would not ever lie to him. Regardless of the cost.

"Yes. At the time, I felt as though I did love him."

She revealed this delicately. She would not apologize for something that had been true and that she did not regret.

He took this in.

"Do you still?" The words sounded measured. The tone was almost gentle.

But his voice was a little hoarse.

She wondered if this brave man had needed to gather nerve to ask it.

And if he was, in fact, braced to hear her answer.

What was the *truest* truth? What happened to love left behind deliberately? Was it like the weather? Did it merely spend itself like a storm, and then make way for new weather?

She wasn't anymore the person who had loved Paul Carson for so short a time. She could not even conjure his face clearly.

But one lingering impression remained.

"What is left of the feeling now . . . is gratitude. He was a refuge during a difficult time."

If Magnus wanted to know more, she would tell him. If he wanted another apology, he would not get one. She had apologized the night she'd kissed Paul. She didn't know what groveling would accomplish. And God help her, she didn't think it was in her to grovel, anyway. Cursed pride.

She hoped this was the end of the questions for now. Her chest felt strangely *sore* from the effort of containing emotions too big, too complex, for her heart to hold. Her arms had suddenly gone cold from nerves.

She felt as though she was awaiting a verdict of some kind.

Magnus's gaze was thoughtful. And while there was nothing censorious in it, there was nothing particularly forgiving in it, either.

Details intruded upon her awareness during this silence. How his lower lip was a little fuller than his upper lip, and the effect was almost intolerably erotic. How if she tipped her head forward now it would likely land where his heart was beating. She imagined the feel of it, thud, thud, thud, like a battle drum, against her cheek. Despite the tension, her body seemed to be pointing out these things to her as if they were critical to know.

The breeze was suddenly a caress on her skin. For all the world as though it was taking a liberty.

Magnus's gaze flicked to her mouth and lingered for the span of about two heartbeats, before returning to her eyes. The result was precisely the same as if he'd dragged a finger along the short hairs at her nape again. That flash of heat between her legs.

That catch in her breath.

He was a dangerously compelling man. She was certain the ways in which he was subtle and the ways in which he was not were also strategic choices.

He noticed too much.

He had taken advantage once before by noticing too much, and look where that had gotten them.

He finally gave a nod. He extended his arm, and lifted an eyebrow.

Relieved, she regarded his arm a moment, then gently, tentatively laid her hand upon it.

In silence that was more pensive than fraught but was a little bit of both, they strolled out of the statue garden, and toward his waiting carriage.

"The weather certainly turned," he said. "Would you like to wear my coat?"

She in fact, irrationally, very much wanted to wear his coat.

"Thank you for the kind offer, but no, thank you. I think I'll be fine inside the carriage."

And as they walked, absorbed in separate but likely similar thoughts, she realized there was a question she had never dared outright ask *him*.

She remembered so clearly his marriage proposal. There had seemed little of ardor in it. It had been grave and stately and earnest.

But she recalled how softly illuminated his face had been when she'd said "yes."

How *satisfied* he'd been with it all. Because he'd known he'd be getting what he wanted. Or was it something else?

Her heart accelerated.

They arrived at the waiting carriage, and Magnus made a friendly gesture to the driver indicating he ought to stay put; Magnus helped her into the carriage, and stood back.

She held the door open. His eyebrows flicked in surprise.

She gathered her nerve. And asked it.

"Why me?"

He froze. Something akin to panic flashed across his features. He looked caught out.

She felt a slightly unworthy little surge of satisfaction that catching him out was at all possible.

The breeze flipped the ends of his coat and ruffled his hair in the long silence that followed.

Perhaps he was deciding what answers to give her. Or whether to answer at all.

"Because . . ." He exhaled, and then she saw something like resolve settle over him. "Because I thought I had never in my life seen anything so lovely as you. It made me feel"—he made a short, pained sound, almost but not quite a laugh—"it made me feel unfamiliar to myself. Entirely new."

She stared at him.

Spellbound by the gift of this information.

By what he was saying and what he wasn't saying. By his subdued, thick voice, and the tension in his features, and by how his words had been traced faintly with resentment and uneasiness at the necessity to reveal any vulnerability at all to her.

For all these reasons, she was certain this was truth.

It didn't mean any of it was *still* true.

For a shining moment in time, he'd basked in the glow of his illusions about her.

And then she'd shattered them.

She could not for the life of her think of what to say.

"And I wanted you in my bed more than I wanted my next breath," he concluded simply.

And as she sucked in a short, sharp breath, he touched his hat to her and firmly closed the carriage door.

The driver snapped the ribbons and the carriage lurched away.

FOR THE REST of the afternoon, every breath Alexandra drew felt just a little hotter than usual. As if *I wanted you in my bed more than I wanted my next breath* had permanently raised her temperature.

She had asked the question, and had somehow failed to anticipate that she might not know what to do with the answer once she heard it.

One part of his answer nearly cracked her heart with its painful beauty, because in it she heard echoes of that battered, unwanted, tender boy who had still dared to admire, to aspire to, something lovely. Who had been laughed at when he'd dared to reveal his feelings.

The other scared her and thrilled her in a way that made her feel, as he'd said, unfamiliar to herself.

Both infuriated her.

As if she'd been handed the pieces of something impossibly beautiful that had been broken long ago.

But he'd asked her: *Do you still love him?*

She found she hadn't the nerve yet to examine why he wanted to know that, in particular.

As promised, Mr. Lawler had sent over documents: copies of the deed of transfer, a detailed description of the property, documents outlining their financial arrangement—he was indeed settling a significant sum upon her—and helpful lists of names of persons and businesses: the bank and banker upon whom she could call, local merchants and craftsman and neighbors and the like, along with letters of introduction from the colonel, now the Earl of Montcroix.

He'd been absolutely thorough and efficient when he set out to banish her.

She breathed shallowly, and tipped her forehead in her hands for a moment and imagined Magnus silently *burning* for her during that house party, and disguising it so well with his intimidatingly controlled, dignified facade. He had simply made his plans. *He thinks you have developed a rapport, and that you will be a credit to him*, was what her father had told her, when he'd informed her of Brightwall's extraordinary offer of marriage. *And I want you to accept him.* They both knew she would.

But perhaps she *had* sensed the intensity of Brightwall's regard. She simply hadn't known what to call it. If she'd known the whole truth of how he'd felt, would she have shied away from it, and from him?

She didn't know. She had been in love with Paul, and this perhaps had kept her from ascribing any significance to the nature of Brightwall's attention. Or to the way he fascinated and unsettled her. To the way he'd inspired something almost like protectiveness, perhaps even tenderness, in her from the first. Yes: as he'd said to her father, they had developed a rapport.

And she'd simply been a different person then.

She'd never had a lover in the literal sense of the word.

She had never . . . *ached* . . . with want in the presence of a man, the way she did now, in Magnus's presence. Not even with Paul, whose kiss had admittedly been lovely. And her first and only kiss to date.

She was still young, and every moment she spent in proximity to Magnus reminded her of how she'd been hiding from herself how excruciatingly lonely she'd been for five years. Because it had been far too painful to confront.

And she was certain Magnus—even as he sent her what she decided she'd call the banishment documents—knew how she felt.

If he'd ever dreamed of exacting the perfect retribution . . . taking advantage of this would be the perfect way to do it.

It seemed wildly unfair, infuriating, that he should hold yet another card. That he should possess the superior experience and all the control.

Then again . . . perhaps he *didn't* possess *all* the control.

What would he do if she were to test his resolve?

That would be a risky game, indeed.

But one, she decided, worth playing.

HE'D INTENDED TO be at the boardinghouse for dinner—the food here was astonishingly good—but he'd been delayed in various meetings and he'd been obliged to take a quick pub meal instead.

He'd dodged the sitting room in favor of the smoking room when he'd returned, as he'd been in the mood for brandy, cheroots, and uncomplicated company.

Also because he was not quite ready to see Alexandra.

Telling her two truths he'd never uttered to another soul had left him feeling conflicted and unsettled and raw.

He hadn't told her the entire truth, of course. He was no fool. One did not recklessly show one's hand.

The second truth he'd shared had been by way of playing a card. It had been a defensive maneuver of sorts. Because the first truth had left him feeling vulnerable and exposed, which was his least favorite way to feel. Shocking her had been a way to retrieve some of his power, an attempt to ascertain something he suspected.

He'd had the breath-stealing pleasure of watching her eyes go dark, which had been his answer. And he'd thought about this for the rest of the afternoon.

Magnus believed the animal-den snugness of the smoking room was a further testament to the genius of the proprietresses of The Grand Palace on the Thames. A handsome yet stain-hiding brown was the prevailing theme, evident in the worn but still-plush carpet, long velvet curtains, and the furniture, which was of the pleasantly battered variety that invited a man to sprawl or prop booted feet upon it. Clearly Hardy and Bolt were fortunate in having wives prescient enough to anticipate a man's occasional need to be unbridledly disgusting in the company of other men.

Captain Hardy, Lord Bolt, Colonel Brightwall, and Mr. Delacorte leaned against the four walls in companionable silence. Brandies had been passed around. Cheroots had been lit and sucked into life. Smoke rose and mingled.

They were all thinking about sex. For different reasons.

"At least he lets her go first every time," Mr. Delacorte finally said. "It's the gentlemanly thing to do."

While Mr. Delacorte was rather pleased to finally not be the only one making untoward noise in the boardinghouse—an irritated guest had once compared his snoring to the sound of a rusty saw dragged across rough bricks—no one who'd heard them was exactly enjoying the sounds emanating from Corporal and Mrs. Dawson's room.

Apart, presumably, from Corporal and Mrs. Dawson.

Corporal Dawson seldom joined them in the smoking room. He and his wife kept a busy schedule behind a closed door.

"Well, there isn't much a bloke wouldn't do for his lady, am I right?" Delacorte pressed, when no one replied, and merely stared at him, warily.

"Tread carefully, Delacorte." Captain Hardy exhaled smoke.

"Of whom and what are we speaking, if I may ask?" Magnus liked Delacorte.

"Corporal Comesalot and his wife," Delacorte said.

Magnus coughed a laugh, startled.

"Delacorte." Lucien stared at him. "For God's sake. Colonel Brightwall is our esteemed guest. If you say things like that . . . he's going to want an affectionate nickname, too."

Magnus smiled. This conversation was the reason Magnus liked smoking rooms in general. Sequestered in such a place, men didn't have to pretend that they weren't fundamentally a bit awful, and at least as gossipy as women, if not more. Any night at White's revealed the truth of this.

"Believe me, I've been called many things other than my name." He paused. He couldn't help himself. "How much is a lot?"

"No one stands by the Dawsons' door to do a count, but five times a day seems to be the outside guess. Judging from the . . . sounds," Delacorte informed him.

This conversation was doing very little to distract Magnus from his self-inflicted sensual torment.

"That's about all a bloke is useful for in his twenties, so hats off to him." Magnus blew smoke toward the ceiling. "Though I'm grateful the French didn't get him so he can enjoy himself now. The army will be hard enough on him."

All the men in the room smiled knowingly, as they were all closer to forty than to thirty years in age.

The days of five times or more a night, however, were behind them. And every last one of them was thinking this, and not saying it.

But Magnus doubted anyone could burn more volcanically than a man who had longed for the same woman for nearly five years. Not even a twenty-year-old man.

She'd once loved a young man of that age. And that man had kissed her, and held her face tenderly. This was indeed burned upon Magnus's memory.

But Magnus had touched Alexandra like a lover today to let her know that he recognized her dawning desire, and that he knew it was all for him. He'd wanted her to know that he not only saw this . . . he knew what to do about it.

But he might as well have set himself on fire. He had restlessly burned for the rest of the afternoon.

Regardless of what he'd told her, he didn't think she could ever truly comprehend how desire could be a form of suffering, or what it had cost him to endure it.

He could not quite shake off a low-simmering anger. Wanting a woman who had betrayed him felt like a weakness. Surely war ought to have drummed all frailty out of him.

And yet he felt weak in an entirely different way when he thought of her kneeling next to Mrs. Scofield, gripping her hand, and, with her inimitable fiery grace . . . defending him.

"Your suite is in the annex, so you may not be

aware of this, Colonel," Delacorte said. "But that little wife of his makes noises like you've never heard in your life."

Captain Hardy sighed. "Delacorte . . . we aren't completely exempt from being gentlemen in here."

"I apologize. But the colonel needs to understand the full picture, I think," Delacorte defended. "Otherwise we wouldn't be discussing it. And I didn't say it was a bad thing. It's just very loud."

Magnus looked at Hardy and Bolt for confirmation, eyebrows upraised.

"It's . . . good God, it's quite something," Bolt agreed, reluctantly. Uncomfortably.

"Ah." Magnus nodded slowly, taking this in.

It was a damned struggle not to shift restlessly at the thought of making a woman moan in pleasure.

"Maybe Mrs. Dawson is doing it because Corporal Dawson asked her to do it," Delacorte reflected. "After all, everyone has different tastes. We're all men of the world. What wouldn't you do for the right woman? A woman once asked me to say '*yes*, Your Majesty' over and over again while we were, ah, enjoying a little jingle bang, and did I do it? Yes, I did."

The other men stared at him.

"I'll tell you the greatest sacrifice I ever made for a woman," Lucien finally said. "After I married her, I moved into this boardinghouse, whereupon I met you, Delacorte, and was subsequently forced to hear that story, which I cannot now ever unhear."

"Ha." Delacorte, secure in Lucien's affections, was always delighted to be teased. He gestured with his cheroot at Bolt and Hardy. "I heard the two of you were standing by their door with your pistols drawn. Very gallant of you to want to rescue the girl from the throes of pleasure, of course. But one would think two worldly fellows like yourselves ought to have guessed what was going on in there. A bloke starts to forget when he gets up in years, I suppose."

Hardy and Bolt fixed him with baleful gazes.

Delacorte smiled at them kindly, wildly amused at having scored a little point.

Chapter Twelve

‎❧❧❧

$\mathcal{P}$RESENTLY, THE smoking room gentlemen re-
joined the ladies in the sitting room.

Mrs. Pariseau and Mrs. Cuthbert had gone out
together to see a play—something *sedate*, Mrs.
Pariseau had assured a fussing Mrs. Cuthbert—
and Corporal and Mrs. Dawson were out visiting
friends for the evening. That left Mrs. Durand,
Mrs. Hardy, Dot, and Alexandra, who had apparently just concluded a rousing game of whist and
had taken up knitting and embroidery in order to
recover their nerves. Alexandra had been loaned
an embroidery hoop.

Captain Hardy settled in at a table with a book
while Lucien headed upstairs, muttering something about a change of clothing.

Alexandra's hands stilled on her embroidery
when Magnus entered the room. She somberly
tracked him with her eyes as he wended his
way toward her and settled almost gingerly
into an adjacent chair. Her expression was both
intent and a trifle wary.

Whatever she saw in his eyes made her briefly
duck her head down to the embroidery.

As if her lost composure could be located in her lap.

She looked quickly up again, aware that they had an audience. "How was the rest of your day?" she asked politely.

"Busy and satisfyingly productive. And yours?"

"It was lovely. I met a striped cat named Gordon."

He smiled faintly. "Any day you meet a cat is a good day."

She began to smile, too. Then her eyes darted away uncertainly, then she looked down at her lap again, and then at the wall.

He watched a flush travel along her collarbone and spill into her cheeks.

He stared at her profile. Ah, yes. He would warrant she'd been haunted all day by his last words to her before he closed that carriage door.

He thought he might have paid another five thousand pounds for her thoughts right at this moment.

Mr. Delacorte had settled in at a table, but his boot toe tapped restlessly. "The night is still young. I don't suppose I can interest any of you gents in a donkey race on in an hour or so?" he asked hopefully.

"I beg your pardon, Delacorte? I hope 'donkey race' is not a euphemism," Magnus said.

"Ha. Two splendid donkeys are on tonight. My favorites! The odds-on favorite is a big hairy chestnut-colored brute, built like a snorting brick on four legs, mean as a cuss, *loves* to run."

"Oh, he sounds *adorable*," Dot enthused. "What is his name?"

Everyone swiveled toward Delacorte when he didn't reply.

He cleared his throat. "Oh, is his name really important, in the scheme of things?" he said finally, cheerily. "He's a donkey."

"The donkey's name is Brightwall, isn't it?" Magnus said.

Every pair of eyes in the room widened.

Delacorte was clearly struggling with the truth. "Does it matter what he's called? He's a splendid beast," he finally decided to say. "You've *never* seen a handsomer donkey."

Magnus was thoroughly amused. "Where is this donkey race featuring Brightwall the Beast?"

Delacorte gave up. "The night races are held on some woods on the outskirts of Holland Park. They get up a makeshift track, it's all lit by torches, and you can make wagers and everything. It's a wonderful time."

"Sounds quite illegal," Magnus remarked pleasantly.

"Oh, it is," Delacorte assured him.

There fell a little silence.

"Who's he racing against?" Brightwall wanted to know.

"Another excellent jenny named Shillelagh."

Dot's embroidery hoop tumbled from her hands. She rose slowly from her chair, her lips trembling, emitting the small airless noises one makes when excitement prevents the formation of words.

"Fate!" she finally squeaked. "It's fate!"

"Oh, Dot, I'm not sure about this . . ." Delilah was beginning to feel nostalgic for the boring nights they'd enjoyed just a few days ago.

"What is Shillelagh like, Mr. Delacorte?" Alexandra wanted to know.

"She's gray, low-slung, has a white muzzle and light legs," Delacorte told them. "Pretty little thing. Scares her competition by sneaking up on the outside, then running like the blazes. Can sometimes be a bit balky, and she once bit me when I was allowed to pet her but she didn't break the skin. But that's the best part of it, right? It's unpredictable! A bit like The Grand Palace on the Thames."

Angelique and Delilah were none too pleased to learn that Mr. Delacorte equated The Grand Palace on the Thames with being bitten at the donkey races.

Dot turned to Delilah and Angelique, her hands clasped beseechingly. "I know it's not my off day . . . and I know it's Mr. Pike's night off, too . . . so there's no one to answer the door . . . maybe we won't get a new guest tonight! I'll give up my next one and the next one . . . I promise . . . *please* may I go to the donkey races?"

"Ummm . . ." Mr. Delacorte was alarmed.

"It does rather seem like fate," Angelique whispered to Delilah, mischievously.

"*Shhh.*" Delilah nudged her surreptitiously.

But because Dot's blue eyes were the size of dinner plates, almost no one could beseech as well as she could. She asked for so little. It was heartrending.

"I just don't think that's wise, Dot," Delilah said, somewhat desperately. "It can be a bit of a rough crowd, isn't that right, Mr. Delacorte?"

"Well. I'd have to say yes, it could be. It's not *usually* a place to take ladies. Although there are, er . . . some ladies, after a fashion . . . there. It's a friendly crowd, on the whole. But mostly everyone just wants to watch a race. You will hear a lot of jar words," he said frankly.

"Which ones?" Captain Hardy asked.

Mr. Delacorte snorted. "I'm not falling for that again, Hardy."

Captain Hardy grinned.

"*But* the jar words are mostly because everyone gets so excited. They sell chestnuts!" Delacorte added by way of enticement. "The fights usually happen later, when everyone is full of drink. And by then I'm home for curfew."

Angelique and Delilah were speechless.

Mr. Delacorte was nearly quivering with the effort to restrain his hope that people he liked would go with him to a donkey race, which was very nearly his definition of happiness.

Alexandra cleared her throat. "I think . . ."

Everyone turned to her.

". . . that I've seldom wanted anything more than to see a race between a donkey named Brightwall and a donkey named Shillelagh."

She said it quietly. But when her gaze collided with Magnus's, an interesting, spikily challenging frisson passed between the two of them.

There ensued quite a long silence, as everyone was very curious about what the colonel would say.

"May I ask what compels your interest in a donkey race in particular, Alexandra?" Magnus said with a certain taut formality.

"Someone once suggested I ought to diversify my pastimes," she replied politely. "I don't feel as if I've had a sufficient variety of experiences. And if Dot thinks it's fate, who am I to argue?"

Dot nodded vigorously.

"And . . . I've never been to a donkey race. It sounds like fun."

She said it almost wistfully.

Tentatively.

This launched a little war in Magnus's thoughts. He frankly suspected he would enjoy a donkey race more than he'd enjoy an opera, for one thing. Alexandra's wistfulness triggered his regrettable itch to give her anything she wanted, and it irritated him that some reflexive part of him apparently still craved to be her vassal. He also still felt a trifle guilty again that she'd apparently been somewhat deprived of entertainments for about five years. Guilt he mostly didn't deserve, but there it was.

And what kind of man took his wife to an illicit nighttime donkey race?

This was not a dilemma he'd ever anticipated confronting.

"I'm a conspicuous person," Brightwall began carefully. He was thinking aloud. "I don't want to put a damper on the occasion if someone recognizes me. Especially if the donkey is named Brightwall. And given that it's illegal . . . talk about being in the belly of the beast. Literally."

Alexandra regarded him evenly. "It will be dark."

He stared at her. Something about that sentence sounded both like a promise and a dare.

Both Delacorte and Dot briefly covered their mouths with their hands, hardly daring to hope.

"Maybe if you wear a disguise?" Delacorte suggested to Brightwall.

"I don't think I have a dress big enough to fit Magnus," Alexandra said.

Everyone chuckled, albeit cautiously.

"It *will* be dark, and if there's a crowd, I doubt anyone will be able to recognize me," Magnus allowed slowly.

Alexandra and Dot and Mr. Delacorte all clasped their hands and crossed their fingers.

They swiveled toward Angelique when she leaped to her feet.

"Delilah and I are just going to have a little private word. We'll be right back," Angelique said briskly.

Delilah looked at her, surprised. "Where are we go—"

Angelique looped her arm through Delilah's and tugged her from her chair, marching her startled friend to stand beneath the chandelier, out of the hearing of everyone in the room.

"Think about it," Angelique whispered without preamble. "Helga and the maids have gone up to their rooms for the night. If they all go out . . . we'll be *alone* here. With Tristan and Lucien. How often are we ever alone here with them? Never."

Delilah mulled this for three seconds.

"I guess Dot is going to the donkey races," she concluded.

They returned to the group in the room and settled back into their chairs.

"You really want to do this?" Magnus said to his wife.

Alexandra nodded. "I'm certain Mr. Delacorte would be pleased to look out for me and Dot if you prefer not to go, Magnus."

For the second time this evening, everyone else's eyes widened in wary surprise. Mr. Delacorte looked downright alarmed. His mouth parted, as if he was about to issue a disclaimer about taking another man's wife to a race.

He clapped it closed again.

Alexandra had said it so innocently. But there was something *just* a little anarchic about the glint in her eyes and the slight hike of her chin.

Magnus's lips moved in a slow, faint, mostly unamused smile. She wasn't quite saying, "I'm going whether you allow it or not, Magnus," but the implication hovered about the edges of her words, and everyone knew it. She was daring him to refuse her in front of these people. And leaving him to wonder whether she might cause a little bit of a scene if he did.

Damned if he didn't admire the diabolical strategy. It darkly amused and infuriated him, in equal measure. She had bloody *maneuvered* him.

It took all of his discipline to tamp all of his colonel instincts and issue a flat "no" on the principle of the thing.

"While I'm certain Mr. Delacorte would acquit himself well as an escort for you ladies," he said, with gentle irony, because he was a diplomat, too, "you will need to contend with my company, too. We will take my carriage."

"And we've decided, Dot, that you can go, too," Delilah said hurriedly.

"Oh, HOORAY! Thank you thank you thank you!" Dot gave a delighted hop.

And Alexandra was suddenly radiant with delight and surprise, even as she looked uncertain.

"Delacorte and I will take good care of the ladies," Magnus assured everyone present.

Thusly earning beams from everyone present.

"Be prepared for lots of cheerful shouting." Delacorte was brisk. "But wear something you don't mind getting splashed."

"Splashed? With what?" Dot wondered.

"Oh, it could be anything, at the donkey races," he said happily.

TWO OLD BROWN wool cloaks were scared up, and these were meant to cover Dot and Alexandra from head to toe, so that they looked a bit like monks or peasant women and less like nice young women who had no business going to a donkey race. They tied aprons over walking dresses and wore their sturdiest walking shoes. Mr. Delacorte apparently kept an old coat and a pair of trousers just for such occasions as nighttime donkey races, but Magnus hadn't brought any very old or worn clothing with him to The Grand Palace on the Thames.

"I'll hope for the best," he said dryly.

This odd little band filed out the door, promising to be in well before curfew.

Angelique went upstairs in search of Lucien.

And just like that the sitting room was quiet at seven o'clock in the evening for the first time in the history of The Grand Palace on the Thames.

Delilah looked at her husband, then went to sit down across from him.

"Well, my love," she said. "Everyone except Angelique and Lucien has gone to a donkey race. What shall we do?"

Captain Hardy clapped his book closed. "Go to church."

Just one of the delightful aspects of being married was the gradual development of their own secret coded language.

"Go to church" meant "make love."

It had as its origins the meandering discussion they'd had one night about the "with my body, I thee worship" part of the traditional wedding ceremony. They had both taken this part of their vows quite to heart.

They'd been married for a little over a year and he could still make her blush.

"You certainly didn't need much time to ponder that."

"Why would I ever need to ponder that when I'm married to *you*, Delilah?"

"Unassailable logic."

He grinned at her.

His grin faded. "The truth is, I'm beginning to feel outclassed by a bloody corporal."

"Oh, it's probably theater. The noises. Don't you think?"

"Perhaps. But let's say it is. How would a girl like that know what sort of sounds she ought to make?" he asked.

"Hmm. Good point."

They contemplated this a moment.

"I'm a little worried they're going to wear it out," Delilah said.

Captain Hardy coughed in shock.

"The *bed*," she clarified. "We may have to buy another bed. Not his, ah . . . or her . . ."

"No, both of those do last a while, thankfully. But imagine if a man only got a finite number of uses out of uh, his . . . ?" he reflected.

"A bit like the genie who offers you a finite number of wishes?"

"If that was the case, I'd spend all my wishes on you," Captain Hardy promised.

"Awww. That might be the most romantic thing you've ever said."

He laughed, and then paused. "I'm sorry I've needed to be away so often lately. I miss you."

She touched his cheek. "Please don't apologize. I know it's only temporary."

"But it's not easy?" It was both a question and a statement, and by way of seeking confirmation that he was missed. He said it almost gruffly. She knew revealing vulnerabilities was his least favorite thing to do.

"It's not easy," she confirmed softly. "I miss you. But I'm so proud of you and the Triton Group and all you're accomplishing."

"The Brightwalls were apart for five years," he said shortly.

This was his way of trying to tell her that he'd noticed their distance, too, and it was bothering him. Her heart squeezed.

"I feel for them," she whispered. "But they're not like us."

He nodded, seeming relieved to have it said aloud. "I had a dream last night that an intruder sneaked into The Grand Palace on the Thames and made off with you, but he let you take your favorite hairbrush."

"Oh, Tristan. Pike is here. And if an intruder should somehow manage to breach our ramparts—and one won't—I'll just follow your example, my sweet, dangerous husband, and bang his head on the table and use a cravat as a sort of garrote."

He laughed. "Good to know I'm setting an example. But back to a burning question. What is Dawson *doing* to get his wife to make those sounds?"

She was amused that he sounded so earnest. "Well . . ." Delilah was definitely feeling a little warm now.

"No, I mean, *specifically*, not generally. Is it a sequence of events, corresponding with each sound? Have new techniques been invented? Is there a pamphlet I ought to be reading?"

"You've given this a lot of thought."

"Men are base creatures at heart, Delilah," he said grimly.

"Perhaps it's the novelty of it all for her. The first time I . . . and you . . . well . . . it was definitely a revelation, I'll grant you that. Very worth shouting about. Although I didn't, because I couldn't, as we were in this very room. But I think mainly it was so incredible because it was you."

"No doubt," he said comfortably, which made her smile. He paused. "Would you have made those sounds if we hadn't been constrained by secrecy? And . . . ah, discretion?"

"I don't know," she said truthfully. "Do you think she even knows she's doing it?"

He hiked and let drop one shoulder. "Impossible to say."

Then something alarming occurred to her. "Do you . . . *want* me to? Make those sounds?"

He pondered this. "I don't know?" He almost whispered it. "On the one hand, I think I would love knowing I had given you so much pleasure that you went right out of your head and started, er, scream-grunting. On the other hand, if you did, I might want to smother you with a pillow."

She laughed.

Delicately she said, "You do know that I go right out of my head every time?"

His smile was slow, crooked, and very gratified. "Every time?"

"Every. Time. Dear God, it's so good, Tristan."

They exchanged sultry, satisfied smiles.

"But *you* aren't very vocal during. Do men ever do a lot of shouting? The last time we . . ."

"Made love," he supplied patiently. He'd married a blue-blooded woman, a former countess, and he'd been a soldier. And while he occasionally enjoyed scandalizing her, he also loved her refinement and was generally quite gentle with her sensibilities.

"All you said was 'Christ. *God*, that's good. Yes, Delilah. God, yes.'"

He froze at this recitation.

She'd even done his voice. A husky, urgent baritone.

Her eyes were dancing wickedly now.

"I have seldom felt so conflicted," he said slowly. "I'm very embarrassed . . . and very amused . . . and very, very aroused. I do believe *you* said . . ." He leaned forward and breathed the words into her ear. "'Harder, Tristan. Please. *Please. Now.*'"

She closed her eyes, awash in lust. She drew in a shuddering breath.

He kissed her. Softly, softly, as if it was the very first time. And desire hit her bloodstream in a rush that made her breath catch.

"That. That little sound you make. Christ," he breathed. "It makes me hard every time."

She trailed her fingers over his thigh up to his groin, and ascertained the truth of this for herself.

Her fingers lingered purposefully and skillfully there, until his breathing was quite rough.

"What if one of our guests needs something?" she whispered.

"Like what? Earmuffs to drown out Corporal Hardcock?"

She stifled laughter. "We're *right* next to the jar."

"Two of them are busy, the rest are out, and Angelique and Lucien are likely enjoying, oh, I don't know, spillikins. It's been two weeks. I need you."

Who was she to countermand the famous Captain Hardy?

She shut the door and locked it and surrendered herself into his arms.

ANGELIQUE FOUND LUCIEN in their room, rummaging through his clothing press for a fresh cravat. He'd discovered that he'd spilled gravy on his. Such was the romance of married life.

"Lucien. Listen."

"No," he said darkly. "I refuse. I'm afraid to stop and listen now in my own home. I am scarred by the sound of Corporal Dawson's ecstasy."

She laughed. "No, *listen*. It's quiet. Everyone is out for the evening, including Corporal Dawson and his wife."

"Everyone?"

"Everyone except Delilah and Tristan. What-
ever shall we do?"

They fixed each other with smolderingly significant gazes.

"Why," Lucien mused, softly drawing out the
word, "do we make love only in our bedroom?"

She was instantly breathless. "Do you think
about making love in . . . other locations?"

"Nearly everywhere I go I eventually imagine you there with me and nude, I confess. The
warehouse, the ship, in a hack, the back room of
White's. But that's how men's minds work."

"I'm so flattered."

"It's how I keep you with me when I need to
be away."

She was, indeed, touched.

"I have an idea now . . . it could be a little
risky . . . but not *too* risky . . ." He arched a brow.

Suddenly a little risk seemed precisely the
thing to offset worry. "Tell me. I trust you."

"Come with me." He seized her hand, snatched
up a folded coverlet and an unlit lantern, and led
her downstairs, through the passage that led to
the annex, and right into the ballroom.

She laughed as he led her up onto the stage that
their former guest Mr. Hugh Cassidy had built,
and pushed aside their beloved green velvet
curtains, the ones they had wrangled out of an
earl who had tried to steal their cook. Mr. Hugh
Cassidy had gone to fetch them. And Mr. Hugh
Cassidy and Lillias, Lady Vaughn, had met their
destiny behind them.

Suddenly the stage felt like their own secret, dark little cave. Laughing softly, they felt their way in the dark to the wall, and then sank down against it. He settled the lamp down near them. Lucien usually had a flint and steel stashed in his pocket. But neither one of them wanted to interrupt the sawdust-scented darkness just yet.

"Here," he said softly. He opened his arms, and she leaned back against him, snuggling in. He wrapped the two of them in the coverlet. They just enjoyed closeness for a moment, letting their eyes adjust to the dark. They were surrounded by props from the Night of the Nightingale, the event featuring opera singer Mariana Wilde: the stained glass moon, rolls of stitched green felt that had represented carpets of grass, folded fishnets dyed blue they had swagged across the ceiling in order to create a night sky, little crates full of the spangled stars they'd hung from the nets.

"What do you suppose he's doing to elicit sounds like that?" Lucien mused.

She didn't need to ask whom. They might not actually be ghosts, but Corporal and Mrs. Dawson were positively haunting The Grand Palace on the Thames.

"Maybe it's the Vicar's Wheelbarrow," she suggested.

They laughed.

"I wonder . . . is it a sequence of events? Is it the same every time? One to go with each 'oh'? Is it different every time?"

"Are you feeling inadequate, Lucien? Because, I assure you, you are not."

"Huzzah for me and my adequacy," he exulted.

She laughed again.

"Perhaps he knows unusual positions?" he suggested. "He doesn't look the adventurous type, but people will surprise you, as you know. Because his wife seemed *very* quiet."

"What sort of unusual positions? I only know forward, backwards, standing, sitting, kneeling . . . have I left any out?"

Lucien grinned at her recitation. "Oh, there are all sorts of acrobatic things one can do. Swings and special chairs . . ." he said vaguely. "I know I tell you nothing you don't already know when I say that men are ridiculous creatures, Angelique. We will try anything, particularly if it's dangerous. It's a wonder there are any of us left."

She snorted softly.

It was lovely and strange to lean against him in the dark, behind the curtains on a stage. Somehow both illicit and cozy.

"Are *you* . . . interested in that sort of thing, Lucien? Er, swings and chairs. That sort of thing."

"No."

"My goodness. You said that a little quickly."

"Well, I cannot say this will be true forever. People do change in surprising ways for surprising reasons, yes? But now, you see, it's very strange. I'm so in love with you, it's like being under the influence of a beautiful drug all the time. Better than anything in Mr. Delacorte's case. I can do this . . ."

With one finger he drew a semicircle about her breast. She sighed, her body stirring.

"And just like that, I am on fire for you," he murmured.

They sat together, quietly burning. They knew each other's rhythms now. They knew they had the luxury of time, of heightening anticipation, of making love however they chose. And they wanted to heighten anticipation.

It was such a pleasure to just be alone and talk to each other.

"Literally everything about you excites me, Angelique. I think of something new all the time. There is a freckle behind your right knee. Perhaps you've never seen it. It is my new obsession."

He was partly teasing. And partly not.

"Do you want me to tell you about those things?"

"I think I would like you to save them up, and tell me one per year, on my birthday. I'll do the same for you."

"Done," Lucien said amiably.

They were quiet. Angelique cleared her throat.

"I think Colonel Brightwall and his wife . . . something is amiss there, don't you think? He was in Spain for so many years without her. And I sense the tension between them when they're in the room. And they never use endearments. No dears. No darlings. No sweethearts."

Lucien took this in. "Not everyone is so fortunate as we are," he said. "But I think there is pain there. Both for him and his wife. Don't you?

And where there is pain . . . well, you and I know that one cannot be hurt if there is no feeling. And sometimes the most implacable people hurt the most because they won't bend. Brightwall is a brilliant, stubborn man and his wife does not strike me as a quiet, biddable creature."

But he'd said this last bit appreciatively, which made Angelique smile. She was hardly biddable, either. "I've noticed how they look at each other. It might be antipathy—I don't think it is—but regardless, they find each other riveting."

"Let's wish them the best."

They silently did that for a few moments.

"It's hard not to notice that we have several phases of married life represented under one roof these past few weeks," she mused. "Corporal Dawson and his wife are the newlyweds. Then there's you and me and Delilah and Captain Hardy. Then there's the Brightwalls. And then I suppose we can count Mrs. Pariseau and Mrs. Cuthbert the widows."

Lucien was quiet a moment. "You're thinking about all of this because you're worried something like that could happen to us one day. The distance between them."

He knew her so well.

"I had gotten so used to people finding love here at The Grand Palace on the Thames, and I love thinking we had a small part in that. It would be sad if it's the site of an estrangement, instead."

"That will never be us, Angelique. Even if I need to be away for work, we will not grow apart that way." As if to prove his point, he gathered her closer.

"How can you be sure?"

"Well, I cannot," he admitted, which made her stomach lurch a little. "But we are friends. I like you better than anyone, even though I'm compelled to spend half my time with Hardy and St. Leger lately and they're admittedly unobjectionable company. But it won't always be like that. One day you may grow tired of having me underfoot all the time. We married because we love each other, and we chose each other after experiencing much of the bitter life can bring. We know what love is and what love isn't. And I love you so much that it is nearly as much of a luxurious pleasure to talk to you as it is to make love to you. Nearly."

"I love you, too. And I like you. And I do miss you when you're away."

"And you see, I do not think I will ever tire of hearing you say it, so I've an incentive to remain lovable."

She laughed quietly. "Do you ever feel constrained by our lives here, Lucien? We need to be so adult and decorous. It would be rude to make loud, grunty love when everyone is trying to sleep. And you used to be so wild."

"Mostly I was wild because I was unhappy. But if we ever wish to be loud, there's the little country house my father left me. The one in which I grew up. We could run about naked and make love in the grass. Take a little holiday one day.

Of course, Delacorte will probably want to come with us."

She sighed.

"Do *you* feel constrained, Angelique?"

She shook her head. "Mostly . . . mostly I just feel grateful for our life here."

"I expect we can find ways to feel wild right here if we choose. Let's see . . ."

She exhaled, and leaned her head back on his shoulder.

"We are young and innocent lovers." She could feel his whispered breath against her ear. "We've only just met. The attraction is powerful and new, like nothing we've ever before experienced. We have sneaked away for a rare moment together, to the backstage of a theater. We only have a few moments together . . . they might pull the curtain any moment. And this is the first time you've ever been kissed like . . . this . . ."

He turned her in his arms so he could kiss her softly, slowly.

"And the very first time either of us will be making love."

He lowered her to the floor, cushioning her with the coverlet.

And when he made love to her, it did feel like the first time.

And even though they were utterly quiet, they both felt as though their passion shook the rafters.

Chapter Thirteen

❦

LIT TORCHES had been jammed into the ground in a circle around a makeshift but nevertheless surprisingly smooth oval track outlined by posts and a rope rail. Overhead, glowing lamps were strung from trees. The cheerfully jostling crowd could have been comprised of dangerous ruffians or the entire House of Lords (although some would claim the difference between those two groups was modest, at best); thanks to the flickering torchlight, everyone seemed made of amber light and shadows and flashing teeth and the whites of eyes. And it seemed indeed it would have been the ideal fertile ground for pickpockets and other scoundrels, except from the fact that everyone looked and sounded so *happy*. Not a sinister expression in the bunch. Laughter, back slaps, and good-natured insults rang in the misty air.

Mr. Delacorte had led them through the park from a secluded entrance, exchanging greetings with other shadowy people whose silhouettes he apparently recognized on the way: "Ho there, Lumpy! Funny seeing you here! Ha ha!" "Greasy Joe, my good man!" and "Nice night to lose your shirt, eh, Frederick? Ha ha! My money's on Brightwall!"

Finally he brought them to a spot near what he said would be the starting line, and he and Magnus flanked Dot and Alexandra, who were both jouncing on their toes with excitement.

"Ohhh, here come the donkeys!" Dot breathed.

Alexandra felt an absurd thrill akin to the first time she'd seen Princess Charlotte from a distance.

Shillelagh pranced to the starting line, tossed her pretty head, and defecated.

"Look! Now she's lighter! Maybe she'll go faster," Dot said.

"I'm not certain that's how it works, Dot." But now Mr. Delacorte looked a little worried.

Everyone except Magnus had placed a wager—two pence for Dot on Shillelagh, half a crown on Shillelagh for Alexandra, and Delacorte, who was socially exuberant but always fiscally thrifty, a crown on Brightwall.

Suddenly a gasp soughed through the crowd.

"Oh look! There he is! Here he comes!" Dot breathed.

Brightwall the donkey was a handsome, chestnut-colored barrel of a beast. He bared his gigantic square teeth at the crowd and stomped hooves like small anvils. His tail lashed the air, and he threw his mighty little head back and brayed, to the cheer of bystanders.

"What did I tell you?" Delacorte said proudly.

"That animal looks like a small, vicious cannon," Magnus marveled.

"Your mother looks like a small, vicious cannon," the jockey called to Magnus.

"She probably did," Magnus rejoindered.

"Oy, sorry mate!" The jockey touched his cap. Magnus touched his hat.

Alexandra laughed, exhilarated. A little more wildness suffused her with every lungful of chill, misty, smoky night air, every second amplifying her awareness of the huge man who hovered near her, a man who had once wanted her in his bed more than he'd wanted his next breath. During the carriage ride, while Mr. Delacorte had regaled them with tales of donkey races past, Alexandra almost felt as though she could hold up her hand and feel the rays of darkly absorbed intensity shimmering off Magnus, all of it directed at her.

She had indeed tested her power over him tonight by suggesting she would go to a donkey race with or without him. He seemed to have ceded her a win. She was beginning to wonder if there would be a cost.

She didn't know why the notion of a cost would fill her with sizzling anticipation.

The donkeys' long ears fluttered and pivoted this way and that in response to the excited crowd, and they tossed their heads and stomped and danced on their little hooves and switched their tails and shook their round little rumps, showing off. They seemed to love the excitement.

All the while their jockeys, slight young men wearing rolled trousers and rolled shirtsleeves with caps jammed on their heads, were cheerfully insulting each other.

"Brightwall's a bastard! Brightwall's a bastard!" Someone in the crowd started a chant, pumping his fist in the air.

Delacorte shot Magnus an uneasy look.

"Not the first time I've heard that," Magnus reassured.

Brightwall the donkey stomped his feet. "HEEE HAWWW!" he bellowed.

"Brightwall only loves it! He feeds on it! Say it louder!" his jockey jeered.

The crowd obeyed with enthusiasm.

"BRIGHTWALL'S A BASTARD! BRIGHTWALL'S A BASTARD! BRIGHTWALL'S A BASTARD!"

A panicked Mr. Delacorte attempted to clamp his hands over Dot's ears.

It was one of the funniest things Alexandra had ever seen or heard.

"BRIGHTWALL'S A BASTARD! BRIGHTWALL'S A BASTARD!" She joined with reckless glee.

She intercepted her husband's askance look with one of unapologetic mischief.

"They make it sound like a compliment," she explained.

His smile was fleetingly brilliant against the dark. He glanced down.

Which is when Alexandra realized she'd reflexively gripped his arm in excitement, and his tensed bicep felt like a boulder beneath her fingers. A thrill shot through her: he was more powerful than her in every way. She didn't understand why it felt wildly unjust and infuriating and erotic all at once.

He'd gone utterly still, as if he was loath to frighten off a wild creature. She could feel the tension humming in his body beneath her hand.

And she let her hand linger longer than seemed wise, simply to revel in his stillness, his fixed expression, the proof of her power to move him.

She uncurled her fingers slowly, and looped her arm through Dot's. Her heart was hammering with a different sort of portent now.

"Shillelagh's not a lady! Shillelagh's not a lady!" someone else tried.

This chant was less successful, as a good portion of the crowd was already drunk and all those syllables tripped everybody up. It eventually devolved into jeers.

Shillelagh lunged to try to snap the hand of someone reaching out to pet her.

"Oy! Keep yer 'ands to yerself!" her jockey warned. "She eats 'ands fer breakfast."

Another compact, nimble young man leaped into the middle of the track. The crowd surged to the railing. His job, it seemed, was to start the race.

"On your marks . . . get set . . . GO GO GO!"

And Brightwall and Shillelagh were off.

The crowd roared.

The little donkeys were nearly blurs, their churning hooves kicking up clods of earth and dust, their ears thrown back, their teeth bared. Their jockeys clung to them manfully. Soon

Alexandra's view was four little rumps—two
human, two donkey—bobbing along, nearly airborne. They were neck and neck as they rounded
the first curve of the track.

Alexandra and Dot screamed, "GO SHILLE-
LAGH! GO!"

While Brightwall and Delacorte bellowed, "GO
BRIGHTWALL!"

After long suspenseful seconds, Shillelagh was
ahead by the tip of her silvery nose. It was absurdly unbearably exciting.

And then the donkeys rounded the bend and a
cluster of people pushed in front of her and Alexandra could no longer see them at all.

"I can't see!" she shouted. "Aaaahhhh I can't
see! Down in front! I—"

She was suddenly airborne, seized by the waist
and launched up like a bird taking flight, hoisted
effortlessly by her huge husband.

She gasped in delight and laughed joyously.
"Go go go, SHILLELAGH! GO!"

Everyone behind her shouted, "DOWN IN
FRONT!"

"Make me!" she shouted, a little too caught up
in the spirit of things and feeling rather powerful,
now that she was tall.

Magnus plunked her to the ground again.

"Are you trying to start a riot?" He laughed.

His hands remained on her waist.

They both seemed to realize this at once.

Then he dropped them and she staggered

backward. "You would just toss them all aside like cordwood."

His laugh was marvelous and rich, the very essence of primal male satisfaction. Torch flames were reflected in his pupils. It was as though he *knew* the heat left behind by his hands on her waist had traveled to the nether regions of her body.

She no longer had breath to shout for Shillelagh.

But Dot did.

And Dot did.

"SHE'S WINNING! OH MY GOOD HEAVENS! SHE'S AHEAD!! GO SHILLELAGH! IT'S FATE I KNEW IT WAS FATE!"

"GO BRIGHTWALL! YOU CAN DO IT, YOU BEAUTIFUL BEAST!" Delacorte bellowed.

The crowd swarmed the rope rail.

And a roar of exultation exploded from the crowd as Shillelagh, by the tip of her silvery nose, won the race.

Alexandra, in a reflex of exultation, turned and leaped into Brightwall's arms.

She felt iron bands latch around her. Briefly she was pressed against the hot wall of his body. Then he released her and they backed away from each other as if she was a grenade in danger of detonating.

Alexandra spun away from him, her heart racing.

When she dared to glance back, it was to discover that Brightwall was utterly motionless. As if stunned.

Mr. Delacorte was cheerfully philosophical on their walk back to the carriage. "Ah, he'll win the next race. He must have known the ladies were betting on Shillelagh tonight, and wanted to be a gentleman."

Alexandra laughed.

Magnus still hadn't said a word.

"Oh, look! Is that Mr. Pike?" Delacorte waved at someone in the crowd filing away from the track. "I didn't know he liked donkey races! I wonder if he brought his sweetheart with him."

Dot stumbled.

Magnus caught her by the elbow. "Careful now, Dot. It's easy to lose our footing in the dark," he said.

Mr. Pike heard his name and obviously recognized the voice.

His hand shot up and his smile was briefly bright in the darkness. And then he was lost to the crowd.

They all filed into The Grand Palace on the Thames before the eleven o'clock curfew, and found Mr. Pike already home, up on a ladder in the foyer preparing to douse the chandelier lights for the night.

He paused to stare in astonishment when Colonel Brightwall and Delacorte entered with two ladies in brown hoods.

"Pike! Did you have money on Brightwall?" Delacorte asked him.

"Shillelagh tonight—I won ten pence!" Pike told him cheerfully.

When Dot and Alexandra shook off the hoods of their borrowed cloaks, Pike nearly fell off the ladder.

"Dot . . . *you* went to the donkey race?" he asked.

But Dot walked right past him and up the stairs as if she had neither seen nor heard him.

Given that it was Dot, it was entirely possible both were true, since her own thoughts were often as vivid as what was in front of her eyes.

Magnus had been silent in the carriage on the way back.

He didn't say a word on their journey through the black-and-white checked foyer, beneath the rather fine chandelier, through the passage to the annex, and up to their suite.

In fact, she realized, he hadn't said a word directly to her since she'd thrown herself briefly into his arms. Paradoxically, the quality of his silence was saying a lot of things rather loudly, and all of them were making Alexandra's heart stutter like a stone skipped across a lake.

She finally broke the silence. "At last I have money of my own." She jingled her twenty-pence prize winnings in her reticule.

It was childish. Pointed. A bit of a taunt. Meant to prod at the gathering tension of his mood and to ease her own nerves a little.

He didn't reply.

Once inside their suite he aggressively divested

himself of both his greatcoat and his hat, then set to work clawing away his cravat until it hung on either side of his neck. He rolled up his sleeves with equal vigor.

She froze, riveted and startled by the almost aggressive rapidity with which he shed his civilized outer shell.

Her eyes flicked to his arms then swiftly away.

His silence seemed to be gathering density.

She removed her cloak carefully, as if to compensate for his vigorous divesting, and hung it up. She unpinned her coiled braid and let it tumble down her back.

She pulled off her gloves and laid them gingerly on the mantel, as if they were a loaded weapon, and paused by the fireplace to warm her hands.

And all the while she was aware that he had paced, slowly, purposefully, across the room, until he was standing just behind her.

She spun about. "Well, I suppose I'll be off to bed—"

She gasped when he seized her braid, which had nearly lashed him when she turned.

He didn't relinquish it.

And now she was his captive, like a ribbon snagged in branches.

He didn't reply. His eyes were mesmerized. His hand slid up the coppery length of her braid until it settled at her nape. He held her, gently, but utterly fast.

They stared at each other.

She swallowed. "First I lash you with my ribbons." Her voice was frayed. "Now my braid."

He didn't reply. But his fingertips had begun to delicately trace the downy hair at her nape. His body heat was sinking into her, lulling her.

"Alexandra," he said softly. "Do you think I'm actually made of stone?"

There was a sort of tender, amused menace in the words.

But it sounded like a serious question.

He could do anything he wanted to her in this moment, should he choose. They both knew it.

But around the edges of those words shimmered something like a plea.

As if, despite everything, he was still at her mercy.

God help her, she wanted him to do things to her.

Anything he wanted.

What madness was this?

She was terrified of these feelings for a dozen reasons. Chief among them: the power the two of them seemed to possess to hurt each other.

"God, yes," she replied, sincerely, on a whisper.

It was too late for her. The wanting was beyond the reach of reason. Her body was already his. She'd gone pliant. Her thoughts dissolved, scattered; she would not need them for what she was hopefully about to do.

As his lips moved in a slow curve his hand slid down, down to cup the curve of her arse.

Her breath snagged in her throat when he urged her abruptly up against his cock.

Which was already hard.

This is what you do to me, was the message.

Her heart kicked inside her.

She shifted her groin against him. Testing herself. Testing him. Teasing him.

He hissed in a breath.

And she found his cock was so hard now it nearly hurt to move against him.

The battle between pride and need drew his features taut. His breath shuddered shallowly, hotly, in and out, against her lips. Mingling with her own.

Her eyes were going heavy-lidded from desire. She fought it, in vain.

It remained a contest of wills.

What if he let her go? Dropped his arms? Decided this was a bad idea? She felt, in that mad moment, that she would crumble into ash if he did. She felt it would destroy her.

Her lips trembled toward each other, desperate to form the word that meant surrender, that word that would let him know he'd won, that would betray to him that she would do anything he wanted: *please*.

He knew. Because she could see the exultation in his eyes.

And when his control snapped it was with a low groan, the sound of someone at last unchained from a dungeon wall.

It vibrated through her body as his mouth at last touched hers.

The rich heat and singular taste of him were a

heady shock. The kiss was at once a carnal siege—the sensual glide of his lips, then the silken stroke of his tongue—the object clearly to arouse her past endurance. ·

She hadn't known a kiss could do this: inebriate like whiskey, render useless the bones in her knees. Obliterate her will.

His hands gripped her arse and he brought her harder up against him just as her knees began to buckle; she fastened her arms around his neck, held on for dear life, and following his lead, they kissed each other to the brink of madness. Until they were forced to lift their heads, their breath bursting from their lungs in hot gusts.

They dragged each other down to the carpet like two people competing to drown each other.

Once their knees were on the floor, he took startlingly swift, efficient command. His arms went around her and he quickly had her on her back in an almost alarmingly businesslike fashion. Getting her into rutting position, because that's exactly what they were about to do. She looked dazedly up at a big man whose eyes were burning like a marauder's, feeling powerful as a sorceress to have so inflamed him. And freshly frightened, too, by her own anarchic desire, her willingness to fling herself into the unknown.

She clawed up her dress to abet him and felt a sense of unreality as the cool air of the room met her bare thighs. With one dexterous hand he managed to free all the buttons on the fall of his trousers and hurriedly dragged them down his thighs, shoving the great swaths of shirt aside.

His huge erect cock curving up toward his belly from its nest of curling dark hair was the most aggressively masculine, primitive thing she'd ever seen, and it nearly shocked her out of her lust fog.

With no preamble or warning, he slid one testing hand between her legs, up through the curls at the juncture of her legs, and stroked. Her breath snagged in her throat when a lightning jolt of pleasure arced through her. Her stunned sob of pleasure evolved into a low moan when he did it again and again. Fierce satisfaction surged in his features.

And then his hands were expertly parting her thighs and she gasped as he guided his cock into her.

It felt at first like a shocking invasion. Utterly foreign. She knew a split second of stark loneliness as she met his eyes, knowing that all this could mean for both of them was an urgent appeasement of a furious appetite. A mutual vanquishing. The faster they got what they wanted from it, the better.

And then his hips moved and it became wondrously clear that of course this was exactly what she wanted: every thrust ramped up the pleasure gathering, threatening to burst the very banks of her being.

She slid her hands under his shirt, her palms savoring the play of muscles under his hot smooth skin as he moved. His eyes flared hotter still when her hands slid down to fit into the scoops of muscle in his hard buttocks, and she gripped him, rising up to meet every thrust. He groaned and muttered a low oath of pleasure as she locked her legs around his hips.

And then all was abandon: the swift collision of bodies, her own sobs of pleasure as he drove her closer and closer to something glorious she could sense, but could not name. He knew what it was. Surely he knew. Surely this was what he was racing toward. She *prayed* he knew.

And then, because she was beyond pride, beyond anything other than need, that word at last rushed past her lips.

"Magnus . . . *please* . . ."

"Tell me . . ." His voice was a rasp.

"Oh God . . . please Magnus . . . I need . . . I want . . . I don't know I don't know . . . *help* me . . ."

He reached down and stroked her hard and expertly where they were joined.

Bliss unimaginable snatched her from her body and hurled her into the heavens like so much blazing confetti.

A scream was torn from her; she heard it as if she were miles away, floating somewhere over London, drifting, drifting. Her body bowed up beneath him.

She was quaking as if lightning-struck.

And that moment he went still with a groan.

He withdrew from her quickly.

He spilled instead on her thigh.

They collapsed, and lay side by side for a time on the carpet like two people flung haphazardly across the road after a carriage accident. She had a new appreciation for the word "sated." She could not move if she tried. Her body felt thoroughly and properly used for the first time ever.

Some absurd, latent reflex toward modesty made her pull her dress down over her hips. It was still furled around her waist.

And that was when Magnus bestirred himself to sit up.

And so she did, too. He'd found a handkerchief in his pocket. He gently, matter-of-factly cleaned her thigh where he'd spilled. He rearranged his shirt; he pulled his trousers up.

She watched all of this, a little abashed. But still dazed and reeling from her trip into the heavens via an orgasm.

And then they regarded each other as if seeing each other for the first time.

Tentatively, he reached out, and cupped her face. "Alexandra . . ."

He'd made her name sound like a question. One tinged with faint regret.

She looked up at him and saw silver and gold. His eyes, his skin. *Gold is a soft metal*, she thought dazedly. He seemed to her, in the firelight, gilded, and dangerously, deceptively soft. A great, battered, beautiful, pagan beast.

And her heart gave a sharp kick that felt perilously like joy.

Oh, she was very afraid of what was happening to her.

The ultimate punishment for her original crime would be to fall in love with a man she had likely already lost forever.

Perhaps her expression reflected her sudden fear. Because he dropped his hand from her quickly. As though in touching her he'd somehow transgressed.

Did he think he hadn't the right to offer affection to her? Or could he not bring himself to do it, since he felt honor-bound or pride-bound to despise her for betraying him?

Or was pride a factor at all when vigorous sex on the carpet was a possibility?

Regardless, she understood ambivalence all too well.

Suddenly the memory of a little pink scrap of ribbon tucked into a box was like a razor cut across her heart.

If she had found him kissing another woman in the garden on their wedding night, would she ever have forgiven him?

She just didn't think so.

And that was the crux of it.

Would bedding her at last satisfy him? After all, she'd been an acquisition. Something to partake.

This thought rang a little falsely. She nurtured it anyway, because somehow it seemed that if she could fan the flames of righteous anger she could protect herself from being hurt.

"Are you . . ." He stopped. Pressed his lips together.

"Yes. I'm very good. Thank you," she said, with almost absurd formality, as if they were sitting across from each other at a tea party. "And you?"

His expression remained pensive. Absorbed. His eyes never left her face.

A long moment later he said, "I'm very good." His voice was a husk.

Finally, absently, he swiped his hands through his hair, pushing it away from his sweaty forehead.

Neither one of them stood yet.

They sat together quietly, listening to each other breathing. Listening to the fire pop and snap.

"He was my brother's tutor."

He went rigid at once. His eyes flared in wary surprise.

"You never met him," she added. More faintly. "He was living for a time with the family in the house behind us. And he left to teach in Africa."

It had taken a lot of her courage to say that.

They stared at each other again. Her heart jabbed at her painfully.

"All right," he said finally. Carefully.

This was the measure and nature of the pain between them, she understood. Of the damage they'd inflicted on each other. That these questions and revelations could only be approached like shrapnel embedded in the flesh. One shard at a time.

She didn't know what would be left when they were done. Perhaps they never would be done.

After all, her husband's leg retained the souvenir of the time he'd saved a man's life. And in rough weather, he limped.

Perhaps the best solution was indeed to put an ocean between them.

"I'll just say good-night now, shall I?" she said softly, but firmly.

She wanted to be alone, so she could take inventory of herself, now that she was forever changed. There wasn't enough room on the floor for her, and for him, and all of her tumultuous feelings.

He was on his feet at once, his hand extended to her to help her up.

Her hand vanished into his, which was warm and rough and as oddly, immediately reassuring as his coat.

He glanced down at it, his face suddenly bemused. Like a boy, who'd been handed something valuable he wasn't certain he had the right to touch.

She didn't want to let go of him, which was why she did almost at once.

His hair was wildly mussed, which amused her. She was so tempted to reach up, to smooth it, simply to touch him. To tend him. How could the people among whom he'd been raised not have recognized the remarkable person in their midst? It seemed a terrible crime.

If she touched him that way and he stiffened, or dodged away, or worse, looked upon her with surprise, she would have died on the spot.

"Thank you," she said. "Good night."

HE STARED AT her closed door for a few seconds.

Then he dropped his head into his hands.

He breathed in, and out.

In and out.

Christ.

Blazing elation and acrid regret. Triumph and fear. An almost helpless tenderness. The dregs of fury and hurt. They all had gotten hold of various tag ends of his being, and he felt as though they might split him apart.

He relived all of it now: The unthinkably silken skin of her thighs as he slid his hands down to spread them. His fingers twining in those damp copper curls over her quim to discover whether she was ready for him. Her uncertain gaze going swiftly hot and hazy with desire. Her pale throat arching back on a scream of release. Her body pulsing around his cock.

He closed his eyes as fresh waves of lust and shame slammed him.

He could not believe he'd taken his beautiful, estranged virgin wife like a soldier rutting with a camp follower. He knew how to properly make love to a woman.

But if he wasn't mistaken . . . dear God, she had bloody well enjoyed it.

He'd thought he'd sensed this between them nearly five years ago: a spark that could be fanned into a conflagration. He'd wondered since then if it had been a delusion born of wishful thinking. Something he told himself to justify his untenable want for this one particular woman.

But maybe, for her, the spark—if she indeed felt such a thing—was entirely new.

Her brother's tutor. Every time he pictured that slim, shadowy man reaching desperately for her, her body blending into his—misery and fury fleetingly slashed the breath from him.

But he found these feelings, for the first time, tempered with sympathy. For all of them.

Even that young man darting away in the dark.

He didn't think Alexandra would ever love an idiot. And that somehow made it both better and worse.

How Magnus had wanted to be her refuge. And yet how odd it was to now feel a little gratitude that she'd had a source of comfort during a challenging time.

If he'd known she'd just ended a love affair, would he have married her anyway?

He didn't know. Everything about her, in fact, reminded him of everything he didn't know about love.

It still felt to him like a deception.

And he didn't think loving someone was something one could simply cease doing at will.

Would it have been more honorable for her to tell him about her brother's tutor? He didn't know that, either. He did know that she had stood up in church and forsaken all others for as long as she lived, and hours later she had passionately kissed another man.

It remained unquestionably a betrayal, by anyone's definition.

And this conviction brushed up against something implacable in him. A wall behind which he could remain safe.

Because if he touched her the way he'd always wanted to touch her, she would understand at once that she undid him utterly. And his pride still rebelled at the idea of her ever discovering the man known for mercilessness was entirely at her mercy.

Chapter Fourteen

꧁꧂

Alexandra hadn't expected to sleep much, given the evening's tumult.

But once she'd gotten into her night rail and crawled beneath her blankets, she didn't open her eyes again until morning. Ecstasy, it seemed, could wear a girl out.

Last night had also been, she realized, akin to a fever finally breaking.

She was awake and dressed before the maids brought in their coffee and scones. She parted the curtains. If she stood on her toes, she could just barely see the sun glinting off the sea and the tall spires of ships. And if she looked off to the left, she could see a man urinating on the adjacent building. Such was life at the docks. She rather liked the contrast. As it turned out, joy and earthy pleasure and chaos suited her. Like a donkey race.

Like sex on the floor with her estranged husband.

She had no time to consider the aftermath, however, because a motion snagged the corner of her eyes. She pivoted to find Magnus dressed completely, snowy cravat and Hoby boots polished to mirror brilliance and all, emerging from his room.

He halted when he saw her.

She inspected him for signs of regret, or wariness, and his somber, somewhat uncertain expression suggested he was inspecting her for the same.

She found neither.

Nor did he appear to be gloating.

Then his mouth tilted at the corner in a faint smile. He settled in at the little table near the window, and she sat down across from him.

He poured a cup of coffee for her and pushed the sugar over.

Neither one of them had yet said a word. The magical bitter black elixir would no doubt make conversation more possible in a moment or two.

She looked across at the Earl of Montcroix and vividly recalled his eyes burning down into hers, as he hurled aside his miles of shirt and steered his cock into her body, and a fresh wash of lust bolted through her like a gulp of coffee. She fumbled with her napkin.

"I'll be out all day today, I'm afraid," he told her. "More long meetings and affairs of state to attend to. I'm to meet with officers of the king to discuss properties associated with the title."

"How wonderful, Magnus," she said pleasantly. "Or Montcroix, whatever you prefer to be called."

He smiled faintly. "Whatever trips most lightly off your tongue."

She was going to blush again, because tongues made her think of the taste of him.

"I thought I'd spend some time today at the town house to officially say goodbye to the servants and to help supervise the packing of my possessions," she said offhandedly.

After a somewhat lengthy hesitation, he nodded.

"I've also a meeting regarding the timing of the Grosvenor Square town house purchase," he volunteered.

The underpinning of their relationship now seemed to be quiet, civil little gauntlets thrown down.

"I'll make the carriage available to you," he added. "I'll take the hack downtown."

"That won't be necessary, Magnus, but thank you. I can take a hack to the town house. I can afford it. I have all my Shillelagh winnings, after all."

He nodded once, acknowledging the little jest that wasn't entirely a jest.

"My carriage is safer. Please take the carriage."

My carriage, she thought. As if the two of them were not really an entity anywhere apart from public appearances, and never would be. Soon, there would be no "our" of any kind.

But there was a slight emphasis on "please." She understood that this was a man who wanted to care, who'd long wanted an opportunity to care, and he specifically wanted to take care of her. What harm would there be in allowing him to do that for now?

"Very well. I'll take the carriage, thank you."

Her breath hitched when he suddenly leaned

toward her, his eyes flaring. His thumb traced her jaw lightly.

"Alexandra . . . your cheek . . . it's a little pink here. It looks a bit like a burn . . . did I do this to you? When we . . ."

She couldn't yet speak. His touch had sent a quicksilver tingle down her spine.

"Oh." She touched her cheek absently. "I think it was because your whiskers scraped . . . when we . . ."

"Ah."

When they kissed each other nearly senseless, was the rest of that sentence.

Judging from the heat, her entire face was pink now.

Why were they being coy?

Because it was daylight, and the coffee and tea and scones were so sweetly civilized and the people they were this morning seemed to have no relation to the animals rolling around and moaning on the carpet last night.

"Anything can be a weapon," she teased, lightly. Just a little ironically.

But he looked nearly stricken. "I'm so sorry. I didn't mean to . . . I never meant to hurt you."

He didn't specify for what. For the raw, unguarded, desperate hunger that inadvertently burned her tender skin with kisses?

Or for . . . everything?

"I'm not fragile," she said shortly.

"I know," he said gently. He sounded a little surprised. "I knew that the moment I met you."

She was surprised.

"But you should have been allowed to be," he added softly. "You should be allowed to be."

Her eyes widened in astonishment.

She dropped her gaze, moved and unsettled. She supposed a man who had once been a boy who had never been allowed to be weak would notice that fragility had never been an option for her, either.

Perhaps this was why his every instinct seemed to be to protect her.

And yet it seemed clear he was still prepared to send her away.

For that matter, she was prepared to go.

Clearly one night of cathartic passion had not magically repaired the deeper wounds between them.

She lifted her head swiftly when she realized he was probably genuinely worried that he'd hurt her. He'd been essentially called a beast the whole of his life.

"You didn't hurt me, Magnus. It doesn't hurt. And if I had wanted you to stop at any point, I would have asked you to stop, I promise. I wouldn't have furled my dress up to my waist."

Amusement flickered in his eyes, but his expression remained serious. "You are certain you wanted to . . ."

"Yes." It was barely a sound, and absent of intonation. But she let her eyes convey the vehemence of the truth of this.

Who was this wanton woman who made these sorts of confessions over coffee and scones?

They let all of those potent words they'd just said hover in the air for a while.

She stirred sugar into her coffee. "Perhaps it needed to happen just the way it happened."

The way it happened. In other words:

Fast. Hot. Deep. Rough. Urgent.

Angry.

Cathartic.

Extraordinary.

But not tender.

And not loving.

And not again.

Never again.

Transfixed, they regarded each other silently.

Neither of them allowed their expressions to reveal a thing.

He turned away from her, toward the window, as if he was concerned she would read his thoughts. Which were likely very explicit at the moment.

She sipped her coffee. "I wasn't aware . . . that extraordinary pleasure . . . would make me scream."

He slowly turned back to her. His expression now suggested a man who had been clubbed in the head.

Finally he said both the best and the worst possible thing:

"It can be even better."

AT THE TOWN house, a crew of cheery men were patching the ceiling where water had begun to drip into the foyer. They greeted her with deference as she made her way up the stairs.

She'd thought visiting the place she'd spent her sort of mild social purgatory might be a little painful, given that she was leaving it behind, but then everything was painful lately, so what would it matter?

She realized as she scaled the stairs to what she already considered her soon-to-be-former bedroom that "painful" wasn't precisely the right word. She was simply suddenly excruciatingly more sensitive to everything, as though an obscuring defensive layer had been stripped from her and she was *fully* seeing and feeling certain things for the first time in a very long time. Grief and fury and regret and epiphany and bliss and joy.

And sorrow.

The reward for the end of this sorrow would be peace, eventually.

She would not stay with a man who could want her, but not forgive her. Obviously, she *could* not stay with him, if he didn't want her to.

And it wasn't as though she'd forgiven him entirely, either. Although she was so much more accustomed to yielding than he was, to finding that way to make everything better for everyone.

And speaking of pain—she hadn't told Magnus the complete truth. She *was* a little sore between her legs. She felt it now as she climbed the stairs.

Ironically, it seemed the kind of soreness that could only be cured by wrapping her legs around his broad back again and digging her nails into his shoulders until they were both out of their minds with pleasure.

This notion sent such a rush of blood to her head and regions south of her head she was forced to grip the banister. She would know in the future not to entertain those kinds of thoughts on a staircase. Death by swooning from lust and tumbling down a flight would be embarrassing.

Had she enjoyed living here? She could not quite say. It was a fine, comfortable house, in a fine location. The floors were marble; crystal and gilt abounded in the furniture and fixtures. He had bought it furnished, many years ago, he'd told her; he'd chosen nothing, as he hadn't had the time or the knowledge to choose the right things. It had never felt like *hers*; it decidedly wasn't. She hadn't allowed herself to feel she had a right to it. It was the place where Colonel Brightwall had stored his faithless wife, and where she'd slept alone night after night. A comfortable, luxurious purgatory.

To her, it would always be the physical reminder of the way in which she'd been punished for kissing another man on her wedding day.

And today, it reminded her acutely of how lonely she'd been here, because the last few days she'd spent with Magnus and everyone at The Grand Palace on the Thames she'd had a taste of the kind of life she might have had.

But like this town house, that life didn't belong to her, either. It was only temporary.

Hence the sorrow.

And yet she could not surrender fully to that sorrow. The stubbornest of all human conditions—hope—was aiming its rays down upon it, threatening to shrink it like a puddle after the rain.

It scared her breathless.

Superstitiously, she refused to turn to examine too closely the reasons for her hope. She could still feel within her a steely filament of resentment and hurt. She clung to that like a lifeline, because it seemed the only refuge from the terrible fear that she had fallen in love with her husband five years too late.

She sat gingerly down on the bed and closed her eyes. She let her hand wander over the coverlet, reliving the smooth heat of his hips beneath her hands as she arched them to take him more deeply into her body. She already knew she wanted to feel the entirety of her skin against his.

That sound he'd made when he'd kissed her last night . . . that primal, anguished relief—the memory swept through her and nearly made her sway. How terribly lonely he must have been all these years, too.

Lust and longing, hope and fear, tightened her chest.

What if he was spending the day regretting the previous evening?

Then again: *It could be even better,* he'd said.

No matter the cost to her, before she left for New York, she wanted to know how.

"WILL EVERYONE BE in tomorrow night?" Delilah asked the general gathering in the sitting room that evening. "Helga is going to market tomorrow morning and we thought we'd get a definitive count for dinner."

The Dawsons were at their usual table, gazing into each other's eyes. The ladies and Lucien had clustered around Mrs. Pariseau, who had plans to read aloud their next nightly chapter of *The Arabian Nights' Entertainments*. Delilah and Angelique were knitting; Alexandra and Dot were embroidering samplers. Alexandra had decided to attempt to stitch a rather complicated fountain from her imagination.

Captain Hardy had settled in across from Delacorte for a game of chess.

Only Magnus was still out when the boardinghouse residents gathered in the sitting room that evening after dinner.

"I think me and the missus will be in and out all day tomorrow," Corporal Dawson replied to Delilah.

"And in and out. And in and out again, I imagine," Mr. Delacorte said pleasantly.

Captain Hardy gave him a little kick under the table.

"How did everyone enjoy the donkey races?" Lucien interjected hurriedly.

"*Donkey* races!" Mrs. Cuthbert exclaimed. "You went to a race between donkeys?"

Everyone in the room stifled a sigh.

"Mrs. Cuthbert, if I may ask . . . what are your

favorite pleasures and pursuits?" Captain Hardy asked very, very mildly. Deceptively mildly. It had probably taken all of his discipline not to emphasize the word "are."

"Well, to tell you the truth, I visited London only to see my old friend Mrs. Pariseau." She said this as though she'd made a heroic sacrifice. Mrs. Pariseau smiled neutrally. "But usually I find it very peaceful and pleasant when things are predictable. If staying in one place is good enough for a tree or a pond, it's good enough for me."

This was so very nearly profound it gave everyone a moment's pause.

"But trees and ponds change with the seasons, often dramatically," Alexandra said gently. "Perhaps it's all right if you do, too. Leaves fall. Blossoms bloom. Ponds evaporate. Tadpoles live in the pond and frogs appear. And I won twenty pence on Shillelagh," Alexandra added, to answer Lucien's question.

He whistled appreciatively, teasing her.

Mrs. Cuthbert reared back. "My dear, gambling *and* jail? I'm beginning to think that Colonel Brightwall must have taken you on in order to reform you."

This was funny, indeed. Alexandra currently had a bit of a burn on both sets of cheeks (the top set from whiskers, the bottom set from carpet) due to vigorous lovemaking.

"I've learned a thing or two from him," she confessed. "And I rather hope to learn more."

"I suspected as much," Mrs. Cuthbert sniffed.

"And Dot won ten pence," she added cheerfully.

Mrs. Cuthbert swiveled her head toward Dot, eyes huge. "Et tu, Dot?"

"Not eighty-two," Dot told Mrs. Cuthbert patiently. "Ten. Ten pence."

Mrs. Cuthbert opened her mouth to correct her, then intercepted a somewhat quelling look from Angelique and apparently thought better of it.

"How did you enjoy the donkey race, Dot?" Delilah wanted to know. "It sounds as though Shillelagh won. How exciting!"

Delilah had lolled in bed after a decadent evening with her husband. Which meant she was awake by six, instead of five. She had not yet heard reviews of the donkey race.

Dot nodded, a little subdued. "I had a wonderful time." Her tone confusingly suggested otherwise. "Thank you for letting me go."

Angelique and Delilah exchanged swift glances. Of the many things Dot was, subdued was seldom one of them.

"I suppose it *was* fate, then," Angelique prompted.

"Perhaps it was," Dot reflected driftily. "Perhaps it was. But I don't know anymore if fate is always a good thing."

Bemused glances ricocheted between Angelique and Delilah and Captain Hardy and Lord Bolt. A philosophical Dot was a bit worrisome, too.

"Perhaps fate is a thing like—oh, the sky, or a

pond or a tree—it isn't fundamentally good or bad. It just is," Alexandra suggested, delicately.

"Very wise, dear," Mrs. Pariseau approved.

"I learned it in prison," Alexandra lied, mischievously.

She had discovered that every time Mrs. Cuthbert disapproved of something, her bosom heaved a bit and her pearl necklace glinted in the light.

Perversely, Alexandra was actually going to miss her, and this room, when she was gone. She loved the odd balance of people—the give-and-take, the kindness and patience and exasperation and humor and clumsiness. It felt so warm, and so alive.

She thought Magnus would enjoy this evening, too. And a little cloud moved over her mood, because what that really meant was that she thought *she* would enjoy this even more if he was here. She missed him, and she suspected this meant she was a fool.

The somewhat queasy suspicion that Magnus was staying out late deliberately so that he wouldn't need to face her when he returned had begun to settle in.

So be it, if so. But even if she was already in bed when he returned, if, like her, he'd been engaged in his own somewhat torturous inner dialogue today about making love to his wife . . . she intended to extend to him an invitation so subtle that even if he refused it, or failed to notice, it would still leave her with her pride.

But thinking about it now sped her heart.

"What are you going to buy with your ten pence, Dot? New handkerchiefs? Save up to buy your own donkey?" Delilah wondered.

Mr. Delacorte's head shot up from the chessboard as if he'd just heard a brilliant idea.

"I bought a little journal today at the stationer's when I went out to get the newspapers. I'm going to write my most important thoughts in it. I'm going to call it 'Dot's Thoughts.'"

A polite silence ensued, during which everyone silently congratulated themselves on not saying aloud what they were thinking about Dot's thoughts.

"I'd never considered ranking my thoughts from most important to least," Lucien said. "You'll be busy, Dot."

Dot nodded somberly in agreement.

"Speaking of written things, Dot, I can't seem to find our copy of *The Arabian Nights' Entertainments*. Do you know where it might be?" Mrs. Pariseau asked.

Dot's eyebrows assumed a distressed position. "Oh, dear! I'm so sorry. I left it upstairs. I wanted to write the word 'Scheherazade' in my journal and I didn't know how to spell it."

"Perhaps you can go and fetch it for Mrs. Pariseau," Delilah suggested.

"I'm sorry . . . I'm very sorry . . . but I don't think I can." Her voice was low and tormented.

They stared at her. Speechless. Not in their wildest dreams had Delilah or Angelique anticipated insubordination from Dot. Perhaps the ten pence she'd won was giving her notions.

"You don't think you can?" Delilah repeated gingerly.

"It's just . . . I'm sorry, but I'm sore afraid to go up alone right now," Dot whispered reluctantly, with a certain despair. She clasped her hands. "Sore afraid" was something she'd heard in a story and had probably been dying to say aloud.

Then Delilah had it. "You're worried about something?"

Dot nodded wretchedly. "I'm afraid to tell you, because you won't believe me."

"We're always interested in what you have to say, Dot," Angelique said. Mostly truthfully.

Dot glanced around the room at the encouraging expressions, and pulled in a deep breath. "Last night . . . as I came in from the donkey race . . ." She swallowed. "I think I heard a ghost."

Nearly everyone in the room was riveted now. This was better than *The Arabian Nights' Entertainments*.

But wary, meaning-saturated glances surreptitiously ricocheted between the people in the room who were fairly certain they knew what Dot had actually heard.

Delilah cleared her throat. "Dot," she said gently. "We've had this conversation. About the wind and drafts. And the fact that we have no ghosts."

"That you know of," Lucien muttered wickedly.

"That's why I didn't want to tell you!" She

wrung her hands. "I knew you would say that, but I'm not a looby, I *promise*, and I swear to you on our chandelier that it wasn't the wind. The wind can't make a sound like Ohhhhh . . . *Ohhhhh . . . Ahhh Ahhhh AaaaAAAUUGGGGGHSimon!*"

Her raspy cry of ecstatic anguish seemed to echo endlessly in the ensuing silence.

No one was prepared. In the aftermath, everyone looked around to discover they were all variously covering their heads with their hands or gripping the arms of their chairs as if a hurricane had blown through the room.

Eyes were unanimously bulging.

Except for Mrs. Cuthbert's.

Alexandra noticed that Mrs. Cuthbert's eyes had rolled back in her head and her chair was teetering.

"Smelling salts! We need smelling salts!" Alexandra sprang up just as Captain Hardy and Mr. Delacorte leaped forward. They caught Mrs. Cuthbert just as she toppled out.

Her swoon had a soft landing on the carpet, cradled by men.

"I think Dot may have solved our problem," Delilah whispered to Angelique just before she leaped from her chair.

"The Dawsons, or killing Mrs. Cuthbert?" Angelique replied on a whisper.

They hastened to her side with smelling salts.

Alexandra patted her wrists gently. "Mrs. Cuthbert? You're all right. You're safe."

Mrs. Cuthbert gazed up from the carpet at the

worried faces ringing her. Two of them, belonging to the Dawsons, were scarlet.

"You are either the strangest kind people I've ever met, or the kindest strange people I've ever met," Mrs. Cuthbert finally said to them all, woozily.

"I'll get the sherry," Delilah murmured.

"And glasses, too?" Angelique asked her. "For all of us, I think."

"I'm going to drink mine straight from the bottle," Delilah said, only half jesting, as she swept from the room.

After a few moments of tender fussing by the crowd, Mrs. Cuthbert sat up, and seemed to be genuinely enjoying the attention.

"Prudence, dear, I'm so sorry you had a fright." Mrs. Pariseau's knees cracked when she crouched next to her old friend.

"Do you see?" Dot felt vindicated. "I'm not the only one afraid of ghosts. Mrs. Cuthbert is, too!"

Alexandra recalled again what Magnus had said about Mrs. Cuthbert, and it struck her forcibly now as profoundly, matter-of-factly insightful, compassionate, and frank: *Frightened creatures use whatever defenses they have at their disposal.* Her throat went thick as she freshly understood where and just exactly how he'd learned that, and how he'd understood her little episode of throwing things.

"It's very brave to confront so many new things at once," Alexandra told Mrs. Cuthbert. "Anyone might feel a bit overwhelmed." She shot a look at Mrs. Pariseau, who understood that this was her cue.

"Yes, you're very brave to do something new, Prudence, and a lot of new things at once can be hard on a person when it's been a little while since you've ventured out," Mrs. Pariseau added firmly.

"Do you really think I'm brave?" Mrs. Cuthbert lit up at this notion.

As everyone had noticed the magical reviving effect of the words on Mrs. Cuthbert, they nodded solemnly.

"Dot," ventured Mrs. Dawson, her volume and pitch scarcely above that of a field mouse.

As it was the first voluntary word Mrs. Dawson had ever uttered in the sitting room, everyone's head swiveled toward her.

"Please don't be afraid. It was us. It was Simon and me, you see. We was just being silly and making noise. We didn't mean to frighten you." Her voice was shaking.

It was a brave, kind thing for Mrs. Dawson to do, as everyone in that room save Dot knew exactly what the Dawsons were doing. She'd said it because she didn't want Dot to be afraid for a moment longer.

Dot's immense relief was clearly tinged with just the slightest bit of disappointment.

"Oh! I'm glad you're enjoying yourselves here at The Grand Palace on the Thames," she said more cheerily. "I'll go fetch the book."

She whisked out of the room just as Delilah returned with the sherry and glasses.

MR. PIKE WAS bringing in the lamp from its hook when Magnus finally returned to The Grand Palace on the Thames for the day.

As his footsteps echoed across their black-and-white marble foyer, he cast a somewhat wistful glance at the sitting room, which was quiet and dark now.

In every quiet moment, the aftermath of last night visited him in fleeting, blinding surges: Exultation. Lust. Wonder. Uncertainty. Fear. Anger. Lust again. The kind that tensed his every muscle and seized his lungs and made his head feel as though it might launch from his body. It had seemed almost sacrilegious to go about his day on the heels of an event that felt as life-altering as buying his commission or getting shot in battle. But perhaps he was only mythologizing what had just been a very satisfying tumble.

For a man accustomed to making clearheaded decisions and moving on from them, he felt hobbled by his uncertainty, as if it was a dislocated limb. He was wise enough to know that no man could be trusted to be clearheaded about anything after a night of extraordinary sex.

Two days ago he had not been an earl; today he was. He felt no different. How odd it was to know that he was now the owner of estates in Kent and Surrey associated with his new title, and wealthier than even he had ever dared dream.

And yet rather than dwelling on this, more than anything he'd wanted to know whether Alexandra's day had been similarly haunted by the memory of last night.

He'd meant to return to the boardinghouse much earlier. Five years was a long time to be away from London, and it seemed everyone wanted something from him: a meeting to discuss affairs of state or parliamentary affairs, or just to thank him, or to reminisce, and he found it difficult to deny them the time. He'd been briefly to White's, and there he'd been compelled to hold court for a time by young men who'd hung on his every word. How grateful he was that he'd become someone who was considered to possess anything like wisdom, as well as skill.

He supposed that eventually all the disparate details of his life would assume some sort of routine. He could do some good in parliament.

Ironically, he found himself instead wishing he could go to New York and stay awhile, in a place civilized enough to be comfortable, but where few people would recognize him at first sight. A blank canvas of a place, where he could discover who he might be if he wasn't leading men into battle. Who he might be if he wasn't mourning a marriage that had never bloomed.

He found it difficult to imagine any future right now, in this moment.

His most important—and fruitful—meetings today had been with an editor of *The Times* and the Duke of Brexford to sort out a bit of business. He had accomplished what he'd hoped to, and oh, it had cost him. But in the end, he had simply been unable to help himself.

He had also, for reasons he refused to examine too closely, stopped into his favorite London barber today for a close shave.

Save from the low glow of the remains of the fire, the suite was dark when he entered. So Alexandra had gone to sleep.

Perhaps this was for the best.

He set to stripping off his coat and cravat and waistcoat and shirt in preparation for toppling into bed, and put them away in his room. He briefly closed his eyes and paused by the fire instinctively as a cat to savor the last of its warmth on his bare skin. To this day it remained a reflex to snatch up every fleeting sensual pleasure he stumbled across as if it was a coin shining in the street.

When he opened his eyes again, he looked toward Alexandra's door.

It was ajar.

His heart gave a single, hard jolt.

He stared at that hand's span width of darkness like it was the entrance to Aladdin's cave in *The Arabian Nights' Entertainments.*

He suddenly, absurdly resented that everything here at The Grand Palace on the Thames was so well maintained, so smoothly oiled and meticulously dusted. He would never have heard the door creak.

But his instincts told him it wasn't an accident.

And now his heart accelerated.

If it wasn't an accident, was it an invitation?

A test?

Or . . . a trap?

The bear trap sort of trap, that would clamp over his heart?

Christ. It was just a door.

But he now couldn't breathe for yearning toward that dark space and the possibilities that lay behind it.

He didn't see how touching her again would lead to anything but more confusion and pain for both of them. He knew definitively that she still possessed the power to hurt him. This had been an unwelcome revelation. Only fools courted pain. He'd had enough for a lifetime.

And thus began a dialogue between want and reason. Sex was bliss and forgetting, wasn't it? A function of biology. It needn't have meaning or import. It needn't be part of the arc of a *story*, with ramifications.

He thought of Corporal Dawson and his wife, who made love like they'd discovered it, like they were the very first humans, and suddenly he had his answer: Life is short. Pleasures are for seizing.

The next breath he pulled in was hot.

It shuddered out slowly as he moved toward the door and pushed it open.

The fire in her room had burned down to embers, too; an orange glow traced the far edge of the bed. Everything else was lost in velvety, inky shadow.

He hovered just inside the doorway indecisively, and listened for the sort of steady breathing that would tell him whether she was sleeping. Waiting for the shadows to evolve into shapes. Waiting for a definitive sign.

But he could hear nothing. Apart from—he could have sworn—his own heart beating.

He inched toward the darkest edge of the bed and stopped as his thigh met the edge of the mattress. And there he stood, held in a vise of indecision and lust.

If he were any other sort of man there would be no hesitation: he would climb into bed and demand that the woman he'd married satisfy him.

With the increasing chill on his bare torso came the dawning conviction that he'd deluded himself. The open door meant nothing. And this tiptoeing into the room and agonized pondering was unworthy of him as a man.

He tensed his muscles to turn to leave.

His breath arrested in his lungs when something brushed the fall of his trousers.

He froze, breathing shallowly.

The bedding rustled as she stirred, raising herself up on her elbows.

And he stood absolutely motionless, scarcely breathing, as Alexandra worked open a button on his trouser fall.

And then another.

And then the next.

His cock stirred against the brush of her fingers as, one by one, she freed the buttons from their buttonholes. Neither one of them said a word. He didn't assist, move, or breathe. As though if he did, she might change her mind.

The last button freed, he pushed his trousers down to the floor and stepped out of them. She raised the blankets so he could slide beneath.

They turned to each other immediately.

Which is when he realized that she, like he, was completely, gloriously nude.

He gathered her into his body, claiming her completely at once. They laced their limbs. She draped her leg over his thigh. Groin to groin, face to face, they merely held each other like this for a moment, shocked by and drunk on the feel of skin against skin. It almost seemed to him like enough, forever. If he died now, so be it.

He set his hands free over the warm, smooth heaven of her: the sharp wings of her shoulder blades, the satiny slope of her arse, the soft, fuzzed curve outside her thigh and the petal of vulnerable skin inside, skimming the curls of her mound, then dipping to play in the slick heat they covered.

Her breath fell swiftly, hotly on his neck, where she'd tucked her head; he felt every catch of her breath, every sigh, as she received pleasure, reveling in it, rippling and arching beneath his hands. He laid his lips against the pulse at her throat, softly, then drew them up to her ear, and with delicate, purposeful tracings of his tongue and breath, soon had her moaning softly.

He wanted her to understand just how much

pleasure he could give her. How she was made to be touched like this. How he, specifically, knew how to make her writhe from the surfeit of bliss. He brought his skills, his lips, his fingertips, his earthy, sensual hunger to her like offerings.

He filled his hands with the silky weight of her breasts and with his fingers traced hard shapes over her ruched nipples, and exulted at the sound of her stunned *oh* as her breath left her. The arch of her body as pleasure pierced through her.

Apart from that, no words were uttered.

In the dark, they could be anyone: any man, any woman, any two creatures who'd stumbled across each other and had gotten it into their heads to fornicate, rather than two people who had inadvertently ruined each other's lives. It needn't have significance. It needn't mean surrender. It didn't change a thing.

But she might have noticed that his fingertips trembled as they slowly glided over her skin, mapping out the magical terrain of her, showing her the secret places where pleasure hid: the crease of her elbows, the fan of her waist into her round hips, the pearls of her spine, and the little dimple at the base of her spine as it dipped to her arse.

But the way she slowly dragged her hands across his chest, tangling her fingers in the curling dark hair; the way she found and traced with her fingertips the deep gullies between the muscles of his abdomen; and the way her toes dragged along the diamond-hard contours of his calves suggested she had imagined doing all of these things for some time.

Her wandering hand stopped over his heart.

And surely there she discovered for certain what touching her and being touched by her did to him.

So he laced his fingers through hers and guided her hand down to his cock and silently showed her how he wanted to be stroked.

As she dragged her fist again and again along his rigid length, they kissed each other with a tender, searching leisure that undid him. Surely she felt his groan of helpless pleasure vibrate through her body.

He knew she was close, so he slipped his hand between her legs and stroked until she cried out, her body bowing beneath him, and he let his hand linger there, savoring every pulse of her release.

He pulled gently from her arms and bridged her with his body.

Instinctively she shifted her body beneath him and opened her legs to welcome him.

With a thrust they were joined, and he moved, this time more deliberately.

In the dark, they could almost pretend all of this was a dream.

And in the morning, if they wished, they could pretend it had never happened, and meant nothing.

But he said her name in a sort of anguish of bliss when he came.

And she held him until he stopped quaking.

For a moment they held each other. This was all he would allow himself: this moment.

Finally, he pulled from her arms, slipped from the bed, and closed the door behind him when he left.

Chapter Fifteen

❦

OVER COFFEE and scones the following morning, Alexandra handed to Magnus the trousers he'd left on the floor next to her bed.

He took them wordlessly, and laid them over the chair.

They settled in at the table across from each other.

He poured her coffee and passed the sugar.

He was still in shirtsleeves. His forearms were on display. Alexandra watched his hands—strong, rough, long-fingered—as he poured her coffee.

Those hands that had loaded countless muskets and emptied slops had touched her in gloriously, skillfully intimate ways.

And they had trembled as they showed her the secret pleasures of her body.

Her mind blanked for an instant, her thoughts momentarily replaced by what felt like sparkles and sunset colors.

"Dot brought the newspaper up."

His voice was still graveled from sleep.

She shook herself from her reverie.

He pushed the newspaper over to her.

She glanced down at it.

CARRIAGE INCIDENT A PRANK, SAYS BREXFORD

Lord Thackeray is a free man after a series of errors incorrectly resulted in his detention for carriage theft.

Apologies have been made to Lord Thackeray by both the arresting authorities and the Duke of Brexford.

All parties are satisfied that the incident resulted from a miscommunication, particularly with regards to the name of his alleged accomplice, who was misidentified as Mrs. Brightwall.

All parties indicate that no hard feelings remain.

The sheer, cool brilliance of it. What it didn't say was more important than what it did say. It was yet another strategic little lie that wasn't a lie.

A warm, radiant gratitude took her breath away.

She did not quite trust herself to look up yet. "That can't have been easy for you."

She meant logistically *and* emotionally.

She looked up in time to catch his rueful, faint smile. "Oh, it wasn't."

"That's where you were yesterday? Sorting this?"

"For much of it," he confirmed.

They were smiling at each other now.

"Thank you," she finally said. Fervently. Almost shyly.

He nodded.

"He's . . . sound?" She meant Thackeray.

He nodded again.

She sighed in relief. She adored her stupid cousin.

"I don't know how Mrs. Cuthbert will take the news that I was never actually in prison when she reads the article," she mused. "Part of me hopes she never discovers it. I'm having a little too much fun with it. She thinks you took me on in order to reform me."

His smile began slowly and spread. "She said this last night? What else did I miss?"

"Mrs. Cuthbert swooned when Dot imitated the sounds of a ghost, which were apparently actually the sounds of Mrs. Dawson in the throes of passion, although Mrs. Dawson told Dot she was merely having silly fun with her husband. Then Mrs. Hardy and Mrs. Durand passed around sherry, and we all discovered that Mrs. Cuthbert is entertaining when she's tipsy. She voluntarily launched into song."

His eyes went wider and wider as this recitation went on.

"Damn," he swore softly and fervently. "I wish I'd been there."

She laughed. After a moment, she said, "I thought of you." Softly. Tentatively.

It had felt risky to say such a thing aloud.

But suddenly the air fair shimmered with heat as their eyes met.

He ducked his head. A little silence followed as he applied himself to their breakfast-before-breakfast.

"These scones . . ." he murmured, with a head shake.

". . . are heaven," she confirmed. "Their cook is named Helga, I'm given to understand."

"Mmmm."

She refreshed their cups of coffee.

"I think my preparations for my move to New York are complete," she offered casually.

She sipped her coffee as he took this in.

They fixed each other with thoughtful, unreadable gazes.

"Very well." He nodded politely. His voice, however, sounded somewhat frayed.

They ought to open a gaming hell, she thought. The two of them had brilliant game faces.

"I'm sorry to have missed dinner here last night. The food here is delicious. How was it?" he said finally.

"Eel pie, potatoes, and peas with a treacle tart. All delicious. Mr. Delacorte sped through his potatoes the way Shillelagh sped around that track."

Magnus went still, his eyes briefly misty, imagining it.

"Good man, Delacorte. I'm sincerely sorry we'll have to miss tonight's dinner, too. As you no doubt recall, we've the banquet and reception at the Earl and Countess of Scottsbury's home this evening. Followed by musical entertainment, I'm given to understand. A soprano of some sort, again."

"Hopefully she won't be warbling about yearning."

His smile was slow and brilliant and for the second time this morning her mind filled with what felt like sparkles and nothing else.

"I'll wear my pearl-colored satin," she finally said.

As FAR AS Dot was concerned, the world was made of magic. How else to explain how she'd been promoted to lady's maid for the Duchess of Brexford, after her own mother, the previous lady's maid, had run away with a footman? Magic! And surely it was thanks to magic that she'd been hired by the tremendously kind Lady Derring, now Mrs. Hardy, when the duchess had fired her. It was magic when Lady Derring had kept her on as a lady's maid, even after she'd accidentally burned and dropped so many things.

And it was magic that Dot had been present the moment Mrs. Hardy and Mrs. Durand had decided to turn a tumbledown building by the docks into The Grand Palace on the Thames—right after they'd lost their other home forever. Magic had happened on the heels of terrible trouble so often in her life that she never missed an opportunity to wish on things: stars, dandelions, ladybirds. And now she mostly wished that things would stay precisely the way they were, because she'd never felt happier than she was answering the door and bringing the tea and meeting new and lovely people, and she'd thought she'd never want another thing as long as nothing changed.

And then Mrs. Hardy and Mrs. Durand had gone and hired Mr. Benjamin Pike.

She had inadvertently done violence to Mr. Pike twice: she had trod on his foot in a race to the door (which was why he always wore boots in the house now) and on another occasion she had hurled her fist into his jaw and knocked him to the floor. But that was when he'd sneaked up on her in the kitchen because he'd *known* she would think he was a ghost. And though she'd been filled with crippling remorse and he had been too filled with admiration for her aim to be too outraged, he'd been remorseful, too, and they both agreed the whole business was mostly his fault, and it remained their secret.

He had also held her hand very gently as he'd inspected her knuckles for bruises. She remembered well the feel of her stinging fingers resting in his big warm palm, the pain contrasted with a sort of tender care that made not just her face but the entirety of her being fleetingly warm.

He'd gotten his revenge, however inadvertently. Because when Mr. Delacorte had said the night before as they walked back to the carriage, *I wonder if Pike brought his sweetheart*, it had felt as though someone had punched her in the heart.

Which had been quite a shock. Because as much as she appreciated handsome men—honestly, who didn't?—she hadn't decided whether she was able to actually *like* Mr. Pike, given that he was her rival. She'd somehow failed to imagine he might have a life outside of The Grand Palace on the Thames, even though imagining things was what she did best. Which made her realize how large he had come to loom, in every sense of the word, in her life in so short a time.

She was a great believer in signs and portents, too, and she'd always thought the word "fate" implied magic, too; she'd always considered it a romantic, triumphant sort of word. And it was jarring to discover she might have been wrong about it. Because even though Shillelagh had won the race, which had seemed very much to prove her assumption about fate, when Mr. Delacorte had said, *I wonder if he brought his sweetheart*, the night had seemed to take an almost sinister turn.

She didn't know whether Mr. Delacorte knew something she did not or was merely idly wondering aloud, and there seemed no way of discovering this.

All of this was all disturbing to her peace of mind, and she realized she hadn't anyone in which she dared confide—the other maids were amusing, in their way, but a bit silly, and not nearly as conscientious about their work as she was. They were not *thinkers* like Dot.

She would need to turn to her journal and write about it.

She suddenly realized she'd just nearly marched all the way to the third floor, toward her room where her journal was, when she was meant instead to be replacing the flowers in the vase in the sitting room. So she turned around.

On her way downstairs she encountered Mr. Pike himself, doing what he was hired for: effortlessly putting new candles into the sconces, because he could reach them, because he was so very tall and *useful*, which was in part what Delilah and Angelique appreciated about him.

He turned and smiled at her. "Well, good morning, Dot. It's the oddest thing, but I could have sworn I heard you in the crowd the night before. And I thought, surely not. It's not her night off, and . . . well, it was a *donkey* race."

"I don't know how you could have possibly heard me," she said stiffly. "There were so many people there."

"I suppose it's because the only person I could imagine shouting 'Oh my good heavens! It's fate I knew it was fate!' at a donkey race . . . is you."

It was a revelation to hear that Mr. Pike had formed ideas about what she might say, which suggested Mr. Pike was thinking about her when she was not around.

She wondered what his *sweetheart* would have to say to that, if she knew.

If he indeed had a sweetheart.

As if she cared.

"Anyone might have said that," she said quellingly.

He shook his head. "No one sounds like you, Dot." He paused, as though he was considering what to say next. "I suspect that's because there is no else like you."

He said this so carefully it was impossible to know whether he considered this a compliment. She didn't know whether she was pleased to hear it. She did suspect it was the truth. She had never considered herself in this light before, and so Pike had just given her a gift of sorts, something to ruminate upon. She generally considered herself the heroine of her own story, and this observation seemed to confirm it.

But Mr. Pike seemed to be searching her face for something. And his eyes, which were often full of amused glints when he talked to her, were somber. Even a little uncertain.

This uncertainty made her heart pang with sympathy, though she could not have quite said why. He seemed the last person on earth who would need it.

Her cheeks began to warm.

"Also, you're remarkably loud when you want to be," he added. Wickedly.

She sighed. She had indeed shrieked *BOL-LOCKS!* without meaning to when he'd surprised her in the kitchen. Before then, she'd never cursed aloud in her life. She blamed him for this, too.

"I've been told it's a useful skill," she replied loftily. Their former guest Mr. Christian Hawkes had told her she could lead armies into battle with her screams, which he'd heard when he'd toppled bleeding through their door.

Then again, Mr. Hawkes was how Mr. Pike came to be hired at The Grand Palace on the Thames, thereby introducing a note of turmoil into the sprightly tune that had previously been Dot's life. "And I thought we agreed we wouldn't discuss that anymore, Mr. Pike."

He cheerfully ignored this. "What made you decide to go to the donkey races?"

She was a bit embarrassed to tell him now, given that her belief in fate had been shaken. But then she recalled what Mrs. Brightwall had said, about how things like ponds and trees transform even when they stay in the same place. And she wondered whether fate was like that. Whether a donkey race might indeed have been fate, but the kind of fate that would unfold a bit at a time. Beginning with the journal she'd been able to purchase with the money she'd won on Shillelagh.

And then on to the startling knowledge that she could not bring herself to ask whether Pike might indeed have a sweetheart, because, like punching Mr. Pike and then surrendering her hand for gentle inspection, it might be both too painful and too pleasurable to know.

Leading next to that uncertain expression on Mr. Pike's face that made Dot's heart twinge.

Fate might in fact have as many plot twists as *The Ghost in the Attic*.

"Because I liked the word 'shillelagh.' And I knew it was fate," she told him, with great dignity. "Exactly as I said."

His eyes crinkled at the corners. "I see," he said gravely.

"I've work to do, Mr. Pike, and I expect you do, too."

She swept past him to replace the draggled flowers in the vase downstairs.

"You MUST BE overjoyed to be reunited with your husband, Lady Montcroix. More champagne?"

Lady Scottsbury was an attentive, and perhaps strategic, hostess. The free-flowing champagne loosened tongues. Gossip was currency, entertainment, and nourishment for the ton, and parties like this one were like watering holes.

Her dark eyes were sharp and merry, her dress was stunning green velvet and silk, and her breath smelled of champagne when she leaned ever closer to Alexandra to speak to her.

It seemed to Alexandra that every time she turned away from her glass it had been magically refilled, and she realized this before she was good and drunk, but not before she was a trifle tipsy.

"Oh thank you, I think not," she said to the footman hovering behind her.

"The separation was not easy for either of us," she told the countess, "but as usual he considered me above all other things, he made the gallant sacrifice in support of what was best for me and my family."

Every bit of this was, on the face of it, true. Over the past few days she had, in fact, become adept at telling truths that weren't precisely true. And at first it had been an interesting challenge, a test of her social dexterity.

But the more champagne she drank, and the more times she repeated this, the more it abraded her soul as though she'd a pebble in her shoe.

"I recall the years when the newspapers sometimes referred to him as Brightwall the Bachelor Beast! All those lovely 'B's together—the gossip sheets seem to revel in that sort of thing, don't they? I have been featured there more than once,"

Lady Scottsbury shared. "Both before and after I married Scottsbury."

"I'm sorry you endured it, or happy if you benefited from it," Alexandra said, which made Lady Scottsbury smile. "They do love their alliteration. I hope you noticed the article in the newspaper in which they called him the Magnificent Montcroix."

She considered that little article a triumph. *Well done*, Magnus had said to her this morning over the newspaper, amused. It was just a few paragraphs suggesting London citizens might like to pay a visit to the new statue of the Magnificent Montcroix, but it was clearly progress on the reputation restoration front.

Alexandra had been dropping this little alliteration into conversation every chance she got tonight. She enjoyed seeing the eyebrow flicks and widened eyes that meant her conversational partners would be repeating it.

"Oh yes, I can imagine both you and Montcroix would prefer that to Mr. and Mrs. Beast." She loved the way Lady Scottsbury had so casually said "Montcroix," as if Magnus had been born an earl, and it was what he'd been called his entire life. "When those funny little pictures in the newspaper appeared, featuring his wife grappling with the army and whatnot, I confess I thought—surely it's *all* an *invention*. That dignified man can't have married a woman who is mad enough to steal a carriage from a duke . . . that is, if he's truly married at all. He was so very

discreet about it! We all eventually heard that
he'd married, of course, indirectly, and then there
were a few little gossip items in the newspaper
over the years . . . but we never really saw any . . .
proof. We were beginning to think you were a
myth. You've certainly kept to yourself."

Lady Scottsbury lazily fanned her bodice,
which was no doubt meant to call attention to
either her bosom or her diamond necklace. Alexandra thought both were enviable. As was her
subtlety, even if it was a trifle barbed. Alexandra
understood this sort of person, and sometimes
even rather enjoyed them for the challenge they
presented. It was interesting to hear her refer to
"we"—she meant the ton at large, as if they were
a single organism.

"My goodness," she said sympathetically. "Did
you indeed think I was a myth? Surely you're not
suggesting anyone seriously believes my husband
is the sort of man who traffics in fairy tales?" Alexandra's eyes were wide with wounded innocence. "Or that he would lie to the populace?"

Lady Scottsbury froze. "Oh, my dear, no. I
just . . ."

Alexandra's eyebrow was an arrow shooting
upward.

Lady Scottsbury leaned closer. "I've always
thought that it was a pity, in truth, if it was indeed
not true. I cannot help but take note of everything
that could use a little *spiffing*, as it were—from
homes to clothes—and it always seemed to me
that Brightwall *needed* a wife to take him in hand.

A bit of domestication. He's such an impressive man, but he wasn't raised like you or I, my dear. He was born a ruffian. The hair, for instance. Good heavens, there's such a lot of it. Now that he's an earl, perhaps you can influence his choices."

"Oh, I don't know," Alexandra said with off-hand cheer. Her temper was stirring on behalf of Magnus. "I thought it would be more efficient to take a husband who is perfect exactly the way he is. That way, instead of attempting to improve him I can instead simply enjoy his company. The hair, by the way, on the statue recently dedicated to him in Holland Park, is positively immaculate."

Lady Scottsbury's head went back a little, which was how Alexandra realized her delivery had been a bit vehement.

Finally, her hostess smiled fondly at her. "It sounds as though you are very proud of him, and rightly so. The whole of England is grateful to him, not the least for saving the life of General Blackmore."

Alexandra suddenly felt deflated, as if she'd spent the last of her bravado. These moments in particular had begun to wear on her. She *was* proud of him; she felt she hadn't the right to her pride, reflected or otherwise.

And yet she was saying it over and over again this evening, just as she had the previous evening. And the more time she spent with him, the more she viscerally understood his genuine greatness, even if, between the two of them, they had managed to bungle their marriage. Ought she to have understood this five years ago, and been merely grateful to marry such a man? Did his greatness negate completely what she might have wanted, or dreamed of, for herself? Did her feelings matter at all, did *she* matter at all, in light of this? What sort of selfish madwoman kisses another man on the day of her wedding to a national hero?

The champagne was again blurring her reasoning.

Because if she'd had the keeping of him for the past five years, as a wife naturally would, she would have done it brilliantly.

And still she might have never stopped resenting him.

"I cannot take any credit for his accomplishments. I am confident in saying they arise wholly from his stellar character. But it is an honor to bear his name," she said shortly.

"But surely you are a comfort and an inspiration to a man who has borne such weighty responsibilities. He must be proud of you as well."

She could not reply. Her throat suddenly felt tight.

Alexandra whirled at a movement at the edge of her vision.

It turned out to be Magnus and the Earl of Scottsbury. She wondered how much of this conversation Magnus had heard.

Scottsbury was a handsome fellow, gone a bit gray in the hair and ruddy in the face, suggesting he loved both the outdoors and his liquor.

"Good Christ, Brightwall, I suppose all one has

to do to get such a pretty piece for a wife is win a war or two. Ha ha!"

Alexandra went rigid with astonishment.

Lady Scottsbury's tight, studiedly blank expression made Alexandra's entire being contract in sympathy. She would warrant it wasn't the first time Lady Scottsbury had needed to disguise some sort of pain or embarrassment caused by her husband.

Magnus looked ready to split the man in two.

Which was alarming, because she thought him fully capable of it.

Alexandra laid a gentle hand on Lady Scottsbury's arm. Magnus clearly had things he wanted to say to the Earl of Scottsbury that couldn't be safely uttered in front of ladies.

"I wondered if you would show me the way to the withdrawing room, Lady Scottsbury. Your taste is so exquisite, and I should like to ask your advice about modistes. I've heard Madame Marceau is gifted, but she is always so very busy. I wondered if you might have some secrets you'd be willing to impart about where to find a wonderful seamstress."

Lady Scottsbury's face softened into gratitude. She looped her arm through the lady's and they strolled off together.

MAGNUS UNDERSTOOD MEN. He understood liquor.

But an actual screen of red had dropped down over his eyes when the earl had spoken to Alexandra that way.

Magnus slowly turned to the earl. "I comprehend you are foxed, Scottsbury. But I wonder if
you would find it sobering to imagine the consequences if I ever hear you referring to my wife
as a 'piece' again, or as anything other than Lady
Montcroix. Why don't you take a moment to do
that now."

All the blood fled Scottsbury's complexion as he
obliged Magnus by looking at him and accurately
reading his expression.

"Nod if you understand me," Magnus de-
manded.

The earl's head bobbed. "Good God, Brightwall.
I apologize. No need to go *beastly* on me."

Magnus's jaw set. "For God's sake, Scottsbury.
You know better. I don't care if you're foxed.
Please stop."

Scottsbury sighed. "You're right. I'm very sorry.
I will apologize to your wife, as well. I'm foxed
and I'm sorry. I suppose I'm envious. You seldom
took your eyes from her all during the dinner, old
man, and now you look ready to do murder because I called her 'pretty' a trifle too casually, and
again, I'm sorry. What was it Byron said about love
being more dangerous than the measles when it
comes late in life?"

Magnus went silent. He was genuinely nonplussed and not at all pleased to hear that he'd
been so obvious. He hadn't had a clue. About that,
or Byron.

It was just that it was such a pleasure to watch
her. So why wouldn't he? Why wouldn't anyone?

The laughter that rose up around her when she was in the center of a conversation, her bright head gleaming in the candlelight, the flash of her eyes as she aimed a conspiratorial glance in his direction and fulfilled her part of their bargain.

All night, as they had mingled with guests, together and apart, old acquaintances had complimented him on her. He'd witnessed young ladies unconsciously mirroring her gestures when she spoke to them. He'd seen the admiration, both overt and covert, in the eyes of men, and the soft approval in the eyes of dowagers. The slyly probing ones had been put in their place so gently he was certain they'd scarcely even noticed.

He wished Alexandra understood how impressive she truly was. Her nimble social gifts arose from a genuine pleasure in the company of other people, and from her warmth and compassion. From her willingness to *like* them and make them comfortable, even as she saw them clearly.

Did she seem *him* clearly?

What did it mean for the two of them, if she did?

And yet. He could still not reconcile all of the admirable things he knew her to be with the young woman who had passionately kissed another man on her wedding day.

"Thank you for your hospitality, Scottsbury," was all Magnus said finally. Conciliatorily. Dryly.

Scottsbury actually gave him a sympathetic pat. Together they moved on to other guests, and Magnus continued performing his duty as guest of honor, bestowing attention and words and moving on.

But as the minutes wore on, he became aware of what could only be called a gathering panic on the edges of his awareness, for no other reason except that he couldn't see Alexandra anywhere in the reception room.

He knew his sense of unease wasn't quite rational—she had simply gone to the lady's withdrawing room, and was probably merrily chatting there.

But it seemed to him she'd been gone an inordinate amount of time. Or perhaps it merely felt that way. Perhaps time behaved differently when he was with her, paradoxically standing still and moving too fast. Perhaps it was because the difference between a room with and without her in it was like the difference between a meadow and a cell.

It seemed to him this empty panic was a foreshadowing of the rest of his life without her.

And he immediately, almost abruptly excused himself from his conversation.

IN THE WITHDRAWING room, Alexandra and Lady Scottsbury had fussed with their hair and cordially talked of modistes as other ladies came and went. They didn't talk about their husbands.

But they were alone, for now, apart from the attendants, a pair of young maidservants wearing shy smiles.

And in the lull, Lady Scottsbury studied Alexandra, her expression indecipherable. It was a bit as though she was struggling to decide whether or not to say something.

Finally she leaned forward and began soothingly, "I just wanted to tell you, dear, that it's all right if you have one of those modern marriages. I won't tell a soul."

Alexandra froze. "I beg your pardon?"

"Marriage for love is a bit of a fairy tale they try to feed to young women," Lady Scottsbury said frankly. "Almost no one of the upper classes ever does it. You've made a splendid if unorthodox match, but even so, some couples cannot simply abide with each other and that's the way things are. But you are doing a marvelous job tonight— and it's a job, isn't it? Marriage to a man like that?—and he's no doubt proud of you. It's our lot in life, isn't it, to look after these men? To endure their foibles?"

Alexandra was speechless.

Inwardly, she was reeling.

It was a bit like the nightmare she'd once had where she'd entered a full ballroom wearing her slippers and nothing else. She felt as though Lady Scottsbury had whipped aside her social defenses.

"Oh, but I don't. My . . . my marriage isn't modern," she stammered. "I'm afraid you are mistaken."

But this was just another social lie and she heard the moment her ability to sound convincing defected.

Lady Scottsbury tipped her head sympathetically. "My dear, one of you is sailing to America
in a few days. I heard through Scottsbury's niece,
who is related to a gentleman who is related to
the ship's captain, that the name Brightwall is on
the passenger rolls. There is probably only one
Brightwall in all of England. He is so lately returned from Spain, and yet off again to America?
It doesn't seem so; I'm given to understand he
is preparing to undertake his duties in parliament. So it must be you who is off. I know your
charming brother and father are currently in
New York. Both are missed at White's, or so my
husband tells me. And I thought, it seems very
clear that the Brightwalls are not people who are
pining for each other."

Alexandra was bludgeoned by an epiphany:
everything Lady Scottsbury said was true, and it
horrified her.

Because after days of trying to convince herself
otherwise, she realized she desperately wanted it
not to be true.

Infuriatingly, she could think of nothing socially
deft to say, and her silence felt like a self-indictment.

Lady Scottsbury smiled knowingly, ruefully,
not unsympathetically. Satisfied she had im-
parted wisdom to the younger woman, she gave
one last pat to her hair. "Don't worry. We haven't
told anyone else, and we won't. My husband is
fond of your husband. Scottsbury isn't all bad
when he isn't in his cups. And lovers are an even-

tual compensation—for both partners. Remember that. I best get back to him lest he get himself murdered for saying something he doesn't mean. As I said, it's a job." She winked and departed, leaving Alexandra's composure in tatters.

Alexandra wondered how many of the people downstairs were entertaining the same kinds of thoughts about her and Magnus.

And just like that, she felt denuded of defenses. She could not yet imagine returning at once to a crowd of people who insisted she must be proud of her husband, and he must be proud of her. She didn't trust her eyes not to betray her inner turmoil.

And she was so accustomed to smoothing things over for everyone else, to rationalizing and enduring and finding her equilibrium in the midst of upheaval, it was a shock to realize she had no idea how to settle or comfort herself. She could not quite get a purchase on the reason she was so thoroughly upset.

What she wanted was a few moments entirely alone to gather her composure.

Reflexively, she climbed a flight of marble stairs and wandered a bit until she found a little alcove likely normally used to display statuary or ferns. It was about the width of three people standing side by side, and half as deep, but it was currently empty save for a tall, spiky-leafed plant in a pot. If she craned her head one way, she could just about see the top of the stairs. If she craned it the other way, she could look out a large arched window into an endless black night. Clouds obscured the stars. There was no clarity to be found anywhere tonight, it seemed.

In a room somewhere nearby, billiard balls collided on a table to the accompaniment of the murmur of voices and laughter.

Below, she faintly heard the orchestra tuning, in preparation for this evening's soprano entertainment.

She stood for a time like a statue and waited for Lady Scottsbury's particular form of jaded kindness to stop stinging.

Presently, Magnus appeared at the top of the stairs.

Her heart gave a painful leap. She jerked it back like a dog on a lead.

His head swiveled about. He was looking for her, she would warrant. He looked genuinely, nakedly worried.

This, paradoxically, brought her an absurd stab of happiness.

"Magnus," she said softly. To relieve him of his worry.

He pivoted swiftly.

Relief flashed across his features. He approached her slowly. "Why are you standing in a dark alcove like a statue of . . . Aphrodite?"

"Aphrodite, is it? My goodness. I wished I'd thought to say 'Aphrodite' when Mrs. Pariseau was quizzing us about statues. That's better than a fountain."

He didn't reply. He scrutinized her instead.

"Alexandra. Is aught amiss?"

"No," she lied. "Just . . . admiring the view."

He made a show of looking behind him. "Given that I'm currently the view, I'm skeptical."

With a blinding epiphany she realized that he *was* her favorite view. She was momentarily struck dumb as a shy child.

The implications of this frightened her.

She stared at him for all the world like a looby for an instant before she rallied.

"Well, considering I can also see *myself* in the silver buttons of your waistcoat . . ."

He had one dimple that came into view when he smiled and it was bloody delightful.

She tried to smile, too, but she could not quite get the corners of her mouth to commit to it.

"You should wear that plum-colored waistcoat often," she said.

Which is when she realized she was, indeed, a trifle drunk. As a result, the boundaries of her control had gone dangerously porous. Thoughts that would in other circumstances never graduate into spoken words were launching into the world.

He glanced down at his waistcoat, then back at her, puzzled.

"Because it makes your eyes seem very blue, and very bright. Almost as bright as your buttons."

Charmingly flustered, he looked down again. When he looked back up at her, his expression was carefully composed and uncertain.

Did no one ever compliment him? She felt

irrationally furious at this oversight on the part of the world. He was bloody magnificent.

"I can see your eyes all the way across the room. Like a beacon. When you're watching me and you don't think I'm noticing."

Was she brazenly flirting with her husband? Champagne was a menace.

Magnus had gone *very* still. But he was watchful. Wary. No doubt a bit like that boy he'd been who'd always expected to be hurt.

Oh, it slashed her, to see it. And yet she exulted, too. It was better than his cool control.

This uncertain Magnus was one she was positive no one else ever saw.

Finally his smile was slight, speculative.

"So why are you hiding?" he finally asked bluntly.

She gave what she hoped was an insouciant laugh. "What makes you think I'm hiding?"

He snorted softly.

They were quiet a moment.

"Magnus . . . I'm sorry you feel compelled to say that you're proud of me."

She was discovering how alarmingly easy it was to be honest when one was drunk.

His eyes flared in genuine surprise. "Is this what's bothering you?"

Her silence clearly answered the question for him.

He was quiet a moment. Then he gave a soft, stunned laugh.

"Alexandra . . . in a single evening, you have either mildly terrified, captivated, or put into their places, sometimes all at once, most of the titled of the ton. From what I've heard from other guests, the younger women are ready to fall at your feet, as though you're Aristotle and can teach them your ways. All the men are envious and claim to be baffled by why a woman like you would marry a brute like—"

He pressed his lips together.

They both knew why she'd married a brute like him.

"I once said you would have made a fine general, Alexandra. You may have noticed I'm not in the habit of making frivolous statements."

She managed to smile at this. It felt wobbly on her lips.

"That is kind of you to say. And I am still proud," she reflected, somewhat puzzled. "That is, I still have pride. I don't know what the use of pride is to me. I feel at times I haven't the right to any at all. That's all just to say, Magnus, that I'm not proud at all of what I did on our wedding day." Her voice was hoarse now. "Not at all."

"Alexandra . . ." Her name was cracked in the middle with emotion.

And also something like impatience.

She stared at him.

She realized, then, how seldom his voice betrayed any vulnerability at all. He was so fiercely guarded.

And so.

It seemed her husband was fraying, too.

"You are . . ." He gave a soft, almost despairing laugh.

"You are formidable," he finally said quietly. Tenderly.

Almost resignedly. As if this was something so very clear, anyone could see it.

As if she was the conqueror.

As if he was trying to explain to her that he'd never had any choice but to take her however he could get her.

His voice had gone thick.

She could feel some realization struggling to come into focus on the periphery of her awareness. Something she could not quite grasp hold of.

Her skin was all but singing from his nearness. Like all those sirens whose job it was to lure sailors to their doom.

Touch me.

Don't you dare touch me.

These thoughts battled over her.

In this moment she was two girls. The one who had known him only two months, who would have been obliged to submit to him in bed on her wedding night.

And the woman who wanted desperately for him to touch her now.

The first girl had been frightened and innocent. Resentful and grateful. And resentful at the need to be grateful. She had spent her wedding day in a polite fog of unreality, her lips fixed in a remote smile. His hand had rested so often proudly, lightly on her elbow. For five thousand pounds he'd bought the rights to touch her whenever he chose.

This man in front of her would have willingly bedded that frightened girl.

The second girl was tempted to slip her hand right into his trousers to hasten being taken quickly. Now.

The second girl was quietly, furiously angry at the possibility that he'd *known* something about her, about him, about the two of them together, before he'd proposed. That he, with his vision, his gift for seeing the details about people, his superior experience and wisdom and maturity, had somehow known how incendiary, how satisfying, how *right* it would feel to be together. And he'd never said a word. Had not trusted her with his thoughts or feelings. He had not asked for hers. He had merely included her in part of a bargain, the way he was buying a house on Grosvenor Square.

Would they be here now if he had said anything? Would they have hurt each other then?

She didn't know. She didn't know.

I wanted you in my bed, he'd said to her. She was certain that was as true then as it was now.

She didn't think that was the whole truth.

For instance, there was a ribbon scrap in a box that suggested otherwise.

But wasn't it different for men? Didn't they view sex the way Mr. Delacorte had described potatoes the other night, necessary and delicious, to be consumed hastily whenever available?

What man wouldn't take advantage of the

circumstances if he was certain a woman wanted him? No doubt it was easy enough for a man to want a woman and still despise her.

Perhaps he'd touched every woman he'd ever made love to that way.

She didn't really believe so.

He'd likely discovered as he moved closer, ever closer, that she was quivering. Her breathing quickened. But still he didn't touch her.

"I don't feel as if I've the right to be proud of you, Alexandra." His voice was graveled. "Or proud because of you. But I am."

She studied him. It was quite an admission.

"Well, that's because you've impeccable judgment."

One corner of his mouth quirked.

Touch me.

She was a little worried that thought would escape her mouth in a moment.

It frightened her that she wanted him so much, because every time he touched her she lost a little more of herself to him. Or perhaps, in truth, she gave a little more of herself to him. They were unraveling each other a bit more each time they made love.

And he was going to send her away.

This would be her punishment. It was only fitting. She could imagine even now that tearing sensation in the area of her heart as she left.

Oh, but it would be worth it if only he touched her *now*.

No doubt he felt her rib cage jump with the

hitch of her breath when he rested his fingertips against her waist.

The moment his lips brushed hers her blood seemed to travel a slow, hot path straight down through the center of her to pulse in that aching place between her legs.

They watched each other like inquisitors.

And her eyes wanted to close; her body, greedily, wanted to isolate itself with sensation.

But she watched him, as he watched her.

She wanted to see if she could ascertain some sort of truth. To discover what, if anything, he would reveal to her when he touched her.

Perhaps he merely intended to revel in watching her slowly go mad with need.

She hadn't known that kisses could be so infinitely nuanced. That his mouth merely feathering across hers could light tiny bonfires across her nerve endings everywhere in her body.

And as his mouth distracted her with chaste things, his fingers were intent on overtly carnal ones. They glided slowly up her torso, and his thumbs deftly hooked the top of her bodice to drag it down far enough for him to draw his knuckles lightly, teasingly, over her bead-hard nipples. She saw the surge of triumph in his eyes before her head fell back from the onslaught of pleasure. Her breath snagged on a moan.

But he allowed her to see that he was in thrall. His expression was so fiercely, joyfully possessive in response to whatever he saw in hers that it made her knees feel boneless.

And she could feel the lust tense his every muscle; his grip tightened on her.

He kept the pace stately as a minuet. Torturously, dangerously, erotically slow. Laughter drifted in from the ballroom as he furled up her dress. Like a coconspirator, he transferred the folds of her skirt to her to hold so he could unbutton his trousers. A moment later she felt his hard cock press against her belly.

Together they evolved their kiss into something hungry and searching, a clash of teeth, a lascivious duel. She loved the rich, dark taste of him; she reveled in taking as much as he did, in knowing she was driving him mad, too. Below, in the wet heat between her legs, his fingers mimicked the skillful stroke and plunge of his tongue, rhythmically, until her hips were circling against him, until her head thrashed away from him on a surfeit of pleasure, and white heat raced over her skin.

The clack of billiards disguised her muffled cry as her release broke over her with a burst of light behind her eyes.

He guided his cock into her to the sound of billiard balls colliding.

They were locked as closely as two people could be, in this narrow space, behind a spiky plant. His hips moved in deep, languorous thrusts. He scooped his hands under her buttocks, gripping her, lifting her up so he could drive himself deeper. The wall was cold against her bare skin.

She watched a gleam of sweat gather on his brow. Their mingled breath was hot and ragged between them, a storm. Her hands were knotted in the waistcoat she'd just complimented. His eyes were fierce then distant, as his release came upon him.

And she knew when he was close by the shallow, swift sway of his back with his breath. She pressed his head to her shoulder with her hand. His groan vibrated against her neck.

She held him as his great body quaked.

The clack of billiards. The distant echoing laughter of a party. The shockingly close voices of partygoers. All of this was proof.

Sex in a dark alcove at a crowded affair seemed reckless, and dangerous, and absolutely avoidable for anyone, let alone a venerable, famous colonel, and now an earl. One who cared so much about his reputation, and hers.

That was how she knew.

He was not in control of this, either.

They held each other. His cheek pressed against her hair. He murmured something soft and unintelligible, and yes, if she was not mistaken, loving.

And finally she let go of him, because she feared if she didn't do it now she never would be able to again.

Chapter Sixteen

❧❧❧

LIKE so many other things in life, inhibition at The Grand Palace on the Thames seemed to have an ebb and flow.

"This might sound odd, but I'm a little wistful that the Dawsons have gotten so quiet." Angelique said this to Lucien while she sat at her dressing table, pinning up her hair, getting ready for the day. Lucien was sitting on the bed behind her, pulling up his boots.

"Oh, yes. I, too, am wistful that they now feel constrained from making love with the noisy abandon of barnyard animals," he said gravely.

Angelique laughed. "Lucien, don't make me laugh when I'm trying to be profound. It's always a little sad when we lose a bit of our innocence, don't you think? Or maybe the word I want is 'naivete.' They may never make love with that kind of abandon again. And while I don't particularly want to *hear* them do it . . ."

"I do know what you mean. It's that Garden-of-Eden type of innocence, as if they were the only man and woman in the world, and now they've been cast out for being loud. But the loss of innocence is the price of wisdom, I fear." Lucien stood and kissed the top of her head. "At least they were among kind people when they discovered that they're loud."

"We're both profound this morning."

"And I'll miss you profoundly for the next few days." Lucien and Captain Hardy were compelled to go back to the shipyard, but word had it the repairs were nearly done. "Know that I carry you with me in my heart, always."

"Likewise, love."

And they went down to breakfast together.

No moaning was heard in the hall.

But they thought they heard giggling behind the Dawsons' door, and that was good, too.

The unprepossessing Dawsons would likely have been shocked to learn they'd sent philosophical ripples through the lives of all the guests and inhabitants of The Grand Palace on the Thames. Ruminations on mortality and marriage, lust and innocence, courage and seizing fleeting pleasures, had indirectly led to things like lovemaking behind a ballroom stage curtain and Mrs. Cuthbert getting tipsy on sherry and Colonel Brightwall taking a chance that a door ajar five inches was an invitation for him to enter.

In other words, the Dawsons' spirited intercourse had ironically inspired all manner of spirited discourse, even if it wasn't in the sitting room.

Mrs. Cuthbert's blossoming seemed to be underway. Last night her lips had seemed significantly less compressed; she hadn't once sucked in an audible, bracing breath when Mr. Delacorte opened his mouth to speak.

"I think old friends are precious, even when you grow apart," Mrs. Pariseau reflected to Delilah and Angelique as they paused to chat on the third-floor landing that morning. "There's something comforting in knowing that someone else in the world shares your memories and remembers your earlier self. It reminds me of how far I've come, and sometimes I feel like a girl again, for better or for worse."

And then there was the couple who had checked into The Grand Palace on the Thames as Colonel and Mrs. Brightwall, but would be departing as the Earl and Countess of Montcroix when they decided to leave. They certainly weren't the first of their guests to feature both on the front page and in the gossip portions of the newspaper. They were, however, the first guests who had appeared as Rowlandson illustrations . . . twice.

The first had of course depicted Mrs. Brightwall battling soldiers over a stolen carriage.

As newspapers were expensive, it was Dot's habit to bring one from room to room so every guest would have an opportunity to read it, but the previous evening Colonel Brightwall had given her six pence to buy an additional copy meant specifically only for him the following morning.

Dot spread the newspaper out on the kitchen table so the staff, as well as Angelique and Delilah, could have a look, and everyone gazed down at the second Rowlandson illustration. This time it featured both Mr. and Mrs. Brightwall as well as a vivid little paragraph about the Scottsbury ball they'd attended the previous night. The earl and countess had looked ravishing before they departed The Grand Palace on the Thames.

"Well, then," Delilah finally said, speaking for all of them. "This is . . . this is quite something."

Dot lowered her voice. "When I went to bring his newspaper up to them early this morning, Colonel Brightwall was the only one awake. He was staring out the window, wearing a smile. A bit like he was remembering a beautiful dream."

Delilah, Angelique, and Helga exchanged glances. They had a very good idea about what would put that sort of smile on a man's face.

"DID YOU SLEEP well?" Magnus asked Alexandra politely over scones.

It was officially the day before she was meant to leave England forever and live in New York. Tomorrow morning at this time Alexandra was meant to be rolling down the road in a stagecoach bound for Liverpool.

Magnus, still in his shirtsleeves, was already awake and dressed when she emerged from her room. He'd stood up politely from the little table when he saw her. He sat down again as she settled in across from him.

"I did. And you?"

"Yes, thank you. The beds here are so comfortable."

"They certainly are."

Neither one of them had slept a wink.

Yet they did not precisely feel tired, either.

One wouldn't think that making love standing up in an alcove at a banquet would be a sobering experience, but it proved to be.

After they had done exactly that, Alexandra had lowered her dress, and he had matter-of-factly tucked in his shirt and buttoned up his trousers, and they had smoothed each other's hair. They had both returned to the banquet flushed and a trifle dazed, but by then everyone attending was a trifle flushed and dazed thanks to the champagne, so the aftermath of their reckless passion had been camouflaged.

They had departed the gathering soon after. The carriage ride home had been mostly quiet, and the polite retreat to separate rooms tacit.

Each had spent their respective nights staring at their ceilings, enmeshed in a peculiar, almost dreamlike blend of euphoria and tension and fear and nerves, which had lingered into this morning, along with a bit of a champagne headache (for Alexandra).

"Dot brought the newspaper up," he said.

He pushed it over to her.

It was open to the gossip page.

The Magnificent Montcroix and his bride captivated a captive audience of London's cream at a banquet held by the Earl and Countess of Scottsbury, but the two had eyes only for each other. It seems this

beautiful bride of his hath charms to sooth a savage beast.

An illustration was included.

"Good heavens," she said faintly. "Are those meant to be turtledoves around our heads?"

"I believe so," he said mildly.

She couldn't quite bring herself to look up yet. Judging from the heat in her face, she was blushing, exactly as the illustration had depicted her, if the shaded circles on her cheeks were an indication.

She cleared her throat. "It isn't precisely dignified, but hearts in my eyes are perhaps better than swirls about my nose. Although the swirls make me think of Brightwall the Donkey now."

He made a soft sound. Almost a laugh.

In the illustration, Brightwall hovered over her like a behemoth. His hair was impressive, too.

And his pupils were drawn in the shape of hearts.

"Does this conclude our bargain, Magnus? Are you satisfied that dignity has been restored to your besmirched name?"

"I should think so," he said gently.

She nodded without looking up. She took a moment to compose herself. Then cleared her throat.

"Very good then. Well! Everything is ready. I'll set out for the stage tomorrow before the maids are up—you likely already know this since Mr. Lawler submits my expenses, but I've reserved a spot on the coach departing from The Elk & Trumpet Inn, bound for Liverpool, where I'll meet my fellow travelers and chaperones, Mr. and Mrs. Harper. I will stay there for two days before we board the packet. I've arranged to have my additional trunks brought in a separate conveyance. I anticipate that anything else I might need I will find in New York. When my sister returns from Italy, she'll send over on a packet a few mementos that I've kept at my father's house."

He took this in with a sip of coffee.

"You've been very thorough and efficient," he said, after a long moment.

"I generally am," she said, pleasantly enough.

For some reason, this benign little breakfast was beginning to feel a bit like a risky game of roulette.

"So I will depart here tomorrow morning just before the maids come in with our coffee."

He chewed his scone thoughtfully for some time, then had another sip of coffee.

He didn't reply.

It was almost as though he hadn't heard her.

"I'll be out for most of the day," he said. "I've a meeting with Mr. Lawler and my solicitor to attend to a few very pressing legal matters. I should return to The Grand Palace on the Thames by about four o'clock."

"Very good," she said almost hoarsely. "Until then."

"Until then," he confirmed.

SHE'D NEVER HAD a day like this one: utterly fraught. Portent was in every breath she drew.

Something was about to happen; she could sense it. It might be devastating or extraordinary. Either possibility would transform her life completely. After today, she would never be the same person, and she could not say who that person would be. This kind of exquisite torture was unprecedented in her life.

But last night's lack of sleep on the heels of risky, outrageously pleasurable lovemaking proved a godsend, nearly as good as laudanum for blunting that razor-edged anticipation. She drifted hazily through the hours, somehow both dazed and enervated. She lingered in the little garden in front of The Grand Palace on the Thames, marveling at its quiet beauty and resilience in a tiny, gritty patch of London. She visited with Gordon, their fat striped cat, who had been sleeping in the flowerbeds when she'd intruded upon his nap.

She returned to the room, drowsy, and thought she might indulge in a nap.

As the weather was warm, Magnus had left behind his greatcoat, and it hung from a hook near the door.

She buried her face in it and breathed. As if she could pull him into her lungs, into her blood, keep him with her forever that way.

Feeling only slightly guilty, she felt in his pockets again. With trembling fingers removed the little silver box. Superstitiously, she was afraid to open it, as if it contained some sort of verdict.

But the ribbon scrap was still inside.

SHE WAS READING *Robinson Crusoe* in front of the fireplace when the key turned in the lock of the door of their suite.

He smiled when he saw her.

She held up the book. "I was reading ahead to find out whether he befriends the cannibals." She hadn't yet napped.

Magnus didn't reply. He hovered in the doorway regarding her. He doffed his hat, and pushed his hair behind his ears. He shook himself out of his coat, and loosened his cravat.

He swiftly closed the distance between the two of them and stood before her a moment, his gaze fixed, as if memorizing her.

How could she ever have thought his eyes were icy or remote? He could have ignited a thousand candles with the heat in his eyes.

Gently he reached down and lifted her hand from her book. He threaded his fingers through hers.

He drew her to her feet.

And she let him lead her into his room.

WORDLESSLY, HE SET to work at once loosening the laces on her dress; she raised her arms so he could lift it from her. She stepped out of her slippers. She peeled off her stockings while he stripped himself of his shirt and trousers and boots and stockings, all the things that covered up his extraordinary, hairy, scarred, muscled magnificence. They did this with deliberation, as if they had all the time in the world.

The first time had been a reckless catharsis.

The second time—silent, and in the dark—they could almost pretend was a dream. The third, they could, if they wanted to, blame on champagne, though it hadn't been the culprit at all.

This time they left all pretenses and defenses on the floor with their clothes and surrendered themselves to each other.

With a sigh, he gathered her up against his hard, hot body, one hand fanning the small of her back, the other cradling her head. He softly, slowly kissed the pulse in her throat, and then, lingeringly, her mouth. And then he lowered her into the bright rectangle of light the afternoon sun had laid on the bed, as if she was a banquet he intended to slowly, decadently devour.

He stood for a minute before her, and his huge, hard, shambling, scarred beauty flooded her senses and sent such a torrent of blood to her head it was like a blow: the dark hair curling over a torso carved into segments of muscle, like furry tree trunks, and the one in which a musket ball had dug a channel, leaving behind a gnarled, thick white scar that she blessed because it meant he'd lived.

His cock was already curving up toward his belly.

His eyes had gone dark. His faint smile and his dark eyes told her he'd read and understood her expression, and she understood his: she had never felt so beautiful, so alive, so naked in every sense of the word. She had never wanted anything more than she wanted him now.

The bed sank beneath his weight when he joined her there. He stretched alongside her, propped up on his elbows, gazing down. She stroked his hair out of his eyes. Smoothed a finger across one of his woolly brows.

He shifted down the bed, flicked his tongue against her already bead-hard nipple, and when he closed his mouth over it gently sucked. She drew her knees up on a hybrid gasp-moan as the pleasure coursed through her. She threaded her fingers through his hair as he languidly, skillfully sent ripples of bliss through her body with his tongue and lips. And as he did, his hand smoothed across her belly, over the round contours of her thighs, as if committing the shape of her to memory.

Like this he marked her body out in slow, hot kisses, leaving a trail from her breasts, down the seam of her ribs, to the mound of her belly, until he reached the curls at the crook of her legs. And then he parted her thighs, ducked his head between them, and with shocking deliberation and skill slowly drove her to the brink of madness with his tongue and lips and fingers.

She writhed, curling her fingers into the counterpane as exquisite sensation poured through her and emerged as moans and soft oaths and his name, first muttered in shocked appreciation, and then as a plea, because surely no person was designed to withstand so much pleasure.

But he knew what he was about. He led her right up to the edge and over the brink and then suddenly her mouth was open on a silent scream, her body bowing toward heaven, racked by bliss.

And she looked up from her haze of ecstasy to find him looking down at her, his expression all masculine satisfaction and soft wonder and fierce intent.

She shifted beneath him and he rose up on his arms over her, and she thought how beautiful and strange that it was instinctive now to position herself beneath her husband so that their bodies could join, when mere days ago she hadn't known the heady feel of her thighs gripping his back, or how it felt to cling to his shoulders as he moved inside her, as though the two of them were travelers on a rough sea.

Magnus tried to keep this pace leisurely, as if he wanted to ramp and bank his pleasure, to draw out the moment, to make it last forever. She gazed up at him, to find him gazing down at her with the same rapt, wondering absorption, illuminated as he was in raw daylight. But she could see how the pace cost him in the sweat beading on his brow, and in how his arms quivered with tension and leashed desire beneath her gripping fingers. She took advantage of the pace to sweetly madden him a little with pleasure, to savor him: she dragged her palms, then her nails, over his chest in a slow caress; she circled the little brown discs of his nipples with her fingertips, and was rewarded when he hissed in a breath of pleasure. She drew her fingertips over the hard ridge of his collarbone, along his strong throat. *You are beautiful and perfect as you are and I want you*, was what she hoped to show him. She let him see the truth of this in her face. He briefly closed this eyes, as if she was the sun. When he opened them again, they were shining. And if they were tears, he wouldn't let her see; he closed them again.

She slid her hands down to his hips and rose up to take him more deeply and saw the cords of his neck go taut, and his eyes go nearly black, and his control unraveled and his hips moved ever more swiftly until he cried out.

She held him as his body shook with his release.

SHE LAY IN the curl of his arm, her naked body half draped over his. He softly, soothingly stroked her hair.

Presently, she could feel him pull in the breath to ask the question she'd been anticipating all day.

"Why did you do it?"

And there it was.

She knew what he meant was: *Why did you kiss another man on our wedding night?*

Why did you break your vows? was the unspoken accompanying question.

She knew the answer might devastate him. She understood, as did he, that her answer would break this spell.

But there was no hope for it. There was no going forward without saying it. And it needed to be the truth.

She wanted him to hear the truth.

She breathed in, and prepared to say aloud words she'd never spoken to another soul.

And she turned so she could watch his face as she told him.

"Because . . . the point of my life has been . . . it seems it has been to make others happy. From the time I was very small, it seemed all my choices were made for me, because I loved my family and I wanted above all for everyone to be happy, and this determined everything I did, and everything I chose. And I was, for the most part, content to please everyone. But when I chose Paul . . . I knew it would not be a forever love, but it was the first time I'd ever chosen something or someone just for *me*. I didn't know he would come to the garden gate that night. I thought he had already left the country. And when he kissed me . . ." She swallowed. "I didn't know that he would kiss me. I truly didn't know. He had never yet kissed me. And I didn't know that *I* would . . . that I would kiss him."

She could feel that Magnus's breathing had gone shallow.

". . . except that it seemed to me at that moment that kissing him . . . might be the last time in my life I would ever be able to choose who I wanted to kiss."

Magnus closed his eyes slowly.

His lips shaped a silent oath.

He could feel his chest contract beneath her cheek as if she'd shot an arrow right into him.

He pulled in a long, shuddering breath, and pressed his palms over his eyes.

"And I think, Magnus, that you knew that I would have no choice at all but to say yes to your proposal. Because you see things so clearly. You are known to be such a clever strategist. But what *I* wanted didn't seem to matter. You never even asked. I'm not certain you ever gave it any thought. You just assumed you could have me for a price. You were right, of course. You *could* have me for a price."

She felt more brutal than a firing squad aiming at a deserter.

How odd that she could feel his pain in her own body. His suffering radiated from him into her.

She could scarcely breathe for hurting him.

But some pain simply needed to be felt, she had learned.

"And I am ashamed to have hurt you. I am ashamed of what I did. I had never thought of myself as a person who would ever break a vow. But the question you asked was 'why?' And I think . . . I think that was the reason, above all, that I kissed another man on our wedding night. It was a chance to choose one final time."

And she wasn't sorry to have at last said those words out loud.

"But I choose to be in your bed now," she said softly. "And I will, as we agreed, depart tomorrow."

She didn't know whether she wanted his absolution. She didn't ask for it.

She loved him anyway.

So utterly and completely. He had been right about the two of them from the beginning.

Did he know she loved him?

Could he tell? If you were raised without love, did you recognize it when it was in front of you?

The ragged saw of his breathing told her he was suffering.

Finally, he swallowed slowly.

"I'm sorry." His voice was a rasp.

He didn't contradict any of it, because it was all true. It was precisely what he'd done. It was precisely what she'd done.

She didn't reply.

Finally, she laid her head back down on his chest. She listened to the precious, steady thump, thump, thump of his battered, stubborn, vulnerable, flawed, foolish heart.

Her own foolish heart beat in time with his now.

After a moment, his arms closed around her instinctively. They lay together, naked at last in nearly every sense of the word, in silence.

His chest rose and fell in a sigh.

How odd it was, she thought, to feel safest with the one person capable of hurting you the most.

How odd it was to be willing to risk breaking her own heart for the chance to finally, at last, win his.

Because there were a few things left to say.

And he wasn't the only strategist in the room.

THE EARL OF Montcroix, Magnus Brightwall, held his sleeping love in his arms.

No matter what happened to him in life, this moment was real, and he would have this memory forever: her warm, satin skin against his hands, her back lifting and falling with the soft tides of her breath.

His insides felt scoured raw, but the truth will do that to a person.

A wound had been exposed to the light of day.

Had he suspected the truth of what she'd told him? Perhaps he'd somehow suspected it all along?

He believed he had. He just hadn't wanted to think of himself as a man so powerfully, desperately, selfishly afraid of being hurt, so terribly afraid that no one would love him, that he had nearly crushed her precious spirit in order to get what he wanted.

But he trusted himself to plan now, because the truth had been laid bare, and he could plan from a place of absolutely clarity.

It was suddenly simple:

In order to get what he wanted, he needed to give her what she wanted.

How ironic to realize that it was what he wanted, too.

He'd in fact spent the first half of the day preparing for a possibility, because she was right: he was a clever strategist.

Still. He might have once taken a bullet for General Blackmore.

But what he planned to do next would be the biggest risk of his life.

Chapter Seventeen

❧

SHE AWOKE before the maid came in to build up the fires.

And somehow she knew. Because the difference between a room containing Magnus and a room that did not was like the difference between a fire in the hearth and ashes.

They had dozed for a time, then awakened and quietly made love twice more.

She knew she had slept in his arms. But he wasn't in the bed; she slid her foot over to find that the sheets were already cold.

She sat up abruptly.

The pillow still held the indent of his head. She ran her hand gently over it.

She slid from the bed and opened the clothing press.

All of his clothes were gone.

She sat down hard on the bed, pulling the sheet around her, her gut gone cold with shock.

And then she saw, on the little table in the main room, a sheet of foolscap, folded and sealed with red wax.

She scrambled for it and, with shaking hands, broke the seal and read.

My dearest Alexandra,

I know a little about having no choice.

Because I fell in love with you twice.

My heart decided for me when it first saw you. It gave me no choice in the matter at all. I knew nothing about how to love or how to be loved. I only knew I loved you from the moment you crossed to me in that white marble foyer of your home. I had never seen anything so beautiful. My heart recognized its true home.

But here are the things that I did know: How to fight. How to win. I felt my very existence would be imperiled if somehow you were not mine. One of the many things I have learned the hard way is that love is deaf to reason. I did, as you realized, what I thought I had to do. I did not believe a woman like you would ever want or love me, but by God, Alexandra, I meant to make you happy. I meant to try.

So I fell in love with you twice. The very first time I saw you.

And these past few days, all over again.

With all that I knew from the first that you are: beautiful and brave, witty and kind, loyal and stubborn, and proud and passionate. For things I cannot ever hope to put into words. I am not a poet. And I'm not even a particularly brave man. For both you and I have discovered the limits of my bravery. Which is why I am not standing in front of you, speaking, and you are instead reading this letter.

But please never doubt that you are extraordinary.

These are the things important for you to know now:

By the time you read this, I will have departed to board a stage at Rossington Arms Coaching Inn. I am leaving for America, to live in the New York property.

Yes: I am going to America in your place. I made all the arrangements for this yesterday.

I do not know when or if I will return to England.

Mr. Lawler will remain at your service in all matters. He is in possession of legal documents which make possible the following:

All decisions about what to spend, where to go, who to see, where to live, and how to live belong to you utterly. To you and you alone.

The town house is yours, for as long as you live, or until you choose to sell it.

The carriage and horses are yours.

And of course, all decisions about who to love are yours. I truly wish you happiness.

My heart is also yours. I'm afraid there's not much I can do about that. I hope you will not view it as a burden; I shall make no demands upon it. I have no need of it anymore, for I can't imagine giving it to *anyone else ever again. Perhaps you can view it instead as a souvenir of the time you conquered a conqueror.*

I cannot quite ever forgive myself for my selfishness. For not giving you, or allowing you to have, the kind of life you'd likely dreamed of.

But you are a kinder person than I am, Alexandra. Perhaps one day you will find forgiveness in your heart for a man who knew everything about war but nothing about love.

I loved you then. I love you now.
I love you always.

Goodbye and be well,

Magnus Brightwall,

Earl of Montcroix

Glory.

There could be no other name for the golden exhilaration that poured through her now, illuminating every cell, pooling around her wounded, caged heart.

And shattering the lock.

She now took her first full breath of free, loved air.

She gave a soft laugh now, and suddenly she heard again Magnus standing outside of her cell in Newgate: *Let her out*, he'd ordered.

Goose bumps spangled her everywhere. *That*

was what he'd been doing yesterday morning.
Planning, and getting those documents in order.
Ever the strategist.

"Oh, Magnus."

He loved her. She loved him. He *knew* she loved
him, too. He must.

For if she was not mistaken . . .

Her beloved beast had called her bluff.

ALEXANDRA HURTLED OUT of The Grand Palace
on the Thames as though she'd been lit on fire,
startling a pair of yawning maids who were des-
ultorily applying feather dusters to things in the
sitting room. She carried only her shoes and her
bonnet, and a little pocket watch.

She leaped right into his carriage—now her carriage, apparently. It shocked her not at all that it
had been waiting just outside for her, near the little garden. Magnus would have seen to that. Still,
she prayed it meant her instincts were correct.

"Rossington Arms Coaching Inn, please!" she
told the driver, who probably already knew. "Please
hurry, if you can."

She was thrown back in her seat when he cracked
the reins. She finished lacing her dress and smoothing her hastily pinned-up hair and tying her bonnet in the carriage.

At the end of the Barking Road, a slow-moving
costermonger's cart ahead of them ate five precious minutes of the mere seventeen or so she
had to get to him, and it was all she could do not
to leap out of the carriage and run. Instead, she

closed her eyes and prayed. She squeezed her little watch in her palm until it was sweaty and willed time to slow. There was no hope for her heart slowing. It raced ahead of her. It was already with him.

But the driver understood his mission, and he was skillful. At 7:00 a.m., Rossington Arms Coaching Inn at last came into view, and oh thank *God* the stagecoach was still visible, its gleaming red bulk rising above a teeming crowd of travelers and well-wishers and spectators, all threaded through with barking dogs and children and costermongers. The departure of a stagecoach was always a spectacle.

But the horses were harnessed and trunks had been lashed to the top. The driver was clambering up into his seat. He reached a hand down to help up another man who would be enjoying the cheaper, more scenic, and considerably less comfortable ride on top.

And this, if she was not mistaken, meant at least some of the other passengers had boarded. They could leave any second.

When the coach halted, she leaped out and plunged into the fray, which refused to cooperate by parting for her.

"My husband. I'm looking for my husband. Please, sir, madam, if you'd just let me through— it's urgent!"

Surely Magnus would be obvious in the crowd. But her path everywhere was blocked by milling humans around which she could not see, and her voice scarcely penetrated the hubbub.

"I'll be your husband!" a man called cheerily. "Step right over here, miss."

She ignored him.

"He's the Earl of Montcroix. Colonel Brightwall? He's very tall—you really can't miss him! Please, have you seen a very tall man?"

She was babbling. She knew it sounded like lunacy even before people shied away from her wild eyes and shook their heads. An excitedly barking dog nearly tripped her.

A man stepped in front of her. "Of course he's an earl, luv," he called. "And I'm the King of England. You'd best try your luck with me." His fingers scrabbled at her elbow, attempting a grip.

She spun and snarled, "Take your hand off me or I'll stab you with a hairpin."

He leaped backward.

A thicket of people clogged her path in every direction. Every time she feinted to the left or to the right, someone stepped in her way. She couldn't see around them or over them. She'd had nightmares like this: running and running to try to reach someone as the distance grew ever longer.

"MAGNUS!"

If a countess howling his name like a battle cry at a coaching inn caused a scandal, so be it. If they hauled her off to Newgate for jabbing interferers with a pin—well, this seemed unlikely. But wasn't it convenient that she knew how to manage that, too?

Only one thing mattered.

She would shout down the walls of Jericho if that's what it took to find him.

"MAGNUS!" She whirled. Why wasn't she *taller*? She wanted to be taller. The wind tugged her bonnet from her head. But this time her ribbons were secure.

And then it occurred to her: if she didn't see him, he must already be aboard the coach.

And perhaps he was sitting inside, this man who had waited all of his life to be *wanted*, his heart shattered, believing she hadn't come for him.

A cold horror gripped her.

She spun and elbowed her way through outraged people to get closer to the carriage. An employee of the inn was crouching to do a final inspection of the wheels.

"Excuse me, sir—I need to see whether my husband is aboard."

"They all say that, madam. Where is your pass?"

"Well, I haven't a pass for Rossington Station—"

"Then we can't let you on the coach to look," he said maddeningly reasonably.

"If you could just ask—"

"We have a schedule, madam." He sounded nervous now. His eyes cut to a few red-coated soldiers standing on the perimeter. "Please step back." He stood and spread out his arms as if to shield the carriage from her advances.

She was very close to panicking now. What if she was wrong after all? What if he'd sent her here so he could safely depart from another coaching inn? What if he'd never made it here at all because a slow cart had halted his progress?

She staggered back when someone jostled her roughly.

She righted herself and saw a rare clearing about the size of one person in the thicket of people. She instinctively plunged into it and pulled in another breath for another shout, her voice frayed now. "MAG . . ."

And suddenly, there he stood.

Everyone milling about, of course, cleared the way for him and the madwoman who'd been so desperate to find him.

He was an island in a gently heaving human sea.

She feasted her eyes. Held fast by a sort of beautiful terror and exultation. She pressed her knuckles against her lips to stifle a sob of relief.

He didn't look surprised to see her. He was, however, as radiant as a lamp.

He paced to her at once and, without preamble, gently collected her with one arm and pulled her into his body. He wrapped both arms around her, enfolding her completely, and *oh*, thank God, this was home. Here in his arms.

He merely held her tightly a moment. One of his hands fanned the back of her head.

She curled her fingers into his shirt and clung. She could feel the relief in him as he released a huge breath.

"I wanted you to be able to choose," he murmured into her hair.

"I know," she replied. "So I chose. I choose you."

She knew, too, that he'd wanted desperately to be chosen.

For a moment she just savored the feel of him breathing.

"Magnus?"

"Yes?" His voice was a rumble against her cheek.

"I wondered . . ." She swallowed.

"Yes?"

"If you would consider staying here in London."

He lifted his cheek from her head to gaze down at her. "Oh? Why would you like me to stay?" His tone was so gentle. But it was an absolutely brutal question.

His hand trembled as he lifted a strand of hair from her now wet cheek.

She shook her head. "Tell me." Her voice was a rasp. "I want to hear it in your voice. In your words. Tell me."

His shoulders moved as he took on air for courage. Knowing what she now knew about him, she understood laying himself thusly bare required take-a-bullet-for-General-Blackmore bravery.

"I love you, Alexandra."

Oh, it broke her open completely. And inside she was made of nothing but light. Blazing light.

"I love you, too."

Her voice had gone small and cracked and he was at once a beautiful blur made of light, too: it shone from him. He radiated through her tears.

That she could make someone so happy with

those three words seemed miraculous, a gift she hardly deserved.

He groaned softly, a sound of profound joy and relief.

And heedless of the milling crowds, he kissed her. Softly, lingeringly.

"Magnus, don't go to America. Please don't go. I'm sorry I hurt you. If I could undo it all . . . if I had only known . . . I want to stay here with you."

"Oh, my love." His lips brushed her wet cheek. "My sweetheart. I'm sorry, too. But it's all right now. We'll go together one day, if you'd like. But never again will I go anywhere without you if you don't want me to. I am yours, however, wherever, whenever you want me."

"I want you now, I want you here, Magnus, and I want you forever. You were right from the beginning. We *do* suit."

His smile was slow and brilliant. "Very well, then. Forever starts today, Mrs. Brightwall."

He linked his arm through hers, and at long last, the Beast took his bride home.

Epilogue

࿆࿆࿆

*"F*WOG!*"*

With a delighted squeal, two-year-old Magdalena made a lunge for an amphibian friend she'd spotted lounging in their many-tiered fountain in their garden. She'd managed to get a foot all the way in before Magnus swooped in and snatched his daughter up.

Paradoxically, Magdalena was enchanted by every living creature, from cats and dogs to (alas) flies and spiders, and pursued their friendship with gleeful abandon, but she was outraged when she got her clothes dirty or wet, which neverthe-less never stopped her from crawling into shrub-bery, or rolling in the hay with the stable cats, for instance. This mystifying toddler logic was just one of the millions of things Magnus found en-chanting about being a father.

He passed Magdalena to Alexandra so he could settle the picnic hamper he was carrying down on the grass.

"Magdalena, sweetie, frogs live in fountains. Little girls live in houses. It's not polite to go into the frog's house uninvited," Alexandra told her, and gave her a kiss on her round pink cheek, because her cheeks were irresistible and impossible not to kiss.

Magnus and Alexandra exchanged laughing glances over this unique etiquette lesson. They seized opportunities to teach whenever they could.

"Foot wet!" Magdalena extended her leg with playful imperiousness to her father, who dutifully removed her slipper.

"Wet feet are the natural consequences of invading a frog home," he said in the growly voice she loved when he read to her the story of *Goldilocks and the Three Bears* at bedtime. Then he tickled her foot.

She squealed, and laughed, and her laugh was like that fountain: joy *burbled* out of that child.

Magnus felt downright *concussed* by love every time he heard her laugh.

Fatherhood had in fact brutally tenderized his heart.

The world sorted itself into what was important and what was not the night his daughter was born. Alexandra's terrifyingly arduous labor brought a grim-faced doctor to their door and Magnus to his knees, bargaining with God. He had never, ever felt so infuriatingly helpless as he had bearing witness to his wife's pain, the stunning danger involved in bringing a child into the world. It had nearly cut him in two.

But when he at last held his daughter, and kissed his exhausted wife, who was blessedly fine and blissfully relieved and happy, the whole of his life narrowed to a single peaceful certainty:

Nothing else mattered but them. It was as though his time on the battlefield, nearly the whole of his life, was a mere faint echo in comparison.

He would die for his two beautiful copper-headed loves.

They were the reason his heart beat. This was what he was made for: loving and protecting them until the end of his days.

He felt as though he was born when his daughter was born.

In public, he remained a dignified, stern-visaged edifice the country admired and revered.

In private, both he and his wife had become saps. They both teared up easily and shamelessly over Magdalena's first, second, and third words ("cat," "Mama," "Papa"), first smile, first steps, first time she gently picked up a surprised spider by one leg to hand to her mother. Magnus understood fully what an absolute bloody luxury it was to *feel*, and learned that "love" was in fact the over-simple name applied to a universe of emotions. Gratitude swept through him with hurricane force at frequent intervals: gratitude that he was strong enough and smart enough and absolutely ruthless enough to protect his wife and child from any vicissitudes of life. Gratitude for being humble enough to understand there were things over which he had no control at all, and the humility of this knowledge was what delineated every moment they lived together as sharply and brilliantly as a gem.

In bed at night, while his wife slept, sometimes he relived that magical moment Alexandra had told him she loved him, the moment she had chosen him, and then the moments thereafter, that had led up to her breathing softly next to him in a huge, comfortable bed. He did it the way a miser would with gold.

From the coaching inn that day, he had taken Alexandra back to The Grand Palace on the Thames. Straightaway they had sent a trusted messenger on horseback to meet Alexandra's chaperones in Liverpool—a man on horseback would be able to travel much faster than the stagecoach would—with the news that she would not be accompanying them to New York after all, along with short letters from both Magnus and Alexandra for the Harpers to deliver to her father and her brother telling them the same thing: they were well and happy but regretted not being able to visit them, as a result of an exciting complication in their lives—they were now an earl and a countess, in the midst of selling one house and buying another and taking on new roles and properties. They sent their love and promised they would indeed see them soon—together—whether it was on American or English soil.

And then they had settled into living happily for another month at the boardinghouse while they waited for Magnus's town house to be sold, enjoying the spirited discourse and the excellent meals and the truly delightful company. They both wanted a house that would be *theirs*, from the very beginning. Fortunately, Alexandra loved the house Magnus had been in the process of purchasing on Grosvenor Square, and when the sale was completed, they—with more than a little wistfulness—finally bid their friends at The Grand Palace on the Thames adieu and moved into it.

But as it turned out, his new estate in Surrey, amidst greenery and woods, was where they were destined to spend most of their time. They fell in love with it straightaway.

The Earl and Countess of Montcroix set about discovering which pleasures and pastimes they might enjoy. As it turned out, they both enjoyed the works of Miss Jane Austen and horrid novels like the stirring *The Ghost in the Attic*. Magnus found the works of Mr. Miles Redmond enthralling; Alexandra found them ponderous. They loved animals, and so they kept a lot of them: two cats, one fluffy, one smooth, who slept on the bed, and one hound, who slept in the house, and a few others, who slept in the stables along with their cat families as well as their horses. And eventually they adopted a donkey they named Shillelagh, a smaller, gentler version of her namesake, who became their daughter's best friend, and pulled her little cart around the circular drive in Surrey and along the meandering garden paths. (Magdalena called her "Shilly.") Because they both liked gardens that were both a little bit wild and a little bit tame, their grounds were both woolly and cultivated. And in a particularly secluded, enchanting spot in the woolly area, they'd tucked a little fountain featuring a stone boy merrily urinating, because it reminded them of their friend Mr. Delacorte and Magnus thought it was funny.

They discovered they liked entertaining, mostly of the casual sort, so they frequently got up picnics and parties of friends. They invited when they could their friends from The Grand Palace on the Thames, and members of Alexandra's family, and people they had come to enjoy among the denizens of the ton. Both her brother and father startled everyone by returning from New York with American wives, beautiful, spirited, wryly clever women with whom Alexandra soon became fast friends.

They visited museums and parks, and took in plays and operas and musicales, went riding in the row, attended cricket matches and a few more donkey races, traveled across the sea to spend a few months at his New York estate, and spent long quiet evenings at home playing whist or spillikins or making love, and having long, meandering conversations in bed.

And in the process, they did indeed discover what they loved best: being married to each other. As long as they were together, it seemed they could manage to enjoy just about anything. Or at least find a few laughs in it.

Little Griffin, who would be the second Earl of Montcroix, was born two years after Magdalena, and Penelope was born two years after that, and then Maximilian two years after that. And *then* what they loved best was being with their family, and watching their children run about the great lawns and gardens of their estate with their cousins, all those coppery heads and tawny ones glinting in the sun.

And while Magnus made certain their love story was secretly immortalized in the Montcroix family crest—which featured a swan for beauty and grace and love; and for protectiveness and military courage and leadership, a griffin, that terrifying mythical creature cobbled together from other fearsome creatures—no one ever called the Magnificent Montcroix a beast again.

"Do you know who will probably be very loud when the, er, time comes?" Captain Hardy mused to Delilah, as they snuggled into bed for the evening.

They were both feeling a little pensive, as everyone at The Grand Palace on the Thames had just bid genuinely wistful farewells to Mr. and Mrs. Brightwall. The Dawsons had departed a fortnight earlier, and Mrs. Cuthbert had departed a week ago. She had promised to return for another visit, and it was indicative of how she'd blossomed that no one interpreted this as a threat.

Delilah looked at her husband quizzically.

And then she knew.

"Dot," they both said at the same time. Him with grim conviction, her with stunned realization of the likely absolute truth of this.

Delilah covered her head with her pillow, choking with laughter. "I will *not* think of that. You can't make me think of that!" She kicked him playfully.

They both laughed until they were coughing, which was lovely, and helped shake off their wistful mood.

"I hope she never leaves us, and that things stay the way they are now, forever," she said, and he gathered her up and kissed the top of her head, because he knew what she meant, and they both knew full well this was an impossible dream.

The departure of cherished guests was always bittersweet. Much like Planet Earth itself, arrivals and departures were what defined life at The Grand Palace on the Thames. No one left unchanged by their experience. A gratifying number of their guests seemed to leave with a spouse.

And those left behind were often changed, too. The Hardys and Durands felt even closer now, thanks in part, ironically, to the previous distance between the Brightwalls.

"I like to think we had something to do with the Brightwalls' glowing happiness when they left," Angelique had confided to Delilah in their room at the top of the stairs earlier that evening.

All the maids were warned not to ever gossip idly about the guests. But in the kitchen a few weeks ago, Dot had shared with them something she'd sensed they would like to know.

"The Brightwalls sleep in one room now," she'd whispered to them in the kitchen. "They didn't when they first arrived. We never have to make up the bed in one of the rooms now."

And all of them had smiled mistily at each other, feeling enormously relieved and so pleased for Alexandra and Magnus.

"We took good care of them here," Delilah said. "We gave them a safe place to rediscover each other. We forced them to think about what sort of fountain they might want to be. I think we can be proud of that."

The ache of poignant farewells was fortunately already ameliorated by intriguing new guests. A young woman with a modest inheritance had come to London to meet a man with whom she'd been corresponding. This gentleman had advertised for a wife and she was looking forward to being one, and they had arranged to meet for the first time at The Grand Palace on the Thames. Delilah and Angelique were *very* glad they'd be able to keep an eye on her. They knew too well the trouble a young woman alone in the world could find herself in.

And young Lord St. John Vaughn, who occasionally stopped in to play chess with Mr. Delacorte, had told them of a gifted violinist he'd recently happened to meet who was looking for a place to stay. A charming Irish fellow, apparently, by the name of Seamus.

And even as Delilah and Tristan doused their lamps for the night and snuggled in for the sleep of the contented, from various corners of England, indeed, from all corners of the world, the winds of fate were stirring in the lives of men and women, preparing to blow them right up to the front door of a little boardinghouse by the London docks.

And in her little room at the top of the house, Dot opened her journal, dipped her quill into a little pot of ink, and on the top of a page wrote "Dot's Thoughts," followed by the date.

> *Today I found a tiny wooden donkey on the mantel in the pink sitting room. It was sitting on a scrap of foolscap. On it the words "For Dot. My name is Fate" were written.*

In truth, anyone could have left the donkey there. The people with whom she lived were kind and witty. Everyone knew how she felt about fate, and donkeys, and it was possible someone was having one over on her.

But she'd seen that precise little donkey for sale in the stationer's shop for ten pence. She'd in fact nearly bought it instead of the journal.

And she knew Mr. Pike had won exactly ten pence on Shillelagh.

Surely not? Still, the notion caused a pleasant glow smack in the center of her chest.

She briefly galloped the donkey across her little table, making idle clopping noises with her mouth.

Then she carefully settled it next to the inkwell, blew out her lamp, and climbed into bed.

No matter what, she was quite pleased to have a wooden donkey.

DISCOVER MORE BY
JULIE ANNE LONG

THE PALACE OF ROGUES SERIES